Marx, Deceased

MARX, DECEASED

DECEASED

A Novel by
Carl Djerassi

The University of Georgia Press Athens & London

Published by the

University of Georgia Press

Athens, Georgia 30602

©1996 by Carl Djerassi

All rights reserved

Designed by Richard Hendel

Set in 11 on 15 Bodoni Book by Books International

Printed and bound by Maple-Vail

The paper in this book meets the

guidelines for permanence and durability

of the Committee on Production Guidelines

for Book Longevity of the

Council on Library Resources.

Printed in the United States of America

00 99 98 97 96 C 5 4 3 2 1

Library of Congress Cataloging in Publication Data

Djerassi, Carl.

Marx, deceased : a novel / by Carl Djerassi.

p. cm.

ISBN 0-8203-1835-3 (alk. paper)

I. Title

PS3554.J47M37   1996

813'.54—dc20   95-43312

British Library Cataloging in Publication Data available

For

BRETT MILLIER

&

TERRENCE HOLT

CAVEAT LECTOR

Dinner parties based on first attempts to follow the

soufflé recipes in chapter 20 are likely to lead to unexpected

consequences for which no responsibility, legal or moral,

is accepted. Complaints addressed to the author will be returned

unread. Intriguing improvements may be acknowledged.

The death of the author is

what permits the birth of writing.

ROLAND BARTHES

Preface

Why would a scientist-author choose a novelist for his principal character? My avowed purpose in writing fiction is to interpret the tribal culture of science to a general public; I have chosen for this task the genre of "science-in-fiction"—certainly not science fiction, but not quite, either, the "realistic" fiction that knows so little about science. Readers might think that in my work I would stick close to the scientific world, and people that world with figures in long, white coats. This time, I do not, a decision that raises a question. Is *Marx, Deceased* just my transparent attempt to avoid being typed as a narrow science-in-fiction writer?

I claim there is more to it. A recurring theme in my fiction is the compulsive drive of research scientists for peer approval. Name recognition—the struggle to carve out a reputation that is so important to the essential skill of contemporary science—is also related to grantsmanship. While this drive to make a name for oneself has many effects in the culture of science, one effect that has attracted little notice (in the way that most such omissions escape notice) is this: scientists never publish anonymously. Here is where I find a point of contact between two groups we do not often associate: the creative artist and the researcher in hard science. But areas of intersection are not necessarily areas of agreement: this point of contact between the two cultures, while it reveals some convergences, exposes important differences as well.

Most writers also display a need for approbation by their peers. Novelist Stephen Marx's preoccupation with his own image is not very different from describing a scientist's hunger for peer validation. In each instance, that urge is both the nourishment and the poison of a creative mind.

But writers also lust for recognition beyond the community of their peers. Unlike scientists, who live and die by peer review, a writer requires above all else the approbation of the general public. Best-sellers are created by the book-buying public, not by the writer's peers. Even the favorable opinions of book reviewers and critics, though craved by authors, are not essential for elevation to the best-seller lists. Here scientists have an advantage: they need not concern themselves with professional critics, because such a breed does not exist in their intellectual world—which, incidentally, also excludes the general public. But the final difference between these two groups, in this regard, is the one that concerns me most, for it is the one that cuts, I believe, to the heart of the matter. It has to do with individual identity—with ego, the ultimate source of all this hunger for success. Scientists, I have said, never publish anonymously. To do so would seem to rob the entire exercise of its point as I have tried to demonstrate in my preceding novel, *The Bourbaki Gambit*. But a writer? If one's central purpose is to win general acclaim—the kind of celebrity in which one's individual identity is as irrelevant as the actual deeds or personalities of any of the celebrities whose faces grace the supermarket tabloids—it hardly matters if one writes under one's own name or not.

This question of celebrity is not an idle one because, ultimately, it goes beyond ego to the quality of the work itself. What kind of celebrity we pick has everything to do with what we write. If a novelist had to choose between best-seller status, on the one hand, and critics' choice on the other—to sell thousands of books for a couple of years, followed by the oblivion of the remainder bins, or to be neglected by the general public now, but still to be read half a century later—in other words, as Flaubert put it, choose between audience and readers, which would it be? Such a choice is a formidable test of a writer's self-esteem, a test to which my fictional author eventually subjects himself.

But does he pass it?

Marx, Deceased

1

"Rocco's." The voice on the telephone was brusque, the *R* rolling like a Ferrari in first gear.

"I'm calling about a dinner reservation," he said. "For two. Next Thursday, 7 o'clock."

"Name?"

"Marx."

"Spell it."

God, not again, he thought. It's just a four-letter word. "Marx, like Karl Marx."

"With a *C* or a *K*?"

"That's just an illustration: Karl Marx, Groucho Marx . . . my name is Stephen, not Karl."

The brusque voice turned defensive. "Let's start again. Your *last* name?"

"*M A R X.*"

"Ah, gotcha."

Stephen Marx sounded relieved. "I'd like a booth—not a table—and if possible, a corner booth with some privacy."

"Gotcha."

"Saint."

Ambrose McPhearson was smiling as he reached across the table to shake hands. Only Marx's friends or relatives used that nickname. This time he took it to be affectionate.

Nicknames usually start in childhood, yet Stephen Marx had not become "Saint" until he was in his early twenties. Shortly after graduation from Yale, during a year abroad in Zurich, the first envelope addressed to him in German had read "Herr St. Marx." Upon learning the German abbreviation for "Stefan," he'd promptly ordered stationary and envelopes reading "St. Marx, Dreidingstrasse 43, Zürich." By the time he'd returned to the States, fluent in *Deutsch*, the nickname "Saint" had already spread among family and friends.

"It's good to see you," McPhearson said. "It's been months."

"It's good to see *you*, Boz," replied Marx. "I don't usually get to see you on such short notice."

McPhearson smiled. Nobody at the bank ever called him "Boz;" he was too much the boss at the bank. "Oh, you know. 'Busy' depends on who's asking. For you, I'm not busy. How's Miriam? What have you people been up to?"

"She's OK," Marx shrugged. "She's up to here with her catering business." He leveled a hand across the bridge of his nose.

"And how's your work going?"

"Have you seen the reviews of my last book?"

"I'm embarrassed to say I haven't," replied McPhearson. "How were they?"

Marx's attempt at nonchalance vanished in a rising wave of anger. "You know how reviews go: most were good to superlative, but then Noah Berg's got me so angry I almost wished dueling were still in fashion."

McPhearson's eyebrows rose. "Really? What did he say?"

At issue in *Cohen's Dilemma* is what happens when a theory, "sweet" to the scientist, turns out to have been "proven" in a flawed experiment. The drama arises when the culprit turns out to be Professor I. Cohen's (I.C., he is called, and icy he is) favorite assistant, and the tainted results turn out to net Cohen—and the assistant—the Nobel Prize.

The serious side to this story—though its author no doubt thought his book entirely serious—has Cohen trapped morally and personally by his professional dependence on the opinions of his colleagues. The issue of reputation and its shadows and taints is the central theme, but Marx's treatment of it here would lead one to believe that reputation is a single prize, given reluctantly and destroyed completely at the first question. You either have it or you don't. One would have thought Marx capable of greater subtlety.

Perhaps he has too much Nobel Prize on his mind.

That was what the review had said, and through hours of obsessive reading and rereading Marx had almost memorized it. He resisted the impulse to recite it aloud: the words were bitter enough without giving them voice.

"Never mind," he said. "I didn't invite you to bitch about a review. Let's order."

Screened by their open menus, the men missed the arrival of two women who settled in the adjacent booth. Both were in their twenties—one, tall and thin: a fashion-model type; the other, of average height and weight: on first impression not particularly striking—at least not by comparison with the model.

"So what is it, Saint?" McPhearson asked when the waiter had departed with their orders. "What prompted this dinner invitation after all these months? Did you just miss me, or do you need free financial advice?"

Marx leaned forward. "Did you know that Hemingway managed to read his own obituaries?"

McPhearson gave him an appraising look before answering, coolly, "Yes."

"Yes?" Marx looked nonplussed. "How did you know that?"

McPhearson made a dismissive gesture. "I did an honors paper on Hemingway at Dartmouth." He leaned across the table, voice confidential. "Now do you mind telling me why you want to know?"

"Wouldn't it be exciting to read one's own obituary?"

"Exciting? I can just see my obituary: Ambrose Samuel McPhearson, born April 16, 1939, Pocatello, Idaho; educated at Dartmouth and the Wharton School. Then I hope it will say I'd reached some ripe eminence in banking, what a whiz I was at arranging corporate mergers, and how much I was missed by my grieving wife Jessica, my three children, and my many inconsolable friends. All things considered, I'd rather be alive."

"Who's talking about dying? I'm talking about reading your own obituary while you're still alive—just like Hemingway."

McPhearson looked. "Why this sudden interest in Hemingway, Saint? This isn't some competitive writer thing, is it?"

"I'm not really interested in Hemingway. Besides—as you seem to know so well—he blew it: he reappeared so soon, there was no time for anyone to rush to print with a critical assessment of his work. But what if he'd managed it better?" Marx leaned forward, hands planted flat on the tablecloth. "What if you could stage your death and stay dead? Long enough for the serious critics to come out of the woodwork, not the journalistic hacks."

His voice had become progressively louder. On the other side of the partition, one of the women had caught the gist of the men's dialogue. She let her companion do most of the talking, while she listened.

Marx lowered his voice. "I guess a banker wouldn't understand. You're either a financial success or a failure—there's hardly anything in between. The judgment of your peers isn't that important. All that counts are numbers: dollars, profits or losses; the bottom line."

"Come now," McPhearson protested mildly. "Don't be so conceited."

"I'm not being conceited. That's just the difference between bankers and people like me—people whose self-esteem depends on the opinion of others."

"Oh, now you're really talking rot, Saint. Since when does your self-esteem depend on anyone else?"

"You think so?" Marx said mournfully. "Have you ever stopped to think how it must feel to work in a field where success isn't something you can quantify? How much uncertainty that involves? How much insecurity? Well why should you: I didn't. Not until I spent all those months interviewing scientists for *Cohen's Dilemma*. What struck me from the start was the way they were all fixated on the opinion of their peers. The only way Einstein knew he was a great physicist was that other physicists told him he was. If they hadn't, he would have remained a clerk in the Bern patent office to the end of his days. When I was working on *Cohen*, of course, I thought this was some quirk of scientists. Since then though. . . ." Marx leaned back, hands in his pockets, staring beneath the tablecloth at what McPhearson could only guess was his shoe. "Since then, I've seen it everywhere. Playwrights and actors who can hardly wait for the appearance of a newspaper after the opening night. Composers. Architects. And writers, like me, who get ulcers waiting for the *Times* to review their latest book. You even worry about what page they're going to run it on."

Marx fell silent. He realized that he was lecturing—not his normal rhetorical mode, no matter what his friends said—yet he couldn't help himself: he felt a compulsion to make McPhearson—to make anyone—understand. Still, how could he explain the anxiety that had been crawling over him since he'd finished *Cohen's Dilemma*: was his writing worth anything? The reviewer's phrase, *the issue of reputation and its shadows and taints*, had seized on him like a cancer until it had become an almost palpable pain. Stephen Marx, author of thirteen novels: he had a reputation, but what was his true worth? How could he ever know?

"When John O'Hara died," he said quietly, "Cheever wrote about him in *Esquire*; six months after Cheever's death, Saul Bellow wrote an enormously sympathetic piece on him in the *New York Review of Books*; or Philip Roth's reminiscences of Bernard Malamud in the *Times*. I bet O'Hara, Cheever, and Malamud would have loved to have read those words."

McPhearson had listened without taking his eyes off his friend. "What about the critics? You have your Bergs, sure, but there are other critics. Can't you get some kind of consensus?"

"That's just it," Marx said irritably. "I'm convinced most critics judge writers less by what they do than by where they are in their careers—as if there were some standard yardstick of performance. If you're a newcomer, they go easy on you. It's not necessarily out of generosity; critics realize there isn't much sport in demolishing an unknown." The gnocchi on Marx's fork had nearly reached his mouth, but at the last moment he put it down. "The second phase starts when they're covering a well-known author, preferably someone who's written a couple of best-sellers. Then the critics begin to sharpen their knives: some of them try to be clever, others are brutal; some, of course, remain complimentary and you become their favorite."

"Saint," McPhearson interjected, "eat that damn pasta."

"Sorry," Marx said. He looked at his fork, as though uncertain of its purpose, then set it down. "But it's the third phase that intrigues me: the posthumous evaluation. That's when one learns their true opinion. I would like to know what some people—even Berg—really think of me; what they'd write if they knew I was dead." But even as he turned finally to his meal, Marx was left with a doubt. Will I know my real worth even then? He remembered the concluding note of the *Times*'s obituary of John O'Hara, who, during his last years, had been treated rather shabbily by the serious critics: "John O'Hara's huge body of work may be around much longer than we had predicted." Is that what Marx, the fly on the wall, wanted to read about himself? That he won't go away?

McPhearson stopped eating; a bemused expression had spread over his face. "I've a feeling you've something specific in mind," he said, staring at his friend. "Is this why we're meeting here tonight?"

The woman had long ago stopped paying attention to her companion. Who is this man, she thought, who wants to read his own obituary? He's bound to be famous; otherwise no one would bother. She wanted to get a better look at him. Walking to the ladies' room would offer an opportunity. Yet the details were becoming too intriguing for an interruption.

"Saint, you worry me. You've hardly touched your gnocchi. I've heard you talk about your work this way before, but this obituary business. . . ." He shook his head. "I don't know."

Marx tried a forkful of the dumplings, and grimaced. "There's something about cold gnocchi." He shoved the plate aside. "Did you know Agatha Christie once staged her own death?"

"Uh-huh. But that had nothing to do with her wanting to read her obituary. She wanted to revenge herself because her husband was about to abandon her."

Marx wasn't paying attention. "It's interesting," he said musingly. "She arranged her disappearance quite carefully, but she didn't devise a plausible way of returning. In the end, all she came up with was 'temporary amnesia.'"

McPhearson put down knife and fork. "Are you writing a novel about this, or is this for real?"

Marx took a gulp of wine. "Real. That's why I wanted to see you. I need your help."

"You're not seriously suggesting—" McPhearson fixed him with a stare that made Marx feel as though his payments were in arrears. "You're not even *considering* asking me to help arrange your death?"

"Relax, Boz. What I'm about to propose is not illegal. It involves no risk on your part. I simply need your help."

"I'm not sure a banker's help is exactly what you need, old friend." McPhearson grinned as he said it, but it was a grin with teeth in it.

"I'm not joking, Ambrose. I'm convinced it will have an enormous impact on my future writing. Even if it doesn't, I'm so caught up with this idea it's left me with a mammoth writer's block. Please listen." Marx reached across the table to touch his friend's sleeve. "Let's start with the basic premise: if you want to read your own obituary, you need to stage a plausible disappearance: something in which everybody immediately assumes that you're dead even without finding the body. Right?"

"I can't believe I'm having this conversation."

Marx took a grip on McPhearson's wrist. "Right?"

"I suppose so," McPhearson said grudgingly. "Go on. And let go."

Marx let go of the wrist. "As I told you, I'm not interested in a simple obituary. I want to read detailed, critical retrospectives by some important critics—"

"Like Berg?"

"Berg?" For a moment, Marx seemed startled by the interruption. "Fuck Berg," he hissed. "He's a reviewer, and reviewing has nothing to do with criticism. I'm now quoting Henry James," he added in a calmer tone.

"'Critics are the lice in the locks of literature,'" laughed MacPhearson. "It's amazing what sticks in your head from school days. Tennyson is supposed to have said that about critics."

"Or the brilliantine that makes their locks shine. Do you know who said that?"

"Who?"

"Yours truly. Just thought it up. But criticism—lousy or glossy—takes time, at the very least some weeks, if not months. If one goes to the trouble of staging a plausible death, one might as well get maximum mileage out of it—"

"Have you finished, sir?"

Stephen Marx jumped at the waiter's voice.

"I suppose so," he mumbled, glancing at the barely touched food on his plate.

"Any dessert? Coffee?" asked the waiter.

Marx shook his head and waited impatiently while McPhearson consulted with the waiter. "One tiramisu and two forks. And two cappuccinos."

Marx was relieved to see the waiter depart. "Let me continue. The dead author has to stay dead for several months. This is where I need your help."

"What?" McPhearson growled.

"I need about twenty-five grand, but I can't take that sum out of my bank account without it being noticed. I'll repay you the day I return. At prime plus two percent," he added sheepishly. "Furthermore, would you rent a car in your name and let me drive it during that time? I can't very well rent one if I'm supposed to be dead, and I don't want to do anything illegal, like getting a fake driver's license."

"What if you get stopped by a policeman?"

"I'll have to drive carefully and hope no one runs into me. Boz, are you willing to help me?"

"I doubt it," replied McPhearson. "First, explain to me how you'll stage your death. And how you'll reappear after a couple of months without admitting it was simply a farce."

"I've got it all figured out," replied Marx. He leaned forward, staring straight at his friend. "I'll tell you later how I'll get back. First let me explain how I'll die. That's where I need your help."

"Oh no, you don't," interrupted McPhearson. "You're not getting me involved in any death, real or imaginary."

"Please wait," pleaded Marx. "Just listen to me. You know I often sail by myself. The Mamaroneck Yacht Club people all know me; none would be surprised if I went out by myself during the middle of the week. Remember: I'm the famous author who has no fixed hours. Suppose I told them I'm leaving for a day's sailing in Long Island Sound; that I'd be back by five o'clock. You follow me in your powerboat. We'll pick a lousy, windy day when nobody else is out on the water. As soon as we're out of sight of land, I'll board your boat and leave the life-vest behind." Marx's voice had assumed a pleading tone, as if he were begging to be believed. "You know how many sailors don't wear one, especially if they use a safety belt. You'll take me ashore where your rented car is parked and I'll take off. The safety belt will look as if it had torn; it will be obvious that I fell into the water. We're committing no crime, you're not claiming my death. I just disappear, and you simply go home."

"What then?" asked McPhearson.

"I'll take off for San Francisco. I'll drive carefully because I don't want to break any speed limits. I've been on the West Coast only once, years ago. Nobody knows me there. I'll get a mailbox in San Francisco and let you know how to get in touch with me."

"You've got it all worked out," McPhearson said quietly.

"I think so," Marx said.

"What about your friends and relatives? And Miriam?"

2

"Damn you, Saint."

No one would have mistaken for affection the tone with which Miriam spat out the last word. As she continued, her mood was quite clear, even if the direction of the argument still seemed, to Stephen, obscure.

"When you associate food with women—or is it women with food?—it's to provide infantile satisfaction. But, of course, when men are involved, it's supposed to be an expression of genius. 'Home-cooking' is the greatest compliment you can pay a woman, but you'd insult a male chef with it. It's one of the last claims of shameless male chauvinism that there are no great women chefs. What about Julia Child? Alice Waters?"

"Who's Alice Waters?" asked Stephen, not realizing he was stoking the fire of his wife's irritation.

"You aren't just a male chauvinist—you're such a goddamned New Yorker, you don't even know that California cooking exists." Miriam was steaming.

"Come on, Miriam." Stephen tried to placate his wife. "What's wrong with being a New Yorker?"

Miriam stopped to draw breath, suggesting to Stephen that perhaps he shouldn't have provided so large an opening. "So let's take Julia Child," he said quickly. "She teaches cooking. Great chefs don't teach, they have tantrums."

"Like all geniuses, I suppose. You should know."

He had meant to divert her, but the subject had turned his own thoughts from their argument, sent them running in a too-familiar direction. "They protect their secrets," he added.

"And Julia Child—by sharing them—proves that she can't be a cooking genius, just a good teacher? Is that it?"

"Precisely."

"Secrets! What is it with you and secrets? You're impossible."

Miriam Marx was about to slam the door when something changed her mind. She turned and walked toward the sofa where Marx was slouching.

"Let's talk," she said.

"About what?"

"You and me."

With a half-suppressed groan, Marx gestured to the easy chair facing him. "Go ahead."

"And drop that martyr's pout," she added.

"Martyrs don't pout."

"How would you know? Saints like you wouldn't recognize a martyr if she sat right in front of you. But let's drop this bickering. I'm serious. Ever since you got your so-called *office* across town, we don't see each other anymore during the day—"

"True," he interrupted. "But who set up a catering business in SoHo, where she spends most of her day?"

"That came after," she said evenly.

"After what?"

After suspecting that there were other women, she almost said, but then had caught herself. She was certain that if she ever spoke those words, it would be the end of their marriage. Every once in a while, she had gotten close to the flickering flame, but she had always flown away, circling the light but keeping her distance. It was his discretion that kept her quiet. She gave him credit for that, possibly too much credit, for never humiliating her with other women—in public or private. But the time was bound to come.

These thoughts took only a picosecond of Miriam's mental rummaging through her complaint filing cabinet. It was rapidly filling, but it could still be shut. For the moment she locked it.

Instead, she said, "After I discovered that time without money isn't worth as much as money without time."

"Would you be good enough to translate that to me?" For a writer, Marx was rarely subtle in conversation.

Her right hand moved out in a pacifying gesture. "Calm down, Steve. As long as you wrote here and I helped you and read your first drafts, I considered the money you brought in 'our' money.

But not any more. When I write *my* book, I don't want to do it on time paid by *you*. When I've earned enough money on my own, I'll start on the book."

"Book?" Marx realized he had gone into a crouch, as if he were about to jump. "What book are *you* writing?"

"A cookbook."

"Oh." The bubble of concern was punctured, the tension in his legs released. He sank back into the recesses of the sofa.

"So you don't think much of cookbooks, do you?" Of course, she knew his opinion. That was one reason, perhaps *the* reason, why she hadn't told Steve until today about her book. The energy to work is canceled by the knowledge that the work's value is being ignored. So why tell him today? Was she again circling toward the flickering flame?

"I didn't say that," he replied smugly. "I only thought they'd all been written."

"So you know all about it," she said sweetly. "Let's try an experiment." It was her turn to lean forward. "What's the difference between Chinese and Austrian cuisine?"

"Seriously?" he asked.

She nodded.

"All right," he said wearily. "What?"

"Just try."

"There are dozens of differences. For instance, the Chinese stir fry in woks and the Austrians slap whipped cream on everything." He threw her a so-there-you-are glance.

Miriam nodded complacently. "Do you want to hear how *my* book would handle such a question?"

"I can hardly wait."

"In Chinese," she said, "you can do it backward."

"You lose me Miriam."

"It's very simple, Stephen. You can start a Chinese meal with rice or soup, and you can end it with rice or soup. Not in Vienna. You can't start with *Sachertorte* any more than you could end with liver dumpling soup."

"Very clever," said Marx, making it clear he didn't mean it.

She ignored him. "The same," she concluded, "also applies to fucking."

The way she had said the word, saving it for last, showed that she had counted on its crudeness. "You ask a man, who's just had an orgasm, and he'd have to answer 'no.' Now pose that question to a woman. She might well say, 'it depends; in principle, yes.' Incidentally, the question 'can you do it in reverse?' is a damn interesting one—applicable to much more than cooking or coitus."

The eyes of both of them seemed to have discovered the same intriguing detail in the carpet's design. Neither one spoke for the next minute.

"Remember '*wickasechs*'?" Miriam's voice had developed a quaver.

"Yes," he said.

Miriam and Stephen had first met shortly after his return from his year in Zurich. "Why Zurich?" she'd asked. His response had amused her when she had learned that he liked to ski and that James Joyce was his literary god. "If an Irish ex-Catholic, who didn't even ski, could flourish in Zurich, why not a secular Jew from New York?" At that time, Miriam hadn't even considered him conceited, just a tad narcissistic, when he referred to the spelling of Stephen, on which his parents had decided before his birth, as an in utero good omen: clearly, he was destined to follow the path of Stephen Dedalus. (Of course, he never reminded anyone that Joyce's Stephen Dedalus considered Marx "a bloody cod," not to be taken seriously. After all, Joyce's Stephen was talking about Karl.)

For weeks they had smoothed over the awkwardness of a nascent affair with word games of his invention—constructing German-sounding, English words, like *hjuhdj* for "huge," or *hämm änt äcks* when ordering breakfast.

Miriam had done her best to play along. "How do you feel about the *wickasechs*?" she had asked, spelling the word.

"Come again?"

When she translated it as "weaker sex," he'd stepped back a few feet as if he'd wanted a wide-angle perspective. "Will you live with me?" he'd asked after he'd returned to within whispering distance. "Of course not," she'd laughed, but a week later they'd rented an apartment together. "Neutral territory," Miriam had insisted, for a level playing field with the *schtrongasechs*.

Within a month of their cohabitation, and long before they married, Miriam took over all of the trivia of daily life: shopping, cooking, laundry, and paying bills. She did not feel put upon—not then, when both had focused on the beginnings of Stephen's literary career. But as time had gone on, and success had brought money, enough money to take care of the more burdensome chores, there had remained an irreducible burden of domestic tasks—paying the bills, answering correspondence, shopping for gifts—to which she could never get Stephen to attend. Her catering business was booming—demanding far more of her time than his writing ever had of his—and she'd started to demand justification as to why she should still be stuck with the family crap. "What do you mean by crap?" Stephen responded. But silently he thought: That's precisely why I can't be bothered. I've got to be able to concentrate.

Marx's reverie was broken as Miriam's remembered face and voice merged with McPhearson's.

"What about your unpaid bills?" he was asking. McPhearson did not sound so much curious as anxious.

"Miriam pays them all—I don't even see them."

"But that's just one example," repeated McPhearson. "There must be dozens of things you haven't thought of—"

"I've thought of them all!"

"Stop bragging and don't be silly." McPhearson didn't hide his irritation. "What about your life insurance? If you're declared dead, they'll pay your wife—"

"I have no life insurance."

"You're kidding!" McPhearson looked baffled. "No insurance?"

"Why should I? I have no dependents; my wife can take care of herself. Besides she'd get the co-op, the stocks, the car. . . ." His voice trailed off. "We have no kids."

"Is that what all this is about? Your immortality doesn't pass through your children, is that it?"

Marx stared momentarily at his friend. "The written word is man's most precious commodity—it assures immortality." It may sound pompous, he thought, but it's true.

"Words are dirt-cheap," interjected the banker.

"True, but isn't that a marvelous contradiction? The most precious possession consists of an assembly of the cheapest components. You can't steal an individual word—precisely because it's so cheap. But as you string them along, they gain meaning and value."

McPhearson showed no expression. "Is that why you write?" he asked quietly.

"I write because it isn't there."

A moment of silence passed before McPhearson replied. "That's a first-class answer."

"It's not mine. Tom Berger said it. I liked it so much I stole it."

McPhearson smiled. "Plagiarism, Saint?"

Marx snorted. "Plagiarism rarely starts with a sentence. It's as you string them along that words gain value. Which is what I like about Berger's explanation. It says that writing isn't simply words strung together; it must also be new. If it retains some newness, it stays immortal." He shook his head as if to clear it. "I didn't come here to philosophize. We were talking about arranging my demise. I'm an only child; my parents are dead, and as far as Miriam is concerned, she'll be relieved."

Marx glanced up at his friend's face, checking for a reaction, but McPhearson's expression was carefully neutral. "You've probably figured out what our relationship has been like the last couple of years." Marx's voice assumed an increasingly pleading tone. "Our paths have simply diverged. Miriam's business keeps her busy most evenings, and my life. . . ." He prodded the dessert with his fork, but didn't eat. "I don't know why we didn't get divorced some time ago. And as for those friends and acquaintances you're so concerned about, and especially the critics—whom I notice you *don't* mention—their reaction is precisely what I would like to test. Sure, some of them will be sorry—maybe even grief-stricken—but they'll get over it. Remember, I'll be back in a couple of months at the latest."

"If you weren't so caught up in this fantasy of yours, I think you'd realize that there are people who would be devastated if they thought you'd just died. I would have felt that way. How can you inflict this on them just to satisfy your morbid curiosity? Are you really that self-centered?"

Marx continued playing with the remnants of the tiramisu, digging with his fork below the top chocolate layer.

"You've got a point, Ambrose," Marx said lugubriously. "It does tell something about me, doesn't it?" His voice trailed off.

McPhearson finally broke the silence. "So how do you plan to come back?"

Marx ignored the question. "When I don't return to the yacht club by late afternoon or evening, they're likely to notify the Coast Guard. Sometime, within the next day or two, they'll find the boat. It won't take them long to assume there was some accident—after all, we picked a crummy day. 'Died in a sailing accident.' Doesn't that sound plausible?"

"I suppose so."

The woman had heard enough. "I need to go to the ladies' room," she said to her companion and rose to her feet before the other could offer to accompany her.

As she passed the booth, the man facing her said: "Come on, Boz, surely you can help me. You run no risk; there's nothing improper."

The woman's visual camera was in sharp focus as she passed Stephen Marx. He had a good face, she concluded. She probably would have noticed him even if she had never overheard the men's dialogue. His hair was dark with just a tinge of gray on the temples; his eyebrows bushy black; the high forehead slightly wrinkled; sensuous lips; cleanly shaven; the nose perhaps a bit too pug. She guessed him to be in his forties, or possibly a young-looking fifty. The way he sat, it was difficult to tell much about his clothing or his height. All she saw was a tweed jacket and an open-collared shirt. She hesitated a moment, wanting to stay and hear more, knowing it was impossible to linger without drawing attention to herself. Marx and McPhearson were too absorbed in their discussion to notice as she looked around the room, then reluctantly moved on.

"It's certainly improper," McPhearson was saying. "And I can't possibly agree—certainly not on the spur of the moment."

"But you'll think about it?"

McPhearson let out an exasperated sigh. "Why did you pick me? Why don't you ask someone else?"

"Come on, Boz. There isn't anyone else. And just think: I may even get a book out of it. You'd be in it."

"Leave me out of it," countered McPhearson. "And why don't you just leave yourself out of it too? Why do you have to live it? Isn't that what fiction's all about? Making things up that didn't really happen? You've done all this planning: can't you just not do it and say you did?"

"I'm not talking about fiction—I want to know who I really am: not just in my own eyes, not just what my friends or enemies say for effect. I want *the truth*, Boz. Will you help me get it?"

McPhearson gave him a long, unreadable look.

"I'll think about it."

3

In the week after his dinner with McPhearson, Marx found himself unable to write. His literary output in that period was limited to a series of phrases he jotted down in the small notebook he always carried with him: (1) Mamaroneck, Rye, midweek, lousy weather. (2) Meeting place of boats. (3) Rental car location. (4) Coast Guard rescue procedure. (5) Time for obituary. (6) Miriam. (7) San Francisco contact. (8) Ambrose's private number. (9) Return scenario. He studied the list but could not think of any additions.

Putting the notebook back in his pocket, he looked around the studio apartment he had acquired to write in. During the past few years it had become a real home. This was his retreat, where he could work undisturbed, with an unlisted telephone whose number he guarded jealously. At least that was the official version. It struck him suddenly that Miriam, and probably others as well, would come here once they thought him dead. His study would have to look as if it had been left without any planned absence in mind. He hadn't considered that.

To have overlooked this gave him an almost physical shock. He stretched out on the sofa to calm down. He needed to think this through.

There were the files, he reflected. Strange that he'd never thought of them falling under the eyes of another person. What was there to hide? That would depend on who saw them. There was Miriam, of course—the only one with a key. Actually not the only one, but only Miriam would use hers if he were considered dead. What would he do if he were Miriam? What would he do in Miriam's office if she were dead? Would he even go there? Perhaps for an hour or so, out of sentimental curiosity. But he wouldn't have it in him to check all the papers, to take on the responsibility of closing her unfinished affairs. Surely Miriam would feel the same about his things. He realized he needed to appoint a literary executor—maybe his agent. Sedgwick would have the most to gain by becoming literary executor. But this bridge would have to be crossed later, after his return from San Francisco. Doing it now, just before his "death," might look fishy.

He was surprised how many odds and ends suddenly appeared before him. "There must be dozens of things you haven't thought of," McPhearson had warned. Marx stared at the filing cabinet in the corner. What confidential papers were still left in the bottom drawer? The bulk had already been weeded out; the rest would soon be gone. He kept no photographs of women except for the ones in his head. Berg! Had he kept their correspondence—what little there was? Marx hadn't; he specifically remembered not having printed an extra copy. Anyway, the only person possibly interested in such detritus would be a biographer, and no one would write Marx's biography during his temporary demise. He filed the topic in his not-to-worry pigeon hole.

Marx looked around. He realized he'd miss the place, the comfortably upholstered couch where he liked to read, half-reclining; the L-shaped desk which, for years, had only a twenty-five-year-old Olivetti portable. Marx had acquired the typewriter on his trip to Switzerland right after college; he had gotten so accustomed to it, he'd never switched to an electric one. He'd gone right to a word processor, making—what had he called it?—his "Bolivian Jump." He held still, searching his memory for the occasion. When was it he'd called it that?

It was when Felicity Samarand came. She came to his reading. She came up to the podium after his talk. She came almost explosively in the cemetery, and then again in his studio—all of this in about five hours.

"A. Luftig (Achilles L. Luftig in his passport) was sixty-four—at an age when, most would say, a man approaches sexual blandness if not actual oblivion. They could be right, of course, but with Luftig they'd be wrong. He was born sixty-four years ago—sixty-four years, four months, two weeks, and one day ago, to be precise. It wasn't easy to guess his age, because it depended on the scrutinizer. A woman of, say fifty, would think him very eligible—especially if she focused on his face: forehead creased by intriguing wrinkles, cheeks caressably clean shaven, hair pale straw (the kind that never turns gray or white), eyes inquisitive. Fully dressed, his body seemed sufficiently trim that a woman of fifty might take him for a steady jogger or racquetball player. His slimness was genetic, however; when naked, Luftig's muscles were less than impressive.

"Women of, say, thirty-four or even twenty-nine—ages he still collected—would respond differently. If they didn't know who he was, they'd never think of adjusting their stockings. But if they'd learned he was Achilles Luftig, they'd pay attention—and not solely for the oddity of the name. God only knows the many peculiar combinatorial appellations some parents are prepared to thrust upon their children. The whisper, 'That's Achilles over there,' immediately placed him into a special class: like *Henry* among political scientists, *Magic* among basketball players, *Norman* among writers.

"To this second group, on first contact he seemed old enough to be their father. But as they engaged him in conversation, suddenly finding themselves the exclusive object of his attention, the age difference started to diffuse. Contemplating the possibility of bedding with him did not seem so absurd when he asked, sometime after only the barest of preliminaries, 'May I taste you?'

"Once his tongue, moist and experienced, had run slowly along the woman's lower lip, starting near the middle and moving startlingly gently to the right corner, her mouth opened. Invariably so. Only when he reached that right corner did his tongue slowly enter the woman's mouth and then return to the center, where he'd started—except that on the return exploration, his tongue remained deep in her mouth. Then he withdrew—as slowly as he'd started—and moved back a few centimeters until his eyes seemingly merged to convert him into a cyclops somewhat out of focus. 'Now your tongue,' he murmured. And nine times out of ten, the young woman's tongue would enter the sixty-four-year-old man's mouth.

"Her eyes were usually closed, but even if they were not, her knowledge of his age—a datum he never hid, indeed flaunted—had dissolved in the cunty moisture she'd started to feel between her thighs. (Hardly ever did Luftig use four-letter words or derivatives thereof. 'Fuck' or 'fucking' was not part of his spoken vocabulary—not in bed, not in standard conversation, not even in banter among men. The only exception was 'cunty.')

"'What a delicious cunty taste,' he might whisper, after the young woman, thighs open, her legs straddling Luftig's shoulders, heaved violently as his tongue, in that same, gentle, methodical, exploratory fashion he'd used on her lips, had traveled along her labia to find her 'magic button'—another of his quaint expressions that should have dated him, but didn't. He didn't always use 'cunty'—not if the woman's taste was strong or acerb. But he did use it invariably when his lips, mouth, chin, sometimes even part of his cheeks, were slick with the faintly musky aroma of a woman in heat. Only then did he insert his right thumb—a stubby but perfectly shaped substitute for a tirelessly erect phallus—against which the woman could rotate and thrust until her climax. Luftig had turned ageless as the ultimate, unselfish lover.

"Only when the women invited penile penetration (some never did, having been caressed into a state of clitoral sensitivity that had caused them to withdraw into a tight, private convulsion), did he remove his wet right thumb and run it around the inside of his palm, to moisten and massage his penis, so that—even if not totally erect—he could have entered the woman with little effort.

"He could have, but in fact, he rarely did. 'Lead me into you,' he'd command, whereupon she reached down and led his member, lubricated with 'cunty' honey, between her wide open labia—in the same manner in which his tongue had entered her open, hungry mouth.

"From a work in progress," he concluded diffidently, even though the bookstore had announced that Stephen Marx would be reading from his latest novel. This was an unfinished section he'd removed from an earlier manuscript, when he had concluded that explicit sexual scenes had no place in it. But he had retained it as bait.

This was the point when he always stopped, to suddenly sweep the audience with his eyes. Within seconds, he could locate the women to whom he had become Achilles Luftig.

She sat in the second row, left aisle, face cupped in both hands, elbows propped on her knees. She seemed quite tall, but he couldn't really tell by the way she was hunched. Nor could he tell about her legs: they were partly hidden by the other people and besides she wore pants. Of course, he had no way of knowing that they were freshly shaven, creamed, and bare or that she dispensed frequently with underwear and that this particular reading at Shakespeare & Co. on Broadway, within walking distance of his writing studio, was one such occasion.

Suddenly, she stood towering in front of him, with three of his novels in hand. Like an experienced booksigning aficionado, she held open the title page so that he could sign "St. Marx" with minimal delay. He didn't know why he'd used "St." rather than just his initial or "Stephen."

"Write 'To Felicity,'" she murmured.

After repeating the process three times and handing over the third volume, he remarked, "You seem to be quite a reader."

"Yes," she replied. "It's probably the best way to learn how to write. By the way, my real name is not Felicity."

"So why use it?" Marx had acquired the knack of speaking in staccato phrases to his admirers without holding up a booksigning line.

"I'm a believer in felicity."

"What kind?"

"Every kind: from financial to sexual."

"So you write fiction?" He was signing the next person's proffered volume while still maintaining a conversation with his triple book purchaser, whose name apparently was not Felicity.

"Here you are," he said to the elderly lady whose title page he'd just inscribed with "Stephen Marx" and looked up at Felicity. Only then did he notice that her eyes were more than passable. They were quite remarkable in the manner in which they managed to display a multiplicity of emotions: amusement, challenge, interest, even seduction.

"Not yet," she said.

Marx was momentarily confused. "Not yet" could have been her answer to the unspoken question that had just formed in the back of his mind, but she couldn't be a mind reader. "Why not?" he asked.

"I'm not yet ready."

Marx stopped signing. This time, he stared at her. "Why not?"

"You shouldn't keep your fans waiting." She pointed to the line by her side. "I can wait until you're finished."

"So you're not an admirer?" He thought it safest to stick to banter.

"I can wait," she repeated. "I've been one for some time."

"How about coffee and cheesecake?" he asked, while he finished signing the pile the bookstore had stacked in front of him. He was always glad to oblige, knowing such signed copies could not be returned as unsold copies to the publisher. "I need some lubrication," he added.

"I don't, but I'll keep you company."

There was something about their conversation that had kept him off balance. Every answer of hers was short and to the point, yet full of double meaning.

Even when Marx rose from his chair, he still had to look up at this gorgeous basketball player type. But Felicity Samarand was not a player, she was only extraordinarily tall—at least six inches taller than he. "Why aren't you ready yet to write?" he asked as soon as they had settled down with their cups of coffee.

"I mean fiction, like you." She pointed a doubly ringed index finger at him as if it were a silver-plated revolver. "But I write film scripts," she continued.

"What kind?" Marx asked, relieved and also curious. None of his novels had ever been made into a film. Some unexercised options were the sum total of his movie industry connection.

"Porno films. That's why I was so interested in your reading. Do you fantasize when you write such scenes? Do you turn into Achilles Luftig?" She didn't even give him a chance to answer. "But you must. I do it all the time. Incidentally, Achilles is quite a name. I also like the combination 'Achilles and Felicity.' It could work in my latest fantasy."

"Which is?" Marx felt his throat becoming dry.

"'To His Coy Mistress.'" She looked at him expectantly, as if awaiting a question.

Marx was irritated. Literary upstaging was an activity he never tolerated in others.

His silence unnerved her, and she hurried on. "I'm working from the line, 'The grave's a fine and private place, / but none, I think, do there embrace.' I want a scene at a cemetery. Have you ever made love in a cemetery?"

Marx had been asked a lot of questions by women—erotic, lascivious, even dirty ones—and he had posed his share. But never one about sex in a cemetery.

"Ah, the pleasures of blasphemy," he laughed, a touch self-consciously, but relieved the conversation was back on track. "Regrettably the answer is no. And you?"

"No, not yet. But remember how Marvell put it? 'Now let us sport us while we may'—"

"'And now, like amorous birds of prey, / Rather at once our time devour,'" he finished the lines in metered rhythm, thanking his Yale literature instructor who had made the students learn some of the Metaphysical Poets by heart.

Within forty minutes, Marx had made love to the tallest woman he had ever met, upright, her back against the stone figure of an angel. Felicity had drawn the line lying supine on a stone slab of a nearby tomb.

Later that night, Felicity, naked after their second coupling—this time on the couch—wandered around his study, examining the working environment of the famous author. Pointing to the Olivetti, she asked: "Is this how you write your books?"

"I did," confessed Marx, "but then I made my Bolivian Jump." He had never used the expression before. Felicity's response was about what one might expect.

"Bolivian Jump? What on earth is that?"

"Oh, you know," improvised Stephen, "like the Bolivian peasant. He went directly from the burro to the airplane without any transition. The same with me. The first nine books were written on this Olivetti, the rest on my word processor." He turned and slid open the closet door. Within, on a small wheeled table, was a computer.

"One day a writer-friend of mine convinced me that the only way to write books was to use a word processor. I just laughed, but he persuaded me to come up to his place and watch him correct a draft. I was so impressed that the following day I bought myself a PC and took a crash course in word processing. I keep the Olivetti for addressing envelopes."

Marx thought that Felicity would be impressed, but she wasn't. He had forgotten that she was of the modern generation, brought up during and after the computer revolution. Typewriters, manual or electric, were an anachronism, Marx realized, and changed the subject; he wanted to become Felicity's contemporary in bed, not a museum piece in her head.

But for once, the decision was not up to him. When he asked for her address, she smiled down on him from her Olympian height and shook her head.

"Achilles and Felicity—maybe. But not Marx and Samarand."

It was the first time Marx could ever recall someone else using him for research.

4

Monday's mail contained a beautifully embossed envelope with a return address that momentarily didn't ring a bell. Marx liked to guess about the contents of letters and the correspondents before opening an envelope. Over the years he'd received a fair amount of fan mail; it was like looking at candy before unwrapping and biting into it. To his surprise he found that the letter was from Ambrose McPhearson.

"Dear Stephen," the letter began.

> I know a quiet corner where we can talk undisturbed in the civilized surroundings you are accustomed to. Meet me on

Wednesday at the Pierpont Morgan Library, at eleven A.M., upstairs, i.e., up the marble stairs beyond the drawings gallery, past
the bookstore, in Morgan's study. You will find me in one of the
red plush armchairs along the west wall, admiring my favorite
painting in that room: The Virgin and two female saints adoring
the Christ child, by Perugino, the Umbrian master who was
Raphael's teacher (ca. 1450–1523). The picture seems to me appropriate for the occasion, due to the particular iconography of
this work: the Virgin and two saints kneel in adoration of the
Christ child, who is shown lying on an expanse of drapery,
asleep, or is he? Any Florentine or Umbrian of this period would
have recognized that the child's pallor and motionless pose refer
to his future death on the cross, a symbolic allusion that was not
uncommon in the fifteenth and early sixteenth centuries.

I shall expect to see you in the other of the two red velvet
plush chairs, and perhaps we'll even have time to study the
Swiss stained-glass panels in the window above and behind us,
as long as I get to my lunch date at the Algonquin punctually. . . .

Stephen Marx was flabbergasted. Was there a hidden message
in that letter: the "dear Stephen" rather than "dear Saint"; the
scholarly, formal, and almost dainty manner in which the setting
for their meeting was described. It seemed to him that this was
the type of note Berenson might have written half a century ago
while scheduling an appointment with Lord Duveen. Hadn't
Duveen been one of Morgan's art dealers? Is he trying to say in
this letter that one is not dealing with a banker? Marx could
hardly wait for next Wednesday.

Stephen entered the marble Renaissance-style palace on East
36th Street and, without stopping in the entrance hall to examine the illuminated manuscripts in their glass cases, followed his
friend's directions to the second floor. He had no difficulty in locating Morgan's study. For a moment he stood at the open door.
The two red upholstered armchairs were unoccupied; indeed, no
one was in the room. Stephen was about to enter when a guard
stopped him.

"Sorry, sir, the public is not permitted to enter. You've got to
look at the room from here."

Stephen flushed. "I don't understand. I've an appointment for eleven o'clock," he looked at his watch. "My friend specifically told me to meet him in this room," he pointed to the two chairs beyond Morgan's leather-inlaid desk in the middle of the room. "In those chairs."

The guard looked faintly condescending. "Sorry, sir, you'll have to wait here."

At that moment a hand clapped him on the shoulder. "Saint, welcome to one of my favorite spots in New York. I like your punctuality." He nodded at the guard, who had suddenly turned ingratiating. "Good morning, Malcolm; this is Mr. Marx." His hand still on Marx's shoulder, he steered him into the room.

Marx's surprise was evident. "I'm not 'the public' at the Morgan," McPhearson explained. "I happen to be one of the trustees. Come, let me show you why I like this room so much. Look at the two Memlings there. That's the Perugino I mentioned. And these," he said as they neared the far wall. "Miniature portraits of Martin Luther and his wife. Cranach. Exquisite, aren't they?"

Marx had already fixed his eyes above the Cranachs, where a large portrait hung. It showed an imposing man in red academic robe. McPhearson caught his look and laughed. "It's difficult to concentrate on the jewels in this room when the Morgans inspect you. It takes some getting used to. This here," he pointed to the red-robed man, "is J. P.—Pierpont's son. I've never met him—he died some forty years ago—but I've gotten to like him. We have our trustees meetings in this room and I always pick a seat on this sofa," he gestured to the red velvet settee across from them, "so that I can look at J. P. when things get dull."

McPhearson showed Marx toward their seats. "Know what I've noticed? If you look at the pictures around this room, you'll find not one smiling face. Now look at J. P. After a while, you actually notice an incipient twinkle."

Marx started to regain his composure. "What on earth are we doing here, Boz? And why did you send me that odd note? You could have phoned."

"Why here?" McPhearson shrugged. "I don't know. I like it."
His face took on an introspective frown. "And maybe because of
the way you overdid it at Rocco's."

Marx started to protest. McPhearson cut him off. "Come on,
Saint. You wanted something from me and you were quite open
in telling me what it was. You hardly spoke about anything else.
But have you any idea of the effect you had as you droned on
about your preoccupation with other people's opinion of you—
actually not just *your* preoccupation but other writers', actors',
scientists', and whoever else you put into your exalted club of
creative types? You made it quite clear that you relegated me to
quite another camp. People like me aren't entitled to such
foibles; we simply haven't earned them. Presumably because our
lives deal only with 'earnings.' I still remember the rather dis-
paraging way in which you told me how easy it is to evaluate
successful bankers—"

"Now wait a moment, Boz." Marx was starting to get angry.
"You've got me wrong."

"No, Saint, I haven't," interrupted McPhearson, "and even if I
had, I wanted to tell you how I perceived your comments, not
how you meant them. I thought a small lesson was in order."

"And what lesson is all this—" Marx waved a hand in the
air— "supposed to teach me?"

McPhearson sat back and looked moodily up at the red-robed
Morgans. To Marx they seemed to be conferring; he saw not a
trace of a twinkle in either face.

"Saint," he said finally. "We're all human, even bankers. And
I believe we serve a useful, sometimes even a creative, function.
Furthermore, I'm not just a banker, even though in all the times
we've met, you've never gone to the trouble of noticing it. There
are times when I'm also interested in the opinions of others. So
maybe I wanted to give you a hint of another part of me—one
you've never noticed. You didn't even catch it at Rocco's when
you asked me about Hemingway. But that's enough—I won't rub
it in. I know you didn't come here to listen to me. You came to
convince me to help you with your crazy scheme. All right, convince me."

Stephen Marx took a deep breath. This was not how he'd envisaged the beginning of their rendezvous. Before he could start with his speech, McPhearson interrupted once more.

"Saint, do you remember how you greeted me at our last meeting? Whether I knew that Hemingway had read his own obituary?"

Marx became impatient. He wanted to get to the point, not indulge in literary chitchat with a banker. "Yes, all right. You know Hemingway. I'm sorry. I wasn't trying to lecture you or anything. I—"

"Look, you con man, make a living out of your death."

Marx flushed. "'Con man'? That isn't fair."

"Hemingway," McPhearson said quietly. "*A Movable Feast*."

"Oh?" Marx said, feeling deflated. "I guess I haven't read much Hemingway recently." For a long moment, the two men fell silent underneath the gaze of Morgan; the figures in the Cranachs and the Memlings and the Perugino stared off in other directions, abstracted with business of their own. "Ambrose," Marx said finally. "Please listen." His voice had dropped as if he wanted to keep their conversation from the Morgans towering above them on the walls. "I haven't got much time."

McPhearson looked at him for what seemed a very long time. "All right, Saint," he said at last.

Marx inhaled audibly, as if he had been unable to breathe for some time. And with a sense of a long constraint at last lifted, he launched into the cherished details of his plans.

"It's the beginning of November," he began. "The sailing season is over by the end of the month. Now is the ideal time: the water is so cold, a man without a life jacket is unlikely to survive beyond half an hour. Furthermore, it gets dark before six. I'll sail from Mamaroneck at two in the afternoon and tell the dockmaster I'll be back before it gets dark."

McPhearson had looked steadily at his friend without a change in expression. Now he said in a quiet voice, "You've already told me all this in the restaurant. Why go over it again?"

Marx had an answer ready. From his jacket pocket he produced a square of paper and unfolded it on his knee. It was a section of a marine chart, marked over with bearing lines that intersected at a point out in the Sound. "I just told you the general outlines then. There's much more to go over." His voice speeded up. "You leave the Larchmont harbor at two. We meet out in the open water—here—" his hand stabbed the intersection of the bearing lines— "and if there is nobody in sight, I board your boat and off we go."

Marx was off. Caught up in the details of his plan, his face had assumed an expression of almost blissful excitement. McPhearson, wary at first, his face still wearing its own much less blissful expression, paid close attention nonetheless.

"The dockmaster will probably wait until 6:30 before notifying the Coast Guard, by which time it will be dark. The Coast Guard will do nothing for the first couple of hours, other than to log the report. The report usually goes to the Coast Guard Station at Fort Totten, on the other end of Throg's Neck Bridge. If a Coast Guard boat is already on patrol, they'll radio them to look out for the lost sailboat, but that late in November it's not very likely that a patrol will be out. All they'll do is issue a 'precom,'"

Marx waited for McPhearson to ask for an explanation, and felt a little inward pleasure when his friend's expression clouded.

"A 'precom,'" he explained, "is a pre-search communication check—they'll radio various harbors around Mamaroneck to see whether anyone has seen a sailboat of a particular description. I would guess that if the 'precom' is negative, the Coast Guard will notify the Rescue Coordination Center at Governor's Island within a couple of hours."

"What happens then?" McPhearson was no longer trying to conceal his interest.

"First, they'll consider the tides and wind conditions during the past few hours and plot the likely general location of the sailboat. Then, they'll send out search boats . . ."

"At night?" interrupted McPhearson.

"You're damn right, at night," replied Marx. "They can't possibly wait until the following morning—the survival time in the water is much too short in November. Actually, they'll launch at least one helicopter from the Brooklyn Coast Guard helicopter station. You should see the lights they have! Even in pitch darkness, they can illuminate large areas of water. Still, looking for a body in water is much more difficult than on land. There are no convenient reference points in the water, so frequently they end up overlooking large areas of water that they thought had been searched."

"Isn't it pretty hopeless to find somebody after several hours in such cold water?" asked McPhearson.

"Alive? Of course. But the Coast Guard would search for a body for at least a couple of days before assuming that the person is dead. Incidentally, that's just a Coast Guard assumption, so as to justify termination of the search. If the body is not found, the legal presumption of death takes seven years, I believe."

"You mean you haven't researched that point?" The mocking tone in McPhearson's question was clear, but Marx ignored it.

"Why should I? I'll only be dead for a couple of months. That is, if you'll help me."

Sabine Diehlsdorf was not secretive; "private" would be a better description. She always had been. Even as a teenager she'd never confided in her peers about her boyfriends, and as an adult she had continued to be reticent about the men in her life. Not that there was an excessive number of them. At least by contemporary American standards, Sabine was not an early bloomer.

The daughter of a conservative, Pennsylvania-German rural family, Sabine had left Gettysburg College at the usual age, with Columbia University's School of Journalism her destination, determined to become a sophisticated graduate student. The decision had marked the most important turning point in her life.

But as she considered the conversation she had overheard at Rocco's, Sabine wondered if another such turning point might be at hand. She realized that if this man "Saint" really decided to pull off his crazy stunt, she would be sitting on a journalistic scoop that could have a significant impact on her career. But who was "Saint"? Sabine had always been an avid reader, but in New York she had stopped reading fiction; all of her reading was now predicated on professional advancement, and fiction had not seemed to figure in that process. Typically, she told herself, the only clue she had caught had been the name of one of the book reviewers, Noah Berg, a name she knew because she saw it in the newspapers. But the newspapers, she realized, would give her the other information she needed. It only was left for her to watch the papers for an obituary fitting the man's scenario.

Three weeks had passed, and Sabine had noticed nothing in her local newspaper staple: the *Times,* the *Village Voice,* or the *Post.* Sabine had just returned from a long weekend to her parents' home in Pennsylvania. A pile of unread newspapers met her in front of the apartment door. She had neglected to inform the super not to deliver them.

Sabine carried the papers directly to the recycling bin. As she stacked the newspapers carefully, she scanned the front pages of each edition, moving with a practiced eye from the upper right-hand column to the central photographs, and finally to the local human interest story at the bottom of the page. She turned and picked up the last paper. It was the Saturday *Times.* In the lower left-hand corner, a small photograph caught her attention immediately. It was "Saint." The headline read "Novelist Stephen Marx Lost at Sea." The subhead: "Presumed Dead."

Sabine rushed back to her apartment with the entire pile of papers. The Sunday *Times* had only a brief follow-up on the first report. The Monday edition of the *New York Times* carried his full obituary, including the titles of his thirteen novels.

At the Doubleday Bookstore three blocks over, the cashier was punching keys at a terminal.

"I'm looking for some of Stephen Marx's novels," Sabine told him.

"Hardcover or paperback?"

"Paper, if you have them." She had been too long a student to consider another choice.

"Downstairs," said the clerk. "If there's any left. Drowning hasn't exactly hurt his sales."

Sabine flew down the stairs, scanning past rows of names she vaguely remembered from college English classes. All she could find were three copies of *Cohen's Dilemma* and one hardcover of *Gasps of Delight*. The *Cohen's Dilemma* paperbacks showed no photograph; but *Gasps of Delight* had a younger Marx in a sailboat grinning at the photographer. As she walked home she studied her purchases. The cover on *Cohen's Dilemma* didn't tell her much. Who was Cohen? What was his dilemma? She had learned a thing or two about titles in journalism school, and she recognized the technique here: a teaser, like a headline, it was supposed to make her pick up the book and look inside for the answer. A bit derivative, though: *Portnoy's Complaint, Humboldt's Gift*—was he copying Roth and Bellow? Sabine opened the book to the first page.

Distinguished scientists should bear distinctive names. But this is not how it always happens. Sure, some Nobel Prize winners are called Lwoff, Dulbecco, or Benacerraf, but there are also Browns and Smiths. The trick is to convert a Brown or Smith into *the* Brown or Smith.

Cohen is another common name in scientific fields. However, Professor I. Cohen, chairman of the department of cell biology in one of the top midwestern medical schools, had arrived at that pinnacle of recognition where a simple "I."—the ultimate understatement—made him *the* Cohen. To cognoscenti he was "I.C."

A scientist, she mused. What does Marx know about them?

The title, *Gasps of Delight*, seemed oddly different; she would have guessed it to be some silly romance or even an X-rated story. Somehow it did not ring true; it certainly did not seem to be the title of a book written by a man. A quick scan of a few pages showed Sabine the trick—the title was meant to be provocative, almost a challenge: "I know it's a pulpy title, but I'll fool you." Later, when Sabine searched the libraries for reviews, she learned that almost every critic had taken the bait and had remarked on the peculiar—indeed trashy—title.

There was nothing sexual about that book unless infatuation with inanimate objects—paintings, sculpture—were sexual. The explanation for the title was in the epigraph, taken from a catalog to a Paul Klee exhibition.

> The size of Klee's works almost requires intimate space, and intimate space immediately leads to intimacy of another nature: close inspection of the work, attention to detail, and the ultimate punctuation mark, the gasp of delight.

The gasps of delight were those of an art dealer, the main character of the novel. When he discovered works he wanted to possess his pleasure was so audible that once, as he held a small watercolor in his hands, his companion had compared his cries to her own on a somewhat different occasion. "Serge, as a dealer, you've got to be more subtle."

Sabine was a good researcher. Two years ago, she had won a summer internship at *Sports Illustrated*. *S.I.* prided itself on its fact checking; the discipline had quickly become second nature to Sabine. Toward the end of her internship, when she had learned she could continue at *S.I.* as a part-time researcher while attending Columbia's School of Journalism, she had written a long and proud letter to her former English professor at Gettysburg College.

> My duties include any footwork required by writers, an occasional interview which I transcribe and give to the writer, and miscellaneous very minor writing tasks handed to me by the writer or editor. What particularly impressed me was that I, the researcher/reporter, rather than the writer, was ultimately responsible for the accuracy of any story that is assigned to me for

"checking." Here is an example of what I had to do recently, when the editor gave me the following paragraph prepared by one of the writers:

> "With no trade apparently in the works, Stabler ended his one-week holdout on July 19, at the curfew hour of 11 p.m., when he drove his $53,000 Porsche 928 into the parking lot of the El Rancho Tropicana Motel in Santa Rosa. He had bought the car the night before."

In a paragraph like this, pretty typical, I was required to verify, with what is called a "red check," the fact that no trade was apparent on July 19, that it was indeed July 19 when Stabler ended his holdout from his contract, that the holdout had lasted one week, that it was at 11:00 p.m. exactly when he actually drove into the parking lot of exactly that motel, spelling verified. The car had to be verified as a Porsche, as a 928, as having cost $53,000, and as having been bought the night before. Most of this kind of verification has to be done on the telephone—*S.I.* is a weekly with insufficient time to be waiting for the mail. As you can appreciate, with the exception of spellings, little of this sort of thing is to be found in books.

In addition to accuracy of fact, I frequently also deal with accuracy of tone. For instance, if the writer describes an athlete as having had "the best game of his career," I check the player's statistics or his coach's evaluation; if these do not concur, I would point this out to the editor (not the writer, who for all practical purposes is supposed to be faceless to the reporter) and would alter the sentence to something like "Smith played effectively." A more subtle example would be "Smith smashed the world mile record." If he only broke it by 1/100th of a second, "smashed" would be inappropriate and I would be expected to catch this nuance and change the word accordingly.

Sports Illustrated considers itself a news weekly, and hence likes to get scoops. Some of the work by reporters is done in secrecy—getting the information without disclosing the ultimate purpose. When a reporter comes up with something really interesting or scandalous, he is sometimes credited in the story. This does not happen very often and, so far, it has not happened to me.

Sabine decided to deal with Stephen Marx as if she were working on a scoop for *S.I.* She knew there was no purpose in trying to write at this early stage. Would anyone believe her? She would have to wait until his reappearance hit the newspapers. Then she would deliver her coup.

The first item she looked up the following morning at the *S.I.* library was Stephen Marx's entry in *Who's Who*:

MARX, STEPHEN JACOB, author; b. N.Y.C., Mar. 20, 1937; s. Harold J. and Anna (Stolz) M.; m. Miriam I. Kaplan, May 18, 1967; B.A. Yale U., 1959; Author: *The Academy of Spite*, 1962, *Oxen of the Sun*, 1964, *Flying from Rio*, 1968, *Mourning Hours*, 1970, *The Bestial Floor*, 1973, *The Mind's Eye* (National Book Award nominee), 1974, *Our Lady of Walsingham*, 1977, *Trials of Meyer*, 1978, *Listen, Sister* (National Book Award), 1980, *A Youth's Companion*, 1983, *Iron Rations*, 1984, *Gasps of Delight* (Pulitzer Prize), 1985, *Cohen's Dilemma*, 1988. Lectureships: Hunter College, 1973; Bard College, 1975; NYU, 1977; U. of Iowa, 1978; SUNY-Stony Brook, 1983. Office: c/o Hunter and Marvel, Inc., 6 West 43rd Street, New York, NY 10036.

She searched for reviews of his last two books, *Cohen's Dilemma* and *Gasps of Delight*, looking through the *Times*, the *New York Review of Books*, and *Book Review Digest*, and then followed the trail through reviews of everything Marx had written over a quarter of a century. The reviews confirmed what *Who's Who* had suggested: Marx was clearly no hack, although she found it odd that after reading all these reviews she still had no clear sense of Marx's overall standing in the pantheon of contemporary American fiction.

Sabine estimated that she had at least two months to do her preparatory work before Marx's return—an event that would likely attract far more attention than his disappearance. She wondered how he would explain himself, what alibi he would use. Judging from what she'd overheard, he would probably come up with something more original than "temporary amnesia." With any luck, whatever story he concocted would add fuel to the journalistic feeding frenzy his return was likely to engender. Demolishing that story would be the final movement of the comprehensive feature piece she was already outlining in her mind. She would have no trouble selling it; every newspaper in the country would want to run it. And after that? Magazines, maybe even a book.

It would be the making of her career.

6

In the weeks after her husband's sailing accident, Miriam Marx drowned herself in work. It was the only way to suppress the memory of that devastating moment shortly before midnight, when her cab had pulled up at the apartment house, on her return from a hugely successful and exhausting catered affair. She had been reflecting contentedly that she was well on the way to financial independence, that soon she might be able to cut back on her hours and get started on her cookbook project. Aside from some scribbled notes on file cards, she hadn't gotten much beyond the title. The moment she stepped from the taxi, she could tell from the doorman's demeanor that something had happened. A reporter waiting under the canopy was the first to break the news.

To Miriam's surprise, the worst of it passed quickly. She wondered about this: Was it the absence of any personal guilt? That Steve was not yet legally deceased—just missing—meant that she was spared the usual traumatic confrontations with lawyers, accountants, and other scavengers of death. Steve's agent, Victor Sedgwick, had been the only one of that guild to call.

"For the time being, you'll have to do nothing," he'd assured her after expressing his condolences, "except for depositing the royalty checks."

She had found the comment in poor taste, and not only because of its essential crassness. Depositing royalty checks, like paying the bills, had been part of the "family crap" she and Steve had argued over. But it was more than that, as well. It was that "for the time being." For the first time she'd started to wonder how long she would be forced to remain in the legal limbo between husbandless wife and widow.

If Miriam had needed any evidence of her husband's literary prominence, the avalanche of condolences descending on her would have provided it. They came in every form: handwritten messages on heavy card stock purchased at Tiffany's, computer-printed letters with their telltale signature of justified right margins, terse telegrams, movingly misspelled notes from readers addressed to her via Marx's publisher, even faxes. To Miriam, this most modern form of communication seemed least suited to expressions of sorrow. Such ostentatious speed was inconsistent with expressions of deep emotion, be they of love or mourning.

Strangers did not find it easy to reach Miriam during the initial weeks following her husband's disappearance. At home, they got her answering machine, even if she was standing next to it. She only picked up the phone when she was certain she wanted to speak to the caller. Weekdays, including Saturdays, she spent in her SoHo office, where Thomasina Rushforth, Miriam's general office factotum and confidante, protected her privacy. Behind that impenetrable buffer, Miriam opened letters and dispensed polite, printed cards of acknowledgment, mechanically separating the correspondents into the large group of anonymous fans and professional acquaintances and the somewhat smaller group of persons Miriam had never met personally but whose names were supposed to be known to her. To this latter group she sent the same card, appending some handwritten variation on "thank you." This process continued smoothly, until one day a letter reached her bearing a name she recognized, although she had never met the sender. The name was Noah Berg.

Berg's letter was well composed, written by hand, and of just the right length. It ended with a few maudlin literary allusions, most of which passed by her undetected. Since the letter required no response other than the printed acknowledgment card, Berg's name should have vanished quickly.

And would have, but that a few days later, he reappeared—this time on her home answering machine. Could he meet her personally? He wanted to discuss the possibility of a major critical piece on Stephen Marx, if she did not consider it premature. The voice was deep and resonant, the message brief but not presumptuous. Miriam jotted down his telephone number, intending to have Thomasina return the call from the office. As happened more than once during that period, the slip was misplaced, Berg's taped message erased by another, and his name lost from Miriam's memory.

But Berg persisted. Three days later, another message, still courteous, though now framed by a thin border of irritation, repeated the contents of the first. Miriam, intrinsically polite and hence embarrassed, returned the call and found herself unable to refuse the requested meeting.

"How will I recognize you?" she asked.

"You won't. I am a Woody Allen type: quite nondescript, with horn-rims and freckles. But it doesn't matter. You were pointed out to me once at an award dinner. I'll recognize you."

Miriam thought she knew the dinner he meant. It had been at the Plaza, Steve getting the National Book Award for *Listen, Sister*. Their first brush with real celebrity—and the last novel to which she had contributed. Steve had been balked in his usual research—as always, he had chosen a subject about which he knew nothing at the start, seemingly everything at the end. But in this case, he had needed her help. She still remembered how they'd made love on the living room carpet after she'd returned from her triumphantly successful research visit to the Carmelite monastery in Brooklyn, a visit that the male author Stephen Marx had failed to consummate. And how loftily ecstatic Steve had been with the completed novel: a modern nun's tale without any sex in all 323 riveting pages. It had deserved the award, she thought. Even the critics had agreed on that.

Noah Berg was not just a book reviewer. He considered himself a serious critic—but most people would have concurred with him in that. More important, he considered himself a *pure* critic.

Pure in Berg's vocabulary meant that he was not a part-timer, or, even worse, a disappointed poet, novelist or other writer manqué. Berg was a dedicated professional. His daily bread came from his position as assistant book review editor at arguably the most powerful paper in the country. But his name could also be found frequently in the bylines of prestigious literary publications, both large and small, on both sides of the Atlantic: from the *New Yorker* or the *New York Review of Books* to the *Hudson Review*— and from the *TLS* to *Paragraph*.

Berg had majored in English at Kenyon College, where he had served as student apprentice at the *Kenyon Review*. Immediately after graduation, he landed a job with the *Plain Dealer* in Cleveland—one of the few midwestern dailies to take book reviewing seriously. During the interview, the book review editor had boasted to Berg about the paper's weekly coverage of at least two dozen books. "But we get at least three hundred during that period," she announced triumphantly, "and it will be your job to come up with a first cut—say eighty of them—that we'll consider more seriously." That's where Berg acquired his skimming habits, which stood him in such good stead during his slow but confident climb in the world of reviewing, first in Cleveland, then in New York. He always left the publisher's costume jewelry for last: the book jacket with the author's biography and blurbs. He started with the first sentence. If that held his attention he'd continue to the end of the paragraph. If that was persuasive he'd go to the end of the page, but never beyond. He'd then flip the pages quickly, glancing at sentences or even just verbal mannerisms (too many "fucks," "shits," or "ain'ts" were automatic disqualifiers), checking whether most of the fiction was dialogue, seeing whether he could find even one clever metaphor in such a lectorial roulette. By the early afternoon he'd shaved the day's book mountain down to a hill. That hill's compost he would examine in more detail, including the jacket material, to generate some written commentary to the shortlist he'd send upstairs to aid in the further reduction to a literary hillock, which would then be divided among various reviewers.

As time passed, Noah Berg made a name for himself as a reviewer, acquiring a byline, and even a reputation in literary circles as a critic of some taste and discernment. But even as his reputation grew, his personal anonymity increased—by design.

In New York, he was careful to get to know as few writers as possible face-to-face. He didn't frequent the usual writer's hangouts, he didn't go to readings (he knew how effectively a good reading could mask lousy writing), he didn't accept invitations to publisher's parties. He wanted above all else to be a professional: to keep personalities out of his work, to keep the lines between the work and the individual behind it—writer and critic—clear.

Yet Berg was far from a hermit. It was just that very few writers ever entered his social circle and when the odd exception was admitted Berg would no longer review that author's books. All of which may go to explain why he could remember so clearly the awards dinner where Miriam Marx had been pointed out to him. It was not the kind of place where one expected to find Noah Berg. He had been making an exception to be there at all.

For Monica Sobremonte, Berg was prepared to consider making exceptions.

Ever since her teenage days, Monica had idolized writers. She had interpreted her relationship with the critic Noah Berg as her first approach to the creative core of writing, but to her disappointment it did not involve the glamorous, personal access— the literary salons she had fantasized about for years. Berg, of course, had explained the reasons—but couldn't he make one exception: "Please, just one?"

"Of course," he had replied, "just name it," and promptly found himself playing Herod Antipas to his Salome.

"I'd do anything for going to the Plaza and being there when they announce this year's winners. Meeting the numero uno of fiction."

When Berg had pointed out Stephen Marx as the evening's likely winner in the fiction category, without further ado Monica had broken through the author's admiring circle to gush her own admiration. It was too crowded and too noisy for Marx to catch her name, but his roving eye had gotten stuck in the cleavage between her breasts. Do they really stand out like that by themselves? he had wondered. Before that question even had time to mature into fantasy, she was separated from him by other devotees. But later, seeing her head for the bar, Marx had followed. In the crush at the bar, Marx's hand inadvertently touched Monica's buttocks, or more precisely, the cleft between them. He had told himself it was inadvertent, but Marx's hand knew what his head had tried to repress. Monica turned slowly—as if she was savoring the tactile foray—and looked him straight in the eye. Stephen, who didn't blush often, turned red. All he could mumble was an apology.

Berg heard none of this when Monica came to him with a fresh drink in her hand. "You don't know Stephen Marx personally?" she asked. Berg started to explain yet again his policy regarding socializing with writers, but Monica's thoughts were elsewhere. "I wonder what his wife's like?" she mused. "Is that her? The chubby brunette over there, who can't stop smiling at him?"

"Chubby?" echoed Berg, following her look. "I'd call her zaftig."

Hours later, when Miriam and Stephen Marx finally left the party, they encountered pouring rain, with not a cab to be had. As they debated alternatives, Monica Sobremonte appeared. "Would you people like a ride? They're bringing my car from the garage." The Marxes accepted gratefully; as they waited for the car, Miriam turned to Monica. "I'm Miriam Marx. I'm sorry I didn't catch your name."

Stephen paid attention as she said, "I'm Monica Sobremonte. You must've been very proud this evening."

While Miriam got ready for bed, Stephen looked in the phone book. He was in luck; there was an M. Sobremonte, 121 E. 61. Two days later Stephen reached Monica on the telephone: "This is Stephen Marx. You're probably surprised to hear from me. . . ."

"No," said the cool voice on the other end, "I'm not."

He never asked Monica about other men; initially, at least, she didn't mention any. Some weeks later, at a reading at the 92nd Street Y, Marx bumped into a poet friend.

"I just ran into Noah Berg," the poet said. He spoke with the lively interest good gossip always engenders. "He looks terrible. Some married man apparently walked off with his woman, and she refuses to tell who it is. I've never seen him like that," the poet said wonderingly. "Ordinarily, he's such a gentle guy."

Before the month had ended Berg had found out. And shortly thereafter Marx found out. Berg's voice on the phone was barely recognizable; the elegant critic's phrases reduced to an avalanche of obscenities. As usual in such discourse, Marx never got a chance to reply. Berg just screamed: "I'll screw you, Marx, thoroughly and indelibly!"

Indelibly? Can one screw indelibly? thought Marx. And even while Berg slammed the phone in his ear he told himself yes. Monica could.

That evening Marx composed a letter. It was brief and to the point: he wanted to answer Berg's charges.

It was one of the first letters Marx had written switching from his typewriter to the word processor. Of course, he hadn't kept a copy. It was hardly a document for his files, temporary or permanent.

Miriam arrived early for her meeting with Berg. Of the few customers in the Whitney's cafe only one was a single man: in blue jeans, not a day older than twenty-five, without glasses, wearing running shoes (one of them ostentatiously untied). Except for the rumpled jacket, he bore no resemblance to Woody Allen. The man looked up at her uncuriously as she passed, and gave no sign of recognition. Miriam ordered coffee and then removed some sheets from her attaché case. The museum had inspired her with some ideas about arranging crudités for an upcoming event—something in an abstract Kandinsky pattern. She was busily jotting notes and sketches, when she sensed she was being observed. Looking up, she saw a man approaching. He was of a medium height, dressed all in black except for an understatedly elegant, cream-colored, extra-long overcoat draped over his shoulders in the Italian manner. He wore an ascot, but no glasses; his hair was well combed and dusted with gray. This cannot be Noah Berg, she thought, there is nothing of rumply Woody Allen in this creaselessly groomed man except for the owlish eyes. Just as she noticed the freckles on his face, the man stopped.

"Miriam Marx?" He reached into his breast pocket to produce a pair of black, horn-rimmed glasses. "I am Noah Berg."

7

"You don't look like Woody Allen."

"I didn't say I *looked* like Woody Allen." Berg carefully draped his coat over the back of an empty chair before sitting down. He hitched his trousers and fussily adjusted the crease. "I just have a Woody Allen face: nothing very distinctive." He took off his glasses. "Try describing me," he challenged her.

Miriam passed the offer. "I'm not very good at verbal descriptions." Seeing his skeptical look, she hastened on. "Really. Not like Stephen. It was one of his strengths—the way he described facial expressions or distinctive features. He'd take one glance and say 'you have rogue's eyes.'"

"Thanks for the compliment," said Berg, replacing his glasses.

"I didn't mean *you*—just some person." Now what made me pick that expression? she wondered. And then she remembered how he'd used it as a one-word epithet: rogue'seye Norman. Even Miriam didn't know that it was one of Steve's Joycean mannerisms. "*Your* eyes are . . ." she searched for the right word. "Big, I would say, sort of owl-like. Like Woody Allen's." They both broke out laughing.

"But I don't recollect seeing you that night at the Plaza. Even with your Woody Allen face. I'm sure I would have noticed you."

"Oh?"

"For one thing: you dress well."

"So I do," he nodded. "It's one of my obsessions. That and writing. I mean reviews and criticism. Nothing wildly original— like your late husband's prose."

Late husband, Miriam thought. I'll have to get accustomed to that phrase. "So why did you want to meet me? To get my permission to write about my 'late husband'?" She tried, only half successfully, to mimic his intonation.

Instead of answering, Berg pushed back his chair. "I'll get some coffee. May I bring you a refill?"

"Not your permission," he said, after he'd returned with the coffee and settled himself with the same careful attention to his pant creases she'd noticed before. He'd answered as if a couple of seconds rather than minutes had elapsed since her question. "That is not yours to bestow."

Miriam was struck by the preciousness of that last word. Somehow, it seemed in character with his general finickiness.

"I don't require anyone's permission for what I have in mind. What I am requesting is your cooperation."

She waited for more, but Berg was suddenly preoccupied with stirring his coffee.

"Cooperation with what?" She sounded wary.

"I've decided on a reflective piece dealing with your late husband's—"

"Please don't call him that," she said.

Berg looked startled. "But he *is* dead."

"I know." Miriam felt silly about the interruption. "I mean it makes me feel so 'widowy,' and frankly," her voice turned firm, "I just don't feel like a widow."

"Acknowledged and understood," Berg said. "The word 'late' will not again cross my lips." He set the spoon down as though it had been instrumental in this exchange and looked at her again. "I want to write about Stephen Marx's writing career—reflect on the totality of his oeuvre, put it in context. . . ." He suddenly stopped, returning once more to his aimless stirring.

"Context of what?" Miriam's wariness had become pure curiosity. She hadn't given much thought to Steve's writing for months—her own work preoccupied her too much, compounded by her attempts to blanket the entire experience. But this seemed different. Berg had said "oeuvre," a word that clearly encompassed the early and middle periods of Steve's writing, when she had still felt an active participant.

"Contemporary fiction, I guess. Over the years, I have reviewed most of your husband's books. The last couple of times, I was tough on him, perhaps too tough."

"Now I remember," said Miriam. "You were the one who wrote the review about *Cohen's Dilemma* that bothered Steve so much."

"It wasn't such a bad review. Kurt Vonnegut once compared a brutal reviewer to a person who puts on full armor to attack a hot fudge sundae or a banana split. At most, I carried a stiletto. And your husband's novel was no sticky dessert." Berg made a face as though he found the coffee unsatisfactory. "It was more like a main course with too much gravy. But that's all past." He waved his hand dismissively. "Once said, some things cannot be unsaid, and reviews fall into that class. What I have in mind now is different: a major critique; wider ranging, interspersed with a personal vignette or two, more—"

"Yes," Miriam interjected, "I imagine Steve would wish something like that."

"The dead can't have wishes," Berg said sharply. "They can have wills but not wishes. That's where I need your cooperation: your husband's will. Whom did he appoint literary executor?"

Miriam frowned. "No one specific as far as I remember."

"Well, who is the executor of his will?"

"I guess I am."

"Guess?"

"It's just a phrase," she said irritably. The man is too precise, she thought. "I am."

"So you're also the literary executor."

"I guess I am." Miriam realized she was repeating herself. And behaving like an inept woman, when in fact during the past few months she had just been disengaging herself from family crap and focusing on her new life.

If she was oozing ineptness, Berg didn't seem to have noticed. "Most literary executors wish to exercise their fortressed privilege in controlling access to the author's papers, behaving like a cow swishing her tail against some biting flies. Even the cow must recognize the uselessness of the gesture, but she does it anyway."

"Now wait a moment, Mr. Berg." Miriam placed both palms against the table as if she were ready to push off. "I don't appreciate being compared to a cow. Not even by a biting—"

"Please!" Berg looked mortified. "Please wait. It was a thoughtless metaphor. It could have been a bull, a steer. . . ." He caught himself. "Let me explain," he said, back in control. "You are probably not aware of the difficulties biographers have faced in recent years, getting access to materials. The Supreme Court's famous 'penumbra of privacy' has started to throw such a wide shadow that you can barely find a literary executor anymore who doesn't treat the materials under his control as his personal preserve." Berg stopped, realizing, perhaps, the tactical mistake he was making. He tried to end on a high note. "Voltaire was supposed to have said, 'we must respect the living, but only truth is good enough for the dead.' And Stephen Marx is dead."

Miriam seemed partly mollified, although the baldness of that last observation made her blink once, emphatically. "All right," she said. "So what is it you want from me? Why don't you see Steve's agent—"

"No," he said quickly. "That's the last person I want to talk to. An author's agent has other agenda. He is invariably biased."

"And a literary executor would not be?" Miriam didn't attempt to disguise her irony.

"Not invariably," Berg said judiciously. "The role is essentially a legal one, after all: providing access to papers, correspondence, unpublished material; giving permission—"

"And if that executor is also the wife? Isn't that the ultimate bias?"

"Of course, it is." Berg leaned forward. "But such bias interests me. It may be positive or negative, but it is deeply personal. And that is relevant to a critic or to a biographer."

"And which are you?"

"With Stephen Marx?" Berg leaned back again, opening space between them, but he kept his eyes locked on Miriam's. "Mostly a critic," he said. "With some minimal biographical touches." He said it offhandedly, meaning to reassure. He had completely misread Miriam's nonproprietary frame of mind with respect to her husband's literary "oeuvre."

"So you're mostly a critic, Mr. Berg—" she began.

"Why don't you call me Noah?"

"All right." She smiled, a little brittlely. "Noah. As a critic—"

"Miriam," he said eagerly. "May I call you Miriam?" Seeing her nod, he continued. "Let me explain to you the role of the critic. To put it quite succinctly, the role of a literary critic is herbicidal rather than horticultural." He leaned back, waiting for her response.

Miriam leaned back as well. "Something tells me you've said that before."

He grinned, his owly eyes wide open, causing her to suddenly note how blue they were, though also chilly. "You're right," he said. The grin made him look, for a moment, boyish.

"I thought so. And now, explain that clever sentence."

"We weed out the authorial crap rather than practicing esthetic literary horticulture." The grin widened, boyish into bad-boy.

"All right," said Miriam, keeping a straight face. "So what do you want from me?"

"Other than getting to know you better?"

"I didn't know that was part of the agenda."

"It wasn't at the outset," Berg said quietly. "It is now."

Miriam narrowed her eyes. "Don't flatter me."

"I'm not."

She gave him a searching look. "Let's defer that discussion for some other time," she said after a pause. "What do you want from Stephen Marx's literary estate?"

"At this point, just a couple of items. One complicated and perhaps personal; the other quite trivial."

"Start with the trivial one."

Berg moved his chair closer to the table, pushing the dishes away as if he were about to unroll a map. "Did your husband keep copies of all of his books? In all editions? Translations?"

Miriam thought for a moment. "He certainly used to. But a couple of years ago he moved his files and books to a studio on the West Side. I presume he's continued the practice, but I really can't say for sure."

"You mean you haven't been to his study?" Berg's surprise seemed almost accusatory.

"Of course, I've visited his study," she answered quickly. Yet you'd be surprised how rarely I did, she was tempted to add, but didn't. "But I didn't check his bookshelves to see what he specifically kept there."

"Did he retain the jackets to his own novels?"

"I think so. Why do you ask?"

"Generally, book jackets are just tattoos—pictorial or verbal ornamentation. But for the piece on your husband, I not only want to see the tattoos of his novels, but especially the tattooists. Who were the people writing blurbs for him? Do you know whether these were important to him?"

"Very," Miriam answered instantaneously.

"You mean the contents or the people who provided the blurbs?"

"Both. The tattoos and especially the tattooists." She'd never heard that simile before and it appealed to her—even the crooning sound of the words. "I don't know about the last couple of books, but he used to talk to me about his choice of potential tattooists before he'd finished the first chapter of a new novel."

"It would be extremely time-consuming to find the jackets of his earlier novels," Berg said. "We keep none at the office, jackets nor books. Could I look at his bookshelves?"

Miriam gave a quick, almost impatient, nod. "And the other question, the complicated, personal one."

"Ah, yes." Berg moved even closer, with both elbows on the table, his chin cupped between locked hands. "Why are there so few overt sexual scenes in your husband's last few books?"

Miriam looked stunned. It was a question no one had ever raised; indeed, one she had never even considered. "Well . . ." she stammered, "*Listen, Sister* is about nuns—"

"*One* nun. And there are plenty of other characters in that novel without a vow of celibacy. But let's forget *Listen, Sister*. What about the other novels?"

Miriam found herself rising to Steve's defense. "Well . . ." she started once more, "*Cohen's Dilemma* dealt with scientists—"

"Are you telling me they have no sex?"

"What are you driving at?"

"Was there any change in his. . . ." It was his turn to hem and haw. His gaze had dropped to his empty coffee cup. "Weltanschauung, his attitude . . .?"

"You mean toward sex?" she asked bluntly.

"Yes, for instance sex."

"Not that I can think of," she replied, trying to sound nonchalant. Why had that never occurred to her, she wondered. Was there really so little sex in Steve's recent novels? The ones he had written in his private pad?

"One last, trivial question." Berg's deep, accentless voice sounded as if it came through a fog. "Does the name Monica Sobremonte mean anything to you?"

8

Sundays were Sabine Diehlsdorf's days to sleep in, but on this Sunday the rain beating against the windowpane woke her. One look out of the window convinced her to skip her regular morning jog. Instead, she turned to New York's greatest luxury waiting outside her apartment door: several pounds of Sunday *New York Times*, which she would bring back to bed together with black coffee and orange juice—the only breakfast she permitted herself. This Spartan morning diet and daily jogs kept her on the attractive side of a firm chubbiness.

Except for the classifieds and the real estate section, Sabine read the Sunday *Times* from cover to cover. First the news, then the weekly summary, followed by a jump to the book reviews before delving into Arts & Leisure and skimming the business section. She saved the sports pages for last, looking them over with a professional, if somewhat nostalgic, eye. Her glory days when she had won her internship at *S.I.* seemed far away now: her half-time appointment at *S.I.* was just a job, her early ambitions almost a source of amusement.

Almost. A year had passed since she had overheard Stephen Marx's conversation with his friend, and in that time there had been no dramatic scoop: Marx seemed, in fact, to be dead. What she had taken for a scheme, she had decided, must have been something else: a death wish waiting to be enacted. He could have gone sailing without telling his friend. Sabine had come to accept this knowledge with real regret. She had never read thirteen books by a single author.

Sabine had reached the book review section. The lead review dealt with a novel, *Middles*, by someone named D. Mann. Sabine had never heard of him/her, but the reviewer's name was familiar enough: Noah Berg. The review was enthusiastic, and Sabine was impressed with the skill with which Berg managed to draw

her in without giving away the story. Berg's last paragraph
started with a question:

> Who is D. Mann? His publisher tells us nothing about the
> author; no pictures, no biographical details—only the cryptic
> statement that he lives in the West and that *Middles* is his first
> novel. My reference to "his" novel actually involves some liberty
> on my part. The publisher's cover blurb is not just uninforma-
> tive—it is genderless. Yet I am convinced that this book was
> written by a male author, a very promising one. Perhaps a mu-
> tated, refined Stephen Marx has appeared in the wings.

At the neighborhood Doubleday's, Mann's *Middles* cost her all
of $18.95, not an inconsequential sum for a graduate student,
even one with a modest supplemental income from a half-time
job with *Sports Illustrated.*

The cover was startlingly uninformative: just the title *Middles*
in script. "D. Mann" was also printed in script: it could easily
have been the handwriting of a woman or a meticulous man. The
title page included an epigraph from Nora Ephron's *Heart-
burn*: ". . . I insist on happy endings; I would insist on happy
beginnings, too, but that's not necessary because all beginnings are intrinsically happy. . . . Middles are a problem.
Middles are perhaps the major problem of contemporary society."

Sabine had never thought of things that way before, and the
idea struck her: it occurred to her that her own life might
become entangled in a middle of its own. She turned the page
and, with a fleeting, guilty thought of an assignment for *S.I.* she
could have been working on, started to read.

By the end of the first chapter she was hooked. She finished
the book by the early afternoon, but long before that she had
concluded that D. Mann must be Stephen Marx. With all thirteen of Marx's books still fresh in her mind, the similarity in
style could not escape her, as perhaps it had struck Noah Berg.
By the end of the second chapter, she had detected in *Middles*
one of Marx's stylistic idiosyncrasies, as distinctive as Breughel
painting himself in every sixteenth-century crowd scene in Hol-

land: the hyphenless, Joycealluding combinatorial adjectives of the wheypale, twinecolored, fatencircled, thoughtenchanted mold. She did not know that this was Stephen Marx's discreet plagiaristic homage to Stephen Dedalus, which he had picked up way back at Yale when first reading Joyce's *A Portrait of the Artist as a Young Man*.

So he really pulled it off, she thought, and then changed his mind about returning to life as Marx. Maybe he'd never intended to return. A literary resurrection as a new author had tempted others, she knew. She remembered the recent notoriety Doris Lessing received upon disclosure that two of her books had been turned down by her usual publisher when she submitted them under the name of Jane Somers. Or Joyce Carol Oates: her *Lives of the Twins* and a couple of other books were published under an alter ego, Rosamond Smith. Oates had been quoted saying how the experience had a purity about it, how "the book might have been reviewed as, simply, a first novel" since no one had heard of Rosamond Smith. She had been disappointed when the secret had leaked out. But if that was all Marx had in mind, why the elaborate ruse? Neither Lessing nor Oates had found it necessary.

Sabine suddenly realized how hungry she'd become. She heated a bagel in her microwave, opened the fridge for some Bulgarian Feta cheese, one of her New York-acquired tastes, and made more coffee. By the time she finished the snack, her mind was made up: she would ask *Sports Illustrated* for a brief leave— a few weeks ought to be ample—to focus on her search for Marx.

Just off Fifth Avenue near the Public Library on 42nd Street, the publisher of *Middles* was one of the most prestigious names in the business. Sabine had expected an imposing entrance: a paneled reception room, the furnishings as distinguished as the authors the firm had published over four decades. What she encountered was a space smaller than her living room, a beaten-up sofa accommodating no more than two anxious authors, a receptionist-cum-typist-cum-telephone operator performing the latter two duties to the virtual exclusion of the first.

Sabine had rehearsed her speech; still she was glad that she'd had a while to adjust to the environment. "My name is Sabine Diehlsdorf and I'm a journalist," she said quickly. "I've come to talk to somebody in your office about Mr. Mann's recent novel."

The receptionist hardly looked at Sabine before dialing a number and then saying, "Jerry, a Miss Dildo wants to talk to someone about one of our authors. Can you see her?" Turning to Sabine, who had flushed upon hearing the devastating contraction of her name, she pointed to the couch. "Wait there; Mr. Gumelkian will talk to you."

From her vantage point on the sofa, Sabine was taken aback by the absence of art or other adornments on the walls, other than framed certificates: National Book Awards, National Book Critics' Circle Awards, Pulitzer Prizes—many bearing the names of authors who had already entered the pantheon of college English courses. She was impressed. The traffic in and out of the reception room was bustling. Most consisted of employees picking up telephone messages that were laid out at the receptionist's desk like cards in a game of solitaire. Suddenly a youngish man appeared: dark-haired, looking as if he needed a shave, with a spectacular Armenian nose and the sort of huge dark eyes usually found in icons. The smile was noncommittal. Before Sabine could rise, he extended his hand. "I'm sorry I missed your name, Miss. . . ?"

"Diehlsdorf, Sabine Diehlsdorf," she said quickly, afraid the receptionist would again relegate her surname to porno level.

"What can I do for you, Miss Diehlsdorf?" He made no gesture to invite her into the inner sanctum.

Sabine discovered that she was nervous. Interviewing strangers was one thing—she'd done it often enough by now to be over any shyness there—but this was something else. She knew a secret—and she wasn't sure if this Gumelkian was in on it or not. And if he was, how she was going to get past his guard?

"I've come for some information on Mr. Mann—the one who wrote *Middles* and got such rave reviews. I'm a journalism student at Columbia and I also work for *Sports Illustrated*." She smiled nervously, and it occurred to her that this might be the most effective tactic of all: the more callow she appeared, the more likely this Gumelkian was to let something slip. "Of course, this has nothing to do with them, it's for the *Columbia Journalism Review*. It occurred to me that an interview with Mr. Mann might be appropriate for our readership—the success story of a new writer. By the way, I feel somewhat silly calling him 'Mr. Mann.' What does the *D* stand for?"

Gumelkian allowed a slightly mysterious smile to cross his face. "I have no idea."

Sabine pretended to look dumbfounded. "What do you mean?"

"Why don't you come to my office." Gumelkian led the way from the reception area into a long narrow corridor, hardly wide enough for two persons to walk abreast. It wound through a maze of crowded cubicles, the desks strewn with paper or books—it was clear that overhead was not spent on furnishings. Gumel-kian ushered Sabine into his cubbyhole, which held bookshelves from floor to ceiling and a single chair in front of his overladen desk. He motioned her to sit, then settled in his own swivel chair. "I can't blame you for being surprised," he said. "I handle public relations for many of our authors. This is the only one on whom we have no photographs, no first name, in fact nothing. I wish I could help you, but I really can't."

Instead of disappointment, Sabine felt elation. An anonymous author who eventually would turn into Stephen Marx was even better. She kept the elation to herself, asking instead, with what she hoped was the right air of confusion, "But how do you communicate with him? How did you get his manuscript? How do you pay his royalties?"

From somewhere amid the paper stack on his desk, Gumel-kian had produced a pipe and was starting the pipe-cleaning ritual which even Sabine, the confirmed nonsmoker, always found quaintly charming.

"We heard from an agent—one of the best in the business—that he had an outstanding manuscript by an unknown. The rest of the story is pretty simple: the manuscript was damn professional, it needed practically no editing, and we decided to make it a rush job so as to make the Fall list. When it came to discussing promotional plans, the agent told us to forget about them. There would be no photographs, no biographical details, no interviews, no talk shows, nothing. The writer insisted on anonymity. Any contact would have to proceed through his office. In a way I was sorry because it's my job to arrange for publicity, but in the end we felt that a mysterious first author might be all the PR we'd need. I hope he keeps it up. It'll help sales on his second book, when there is one." Gumelkian's tone became tinged with surprise. "Now you've got me doing it."

"What?"

"Calling Mann 'he.' What makes you so sure Mann is a man? Usually it's women who use initials, at least in telephone books."

"That's different," Sabine said. "At least for me. All I have in the directory is S. Diehlsdorf, but that's just so the obscene phone callers can't use your first name. But when I write an article you always see my full name. It's the other way around: a man is more likely to use his full name in the phone book, and initials in books. But please go on."

Gumelkian had finally lit his pipe. "Too bad," he said between the first puffs. "I was hoping you knew something." He let out a long stream of blue smoke. "But in that case, there is really nothing more to tell. You know as much about Mann as I do or anyone else in our office. If you could find out who he is, we would love to hear it."

"Even if your mystery author lost his—or her—mystery?"

Gumelkian chortled. "There's a saying in the PR business: 'there's no bad ink.'"

"Then do you think Mann's agent might be willing to talk to me?"

"I doubt it, but it's worth a try. I'll give you his address."

Justin Merrifield did not match Sabine's image of a high-powered literary agent. An imposing man, probably in his early sixties, with silver hair and a genial smile, he settled himself in an easy chair across from her. As Sabine tried to gather her thoughts, the nervousness that had afflicted her with Gumelkian returned with double force; she couldn't meet, let alone hold, Merrifield's gaze.

"What can I do for you?" he asked.

The words came out in a rush. "I'm Sabine Diehlsdorf from the Columbia School of Journalism. I'd like to get some information on your author Mann in connection with an article. When I inquired at the publisher's, they referred me to you. They told me they knew nothing about Mann, not even whether they were dealing with a man or a woman. Which is it?"

Merrifield let out a chuckle. "You certainly don't waste time, do you, Ms. Diehlsdorf? I wish I could help you."

Sabine's eyes finally rose from the floor. "But you're his agent—"

"Maybe I'm her agent," interjected Merrifield with an impish grin.

"Then it's a she—"

"Nothing of the sort." Merrifield seemed to be enjoying himself. "I simply don't know." He peered at her with a humorous imitation of concern. "And surely you don't think we should assume. . . ."

Sabine barely saw the bait, much less rose to it. "You mean you know nothing about him—her—Mann?"

"Nothing." Merrifield's playfulness seemed to diminish slightly.

"But that's so . . . odd, isn't it? Have you ever dealt with an author you didn't know anything about?" Sabine's nervousness was gone now. Was Merrifield really as much in the dark as he claimed? If so, wouldn't that be further evidence that Mann was something more than an unknown first novelist?

Sabine's question had Merrifield rubbing his right temple. "Frankly, no," he replied. "I've been in this business for over thirty years. There have always been recluses, writers who go out of their way to protect their privacy like Salinger or Pynchon— did you know that nobody's even got a photograph of Pynchon?— but this is the first time I've had to deal with a total blank."

"But how do you communicate with him?" probed Sabine. "You've never spoken on the phone?"

"Everything has been by correspondence. To a P.O. box in San Francisco."

"So he lives in San Francisco?"

The earlier amused expression reappeared on Merrifield's face. "I don't know where he or she *lives*. All I know is that the author gets mail in San Francisco. Or maybe someone picks it up for him or her."

"But aren't you curious? Don't you have some preconceived notion whether you're dealing with a man or a woman?"

For the first time Merrifield turned serious. "Why do you worry so much about the sex behind the letter *D*? Who cares whether the author is a man or a woman? What's important is the quality of the writing."

Only a man would say that, thought Sabine. She was tempted to refer to the testosterone-drenched ambiance of *Sports Illustrated* which had sensitized her so much to questions of gender, but she didn't want to go off on that hormonal tangent—at least not now. "Curiosity, I suppose," she offered instead.

"My initial contact with Mann had nothing to do with curiosity," countered Merrifield. "You can imagine that we get a never-ending deluge of unsolicited manuscripts," he pointed to the two piles carefully stacked on his desk. "Most of them rest there unread for weeks on end before I even have a chance to glance at them. Mann's manuscript would have met the same fate except that it arrived on a Friday afternoon. I was almost ready to leave for the weekend—I've got a place on Long Island where I like to read undisturbed. I had planned to take the latest manuscript of one of my authors, but somehow, in the rush, I must have grabbed the wrong one. When I sat down Friday evening to read it, I discovered my mistake. I'm not superstitious, but I thought maybe I was meant to read this manuscript right away, so I opened it." Merrifield leaned forward. "When I finished *Middles*, I wrote Mann a letter with our standard contract. His reply was back within a week. He sounded very sure of himself. In his opinion, *Middles* needed no editorial work and entailed little risk for the publisher, and so he felt a large advance was justified. I could handle that. But then he added that any publisher would have to agree to protect his anonymity: no biographical information on the book cover, no personal involvement in any publicity. He said he wanted to be a 'monk of fiction.'" Merrifield let out a laugh, but it seemed to Sabine to have more than a little exasperation in it. "Considering the character of Nicholas Kahnweiler in *Middles*, I can't blame him—people are bound to assume that some of the contents of that book are autobiographical. Incidentally, that monk remark is why I take Mann for a man." Merrifield gave a grunt of surprise. "You don't suppose that's a clue, do you: 'Mann,' 'man'?"

Sabine barely heard the question. Merrifield's story had assembled itself for her into a picture of extraordinary clarity— and promise. She was convinced she had found the opportunity that would make her career. "You think he's playing some game, then?" she asked. She was surprised at how cool she sounded, wondering if Merrifield could see through her to the secret she carried.

Merrifield furrowed his brow. "I suppose so. Writers do that kind of thing, you know. But what's the point?"

"I suppose I'll have to find out. Could you give me that post office box number in San Francisco?" she asked. "I would like to see whether I can trace him."

Merrifield was silent for some time. When he finally responded, it was to scribble briefly on a notepad. He looked to one side as he tore off the sheet and slid it across the desk.

"You don't know where you got this," he said. He looked at her directly. "If he were to find out, it would probably give him grounds to break his contract. And reason to. But I'd like to know what's going on." He peered at her closely. "But how do you think you're going to find him?"

"Don't worry about that," Sabine said calmly.

As she walked out the door, the piece of paper clutched in her hand, she wondered what made her so confident.

9

Sabine had never been west of Pittsburgh. The agent in the small travel bureau on Broadway and 116th Street suggested she take a cut-rate Newark to Oakland flight and recommended a modestly priced hotel in the center of San Francisco, the Beresford, on Sutter Street. She didn't think twice about raiding her meager savings account—the remnant of a bequest from a favorite uncle—to pay for the ticket. She packed simply. A pantsuit for the plane, a couple of dresses, sweater, blue jeans, extra pair of shoes, her jogging gear, raincoat, and umbrella took care of the essentials. She was so certain about interviewing Marx, she took along her small tape recorder, together with Stephen Marx's *Cohen's Dilemma* and D. Mann's *Middles*. She also decided to wear three rings—two more than usual—on fingers she'd never before considered suitable for rings. She did not own one large enough to go over her thumb and it took her some time to find one at a custom-jewelry store. She'd read about them in *Middles*.

Manya Putnam was the sort of speaker who refused to be chained to a lectern. She paced the podium. Her clear, metallic voice permitted her to do without the leash of lecturers, the microphone cord. She used no manuscript, and as she strode back and forth, microsecond-long flashes of lower thigh registered with Nicholas; then the simple lines of the white silk blouse, the clear imprint of her nipples, the small dangling silver earrings. Almost automatically he looked for a wedding ring, but the two rings on her left hand were on the least-expected fingers: the index finger, obtrusive in her mesmerizing gestures, and the thumb.

The only woman Nicholas had ever seen wearing a thumb ring was an African dancer; but the index finger? Suddenly it came to him: the portraits of Titian he had studied as a young man. There they were: popes, bishops, noblemen, all with the right or left index finger displaying a ring. And Eleonora Gonzaga, Duchess of Urbino, with a ring on *each* index finger. Like Manya Putnam.

He had not thought of that painting for years, but now it had suddenly come back to him. Was it the duchess or the dancer in Manya that had triggered his memory? Did she wear a ring on each index finger—this centuries-old sign of command—to emphasize the twentieth-century gestures she directed at her audience? And the thumb ring?

For Mann to notice her rings she would first have to find him. Her neighbor on the plane noticed them before takeoff. Sabine's seat was in the middle; before she even had time to take out her book, the grandmotherly type occupying the window seat turned to her.

"I hope you won't consider me nosy, but I've never seen this." She pointed to Sabine's thumb. "And rings on both index fingers! Is that some special sign?"

My goodness, Sabine thought, they really work. But she was in no mood for conversation; she preferred to practice dialogue in her mind, the words she and Mann would exchange once she had found him.

"No special reason," she said, and picked up *Middles*.

But what would she say to him when she finally faced him? She couldn't imagine the moment. She would have to play it by ear, she decided. It wouldn't be so hard: she would be the one holding all the cards. It would be nice, for once—and especially with a man more than twenty years her senior. Until recently, older men had invariably generated deference, even compliance, in her. Sabine had attempted to break out of that father-figure preoccupation, but with little success. Go West, young woman, she said to herself. And do it!

The 94114 post office was at 18th and Diamond, in the heart of the Castro area, the gay community's southside branch. When Sabine arrived shortly before nine a long line had already assembled waiting for the service windows to open. In addition to the hopeful patrons, the lobby held a filthy-gray industrial carpet, one rickety worktable holding various postal services documents, a zip code directory, and a couple of pens secured to chains. According to the sign at the entrance, the establishment was open on weekdays from 8:00 A.M. until 5:30 P.M., with the service windows opening one hour later. The lobby wall bore a piceous placard announcing daily availability of mail in the boxes by 10:00 A.M.

Sabine breathed a sigh of relief. It was unlikely that Mann had come earlier. The mailboxes had small glass windows. Number 14079, low down near the floor, was one of the large ones. It was partly filled. To avoid being conspicuous, Sabine joined the end of the slow-moving line. It took nearly half an hour for her to reach the service window, but at the end of that interval, even though over a dozen people had opened their boxes (some calling greetings through their openings to the clerk behind), box 14079 remained undisturbed.

Sabine bought a few stamps for postcards and then stepped aside. For a moment, she wasn't sure what to do next. After determining that there was no other means of public access, she stepped outside. Across the street was a purple-and-burgundy Victorian house, the type featured, with and without cable cars, on so many local postcards. Its clean stone steps were an ideal place from which to monitor the post office door. Sabine took up her post, grateful for the sunlight that cut the morning chill, and waited.

Shortly after ten o'clock, a bearded man in blue jeans and loafers, a sweater over his back with sleeves tied in front, passed her lair into the post office. It might have been his garb, it might have been the travel bag slung over his shoulder, but something about him whispered "writer" to Sabine. She followed him into the lobby where she found him emptying the contents of one of the large bottom boxes. As he straightened and turned, she caught the resemblance to Marx's newspaper photo, in spite of the new, carefully trimmed beard. A quick glance through the glass door of box 14079 confirmed her conclusion. It was now empty.

Marx carried an old Pan Am bag into which he had dumped his mail. He didn't look at it, she noticed; and for some reason she was impressed by this. She followed as he sauntered with the unopened bag toward Castro Street, picking up the *New York Times* on the way before entering the nearest cafe. Observing him through the plate-glass window, she debated whether to join him or wait outside. She decided on the latter course, only to regret it because Marx seemed in no hurry to finish breakfast or the *Times*. When he finally departed, Sabine trailed some thirty feet behind—an unnecessary precaution, given the lack of attention he paid to his surroundings.

He strolled down 18th Street toward Sanchez, past a delicatessen, and then up a few steps into a three-story imitation Victorian, one of a dozen similar buildings on that block. Sabine studied the labels on the entrance mailboxes: one blank, the others reading Iglesias, Bernstein, and Holton. For a moment Sabine panicked: perhaps he was just visiting someone. To enter the locked front door she would have to ring the bell and identify herself through a speaker. But what plausible explanation could she offer for the door to be opened to her? Sabine crossed the street to examine the apartment house in greater detail. She was in luck. In a bay window on the third floor, Marx appeared. He sat down at a table or a desk. Sabine ran across the street, rang the unlabeled bell and waited with trepidation.

"Yes?" she heard after a click.

"Mr. Mann?"

A long pause. "Yes?"

"My name is Sabine Diehlsdorf."

"Who?"

It occurred to Sabine that Marx/Mann might be using another name in his everyday life. She rushed on. "Mr. Mann, I would like to interview you about *Middles*." The few seconds of silence felt like minutes to Sabine until she heard the sound of the buzzer. Quickly, she pushed the door open and climbed the steep stairs to the third floor.

Upstairs, Marx had not moved from the speaker. Standing in a suddenly silent apartment, he couldn't convince himself that this intruder was innocent. She must know, he told himself. Why else would anyone bother? How many others had discovered his identity? How could this have happened?

On the way up, Sabine felt a strange mixture of excitement and composure. Excitement, at locating Marx so quickly, at wondering what the first encounter would bring. Composure, because of the enormous advantage she had over Marx, one she intended to use to its fullest. She knew what he looked like; she had read all of his books; and most important, she was privy to his deepest secret. She knew he couldn't refuse an interview. Clearly he would try to persuade her to keep quiet, but how could he now do so without talking? And what could he possibly say to persuade her to keep the secret?

While Marx waited for the door knocker to sound, question mounted upon question. Who was this woman? What does she want? How do I convince her to keep her mouth shut? Just when I'd become convinced that a new literary career was in the making, that D. Mann would become a rising star, along comes this bitch. It will never be the same, it can't ever be the same. Who the hell is she? What does she look like?

Marx was not aware how threatening a knocker could sound when one's ear is separated from the knocker's impact point only by the thickness of a cheap apartment door. Startled, he threw open the door.

As it happened, neither of them was prepared for this first encounter. To Sabine, Marx seemed much taller than he had while she had trailed him from the post office. But what took her aback wasn't his height; it was the angry stare, focusing exclusively on her face. It was some time before she could bring herself to meet that stare. She stood on the threshold, looking at the floor, unable to move.

On his side, Marx was angry, but also surprised. He hadn't expected anyone so young. He'd anticipated an inquisitor—sharp in features, sharp in approach. Instead, he found a woman with a raincoat over her arm—a woman like Felicity, like other women who had visited his studio apartment, only of more normal height. A woman who seemed content to stand there, eyes turned down as though searching for him there, in the dust of the floor. It threw him off. The moment seemed interminable to them both.

Brusquely, he broke the silence. "Come in," he growled, stepping back into the narrow corridor and pressing against the wall to permit Sabine to pass. "Go ahead," he commanded, closing the door. As Sabine headed for the room at the end of the passage, Marx conducted a second inspection, this time of her back. Firm ass, he concluded as he followed her into the room which served as a combined living and study space. He pointed to one of the two canvas director chairs.

"Please sit down."

The "please" encouraged Sabine to take the initiative.

"Mr. Mann, I realize I'm taking you by surprise. It would have been fairer to write, but I'm not sure you would've granted me an interview."

"You're damn right," he snapped. "But I'd just as soon get to the point: How did you find me?"

Sabine fought desperately not to search for some imperfection on the floor; losing eye contact meant losing the initiative, something she couldn't afford now. She stalled momentarily by pushing the hair off her forehead with her left hand. Through the screen of hair and fingers, she saw Marx's hard expression suddenly change to pleased surprise. Quickly, he glanced at the other hand before exclaiming:

"I'll be damned. Do you always wear rings on those three fingers?"

Sabine held out her hands as if they were some stranger's hands. She had forgotten about the rings. "No, never." Her smile was disarming. "I did this for you."

"For me?" Sabine's answer had the expected effect. Marx was flattered. "To show that you'd read *Middles*? But how did you find me?" It was the second time he had asked the question, but the belligerence was gone.

Sabine hesitated. "I read a review of *Middles* in the *Times*—"

"You read Berg's review? What did you think of it?" Marx's tone was peremptory.

"I thought it was first-class—not only his compliments, but also his style. If I were teaching a course on book reviews, I'd cite this as an example."

How true, thought Marx, and how ironic: Noah Berg, Marx's bête noire had turned into Mann's vicarious advocate through a few printed paragraphs. He could almost recite them, he had read them so often to himself.

There is a certain irony in the studied anonymity of the author of this fine new novel. "D. Mann" arrives on the scene with little other than this cryptic byline and an excellent book. The irony is that this novel's protagonist, one Nicholas Kahnweiler, is an egotist of the largest proportions.

Middles is in fact a study of egotism, and the way in which the thoroughly self-absorbed genius comes to feel the world hit him where he lives, as it were. A scientist with careful scruples, Kahnweiler has inadvertently gotten rich off the defense industry and is left with the means to explore all the facets of his own taste and personality. His wealth also enhances the manipulative aspect of his character as it puts at his disposal all the weapons that money can buy, for use in the most fundamental war of all, that between men and women.

By the time Kahnweiler comes to tell the story that is the novel (and Mann's method of getting this egotist's story out is natural and unobtrusive), he is a veteran of these wars in search of an understanding of their causes, or at least of a truce. Despite his self-congratulation in areas ranging from the knowledge of wines to sexual sensitivity, the reader comes to admire and sympathize with Kahnweiler's struggle to integrate himself into a world from which he has always been estranged.

The person, no, phenomenon, that brings Kahnweiler to his proverbial knees is a woman with the telling name of Manya Putnam, a complicated and beautiful feminist lawyer whose relationship with Kahnweiler tests both their brands of feminism and the limits (not at all close) of sexual domination. As a tale of love between two brilliant and ambitious adults, of the passion of two people so firmly entrenched in the real world, it speaks especially to all of us no-longer-young urban professionals.

Some of the strongest moments in this remarkably mature first novel show Kahnweiler being caught in constructing the sort of egotistic spiral, which rises out of the compelling vortex of the self, that he has habitually created from the time he first began to think independently. Often the spiral concerns his rather overly important sexuality. Whatever its subject, its purpose in Kahnweiler's life has been to construct barriers between himself and other men, himself and his colleagues, even between himself and his most intimate lovers.

The novel's satisfying ending chronicles his earnest attempt at creating a friendship—a non-sexual, disinterested attachment of mind to mind—with another man, something he has not attempted since he reached maturity. The fate of the friendship between Nicholas Kahnweiler and Gerald Bogen is left open, but the story of Kahnweiler's earnest desire to avoid self-interest in their initial extended conversation is a fine achievement. So well delineated is Kahnweiler's character that he behaves, wonder of wonders, like a human being, for whom real change is never an all-at-once proposition. He arrests his own attempts to manipulate Bogen's responses, worries about negating Bogen's personality in the avalanche of his own, and however patronizing it may sound here, succeeds in drawing out the best in both himself and his new friend. This interaction, outside the boundaries of sexuality, is an important sign of Kahnweiler's growth and painful admission of the rest of the world into his innermost consciousness.

If there is a major defect in the Nicholas Kahnweiler character, it is perhaps that he is too well-rounded in the real world sense—too much all the good things a sensitive man of the '80s is supposed to be. How can one man be a feminist, a great lover, a renowned scientist, a wealthy man with a strong sense of noblesse oblige, an oenophile, a reasonable cook (by the end), literate, an art collector, a poet and budding novelist, a man of exquisite taste and master of the perfect gesture, all at once? If this overachievement hampers our identification with Kahnweiler, it also, at its best moments, raises him to the status of a hero in the old-fashioned sense—all the things we are and try to be, only more so.

One gets the sense that Kahnweiler's ego is a burden to him, like the Elephant Man's head. D. Mann, whoever he may be, has clearly pondered this problem of the self in the world, and he presented it in a manner reminiscent of that of the late Stephen Marx, who also understood so well the twin handicaps of ego and desire.

10

"Sobremonte?" Miriam almost sang the word. "What a lovely name. 'Over the mountain?'"

Berg nodded. "Or more succinctly, 'on top.' It suited Monica. Doesn't ring a bell?"

Miriam furrowed her brow. "Not really, but I'm terrible about names. Why do you ask?"

"Nothing important. Just a passing thought when we talked about your husband's study." Miriam missed the forced unconcern with which he dismissed the topic. "But speaking of that, could we visit it . . . to examine the bookshelves?"

"You mean now?" She looked startled. She hadn't been there for weeks. The idea of going there with a stranger seemed intrusive. She looked at her watch. "I have to get to my office downtown. We have a big catering affair ahead of us. I'll let you know when I'm free."

She rose to leave, feeling flustered. Berg's request, the suddenness of it, had unnerved her. But as she awkwardly disentangled herself from the table, and from Berg's attention, she realized what had bothered her wasn't any sense of violation, of impropriety. It was something else. The thought of entering Stephen's study with another man had filled her with a rush of excitement. How very odd, she told herself as she made her way toward the door, the pressure of Berg's eyes a distinct weight on her back.

At the door, she almost stopped and turned. There was no pressing business at her office. But she couldn't. Not today. Maybe another day. Maybe tomorrow.

"I haven't been here for a couple of months. God knows how dusty the place must be."

Miriam strode straight to the window, pulled apart the shades, and threw open the window. A blast of cold March air hit them, before their eyes had even adapted to the sudden brightness of the room. Without taking off her coat, Miriam sat down on Stephen's favorite couch which he'd brought over from their East Side place. It had been good for reading, napping, jotting down notes—and Miriam had never wanted to consider what else. She patted the space next to her. "Come, sit down. Let's talk for a moment before we look around."

"All right." Berg perched on an adjoining cushion. The sofa was perpendicular to the window. Berg's face was silhouetted against the light, an indistinct darkness. "I know it's cold," she said. "Let's keep our coats on until the place is aired out."

Berg tugged his collar closer around his neck and nodded. His head swiveled while he inspected the room, looking everywhere, Miriam noticed, but at her.

"Did he always write here?"

Miriam shook her head. "For the first dozen or so years, Saint—people called him that—did his writing at our place. I used to do a lot of his typing, not first drafts but revisions, and especially the final versions. But then, he earned more money. . . . Our marriage got into a routine. . . ."

Her voice trailed off. She had started looking past Berg toward the bookshelves behind the desk. "One day, he announced it would be better all around if he'd find a writing studio elsewhere; that it would be preferable for both of us if our living space and his work were separated. Initially, I was hurt. Now I realize he should have done it earlier—as soon as we were able to afford it. It would have been better for me, because I probably would have started sooner on my own."

Berg turned to look at her. "Your catering business? When did you start that?" He seemed genuinely interested.

Miriam was pleased. "I've always liked to cook. We had a lot of friends, mostly writers, up to our place and I enjoyed cooking different things: ethnic dishes, trying new recipes. After a while I established quite a repertoire. When Stephen found this place," she pointed around the room, "I decided to do something on my own." She stopped, and the look she gave him was almost shy. "You know what I wanted to do?"

Miriam didn't wait for an answer. "I decided to write a cookbook—an authentic American one. I don't mean just fried chicken and apple pie, but all the ethnic dishes we've adopted. I wanted to interview people—actually mostly women—about those recipes; how they'd learned them; how they'd modified them; some vignettes about their lives. When I told my husband . . . now that's funny, I haven't referred to Stephen as my husband for months . . . when I told him about my plan he just pooh-poohed it. I don't know whether he didn't take me seriously or whether he was jealous at having a second writer in the family. What he said was, he didn't consider it serious writing." She laughed, a little too brightly. "That's how I knew he was jealous. Anyway, it didn't take long before I stopped talking about it."

"You know, that's the only genre I've never reviewed," Berg mused. "We seem to send them out only to women. I've always thought I might like to try one sometime. Did you write the book? Is it out yet?"

"Yes and no," replied Miriam. "Yes, I started it, but no, it isn't finished. I haven't really mentioned it to anyone, not since Stephen made it so plain. . . . But it did lead me into catering." She straightened. "Enough of this." She made a disdainful gesture. "You didn't come here to listen to my story. I think it's time to close the window—I'm getting cold. Anyway, that's how this place changed our lives, or really Stephen's life. Altogether I spent very little time here. In the last two or three years, practically none."

Miriam rose, walked over to Stephen's desk, and slowly ran her hand over the empty desktop. "When Stephen had his accident, I came here—maybe a week after. I was surprised how clean the place was, how few pages were lying around. It was almost as if Stephen had cleaned up. Almost as if he knew." She circled the desk, finally settling down in Stephen's writing chair, to face Berg on the couch.

"I didn't return for weeks, I simply didn't have it in me. I didn't want to intrude into his private world. I wonder whether you can imagine what it's like when a person close to you disappears and the body is never found. There's no closure. You're never sure. Have you any idea how hard it is to rummage through a person's things when you feel as if any minute—" She shook her head. "I would have felt like a thief."

Miriam stared out the window before saying, in a matter-of-fact tone, "I decided to do nothing. Stephen had bought it, all cash! Can you believe that? He rationalized this purchase in a strangely touching way—like some peasant feeling he must own his own land, for security's sake and his self-respect. By paying cash he felt that even if his income would drop ('you never know when I'll get a writer's block,' he used to say), he'd always be able to afford this place. The monthly condominium fee for a studio apartment of this size is not high, and somehow he didn't think about real estate taxes.

"Well, I decided to respect that feeling. Maybe I'm just superstitious, but I won't do anything about this apartment as long as Stephen is not declared legally dead."

"Won't that be a while?" Berg sounded concerned—solicitous even. "Seven years?"

Miriam shook her head. "Not anymore. Now it's five. Still, it's like soldiers missing in action. It's terribly cruel. Thank God, Steve's parents were already gone when this happened. Especially his father, who was incredibly proud of his son 'the writer.' Yet Stephen didn't visit him that often; in recent years, he'd gotten terribly self-centered. You'd think he'd have been just the opposite, given his success."

She stopped for a moment. "Success just made him more and more insecure. I bet he wouldn't have changed even if he'd won the Nobel Prize."

"Was that really one of his ambitions?" Berg was now really mining a biographical vein he hadn't expect to find.

Miriam reflected. "He never talked about it—or about any other awards. Oh, he did, jokingly—early on: 'Wait till I win the Pulitzer and then the Nobel.' But later, when he became a serious candidate for a Pulitzer, he never mentioned it. By that time he had already moved over here," she gestured vaguely around the room. "Basically, he had started to separate me from his professional life. When he did win the Pulitzer, I could see that it meant a great deal to him, though we never spoke about it. I just knew: public recognition was everything to him. And it would never be enough." She turned to Berg, feeling she had opened an important aspect of the writer's life to him, but Berg's interests seemed elsewhere.

"You said he'd removed you from his writing career. How did you mean that?"

"Just that." Miriam's response was abrupt. "He spent his days here—he was a day person, a day writer—it was almost like a nine-to-five job where the husband comes home for dinner and doesn't talk about work in the office. That was when our marriage really started to go downhill. I know it sounds trite, but that's what happened. You see, since the initial shock of Stephen's accident wore off, I've been taking stock of our relationship. Because once the jolt had passed, I realized I wasn't really grief-stricken." She looked embarrassed. "I know it sounds cold-blooded, but I felt almost relieved. Until this moment, I've told this only to Thomasina—my closest business friend. When Steve moved here, we should have separated or gotten a divorce; if we'd done that, we probably would have remained friends. Instead, we let our marriage deteriorate to such an extent that there was very little left."

Berg realized that for the past five minutes he had been struggling to keep from thinking about Monica. I bet she got laid right on this sofa, he thought bitterly. The image kept intruding on his thoughts. But he couldn't hold that against Miriam. They were both victims.

"What held you together?" he asked quietly.

She gave him a long, searching look. "Noah, I don't know what made me tell you all this. Perhaps because I trust you not to misuse my confidence when you write your article about Stephen. Try to be generous. After all, he's dead."

Berg said nothing, his eyes fixed past her toward the bookshelves.

"I suppose it was tact," she said at last.

Berg looked up. "Tact?" He had forgotten the question.

"Yes," she said in a firm voice. "I'm sure it was tact that kept us together. Tact in public, though less in private. But enough of that." She rose from the chair and pointed to the shelves behind her. "You came for this. Let's see what's on those shelves."

11

"Remember how Berg ended the review? By asking whether we didn't have a new Stephen Marx?"

"I do. He seemed to have meant it as a compliment." Marx's mien remained deadpan.

If he can act, so can I, thought Sabine. "Earlier on, I had read a couple of Marx's books—"

"Which ones?" To Sabine, the question seemed suspiciously animated.

Marx seemed to think so as well: he caught himself, rose, saying casually, "Coffee?"

"I'd love some. Black."

While Marx went to the adjacent kitchen, Sabine used the opportunity for some quick reconnaissance. So far she had been locked into a very limited visual space by Marx's attention and inquisition. Now she was surprised by the modest, even Spartan, setting, the paucity of furniture. An old-fashioned gas fireplace seemed to be the only source of heat. Near the bay window stood a long white table, strewn with books and papers, which served as a desk. Perpendicular to it was a small table on wheels carrying a Dell laptop. The two director chairs and the single bookshelf completed the list. No art, no carpet. Except for the mess on the table, the room was spotlessly clean. Through the open door Sabine could see his bedroom—the bed covered with a quilt, the night table bearing the phone and some books.

Marx returned with two mugs and a thermos. As he filled Sabine's cup, she said as casually as he, "*Cohen's Dilemma* and *Gasps of Delight*." She watched carefully: was there a flinch? The coffee poured steadily enough.

Marx looked at her quizzically. The attention made her nervous.

"You asked which of Marx's novels I'd read," she explained.

"Ah," Marx said, "that's right." He busied himself with spoons. "You know," he said finally, "if Berg hadn't made the comment at the end of his review, I don't think I would have noticed. Did you? Notice any similarities?" He looked concerned enough, Sabine thought. And if I didn't know better, I'd just set it down to a writer worrying about the uniqueness of his style.

But Sabine knew better, and the knowledge was making her part of the conversation increasingly difficult. She stalled. "It's difficult to tell. But once Berg put the idea into my head, I did think there were some similarities. Like the way Marx's characters have problems with their names. You do the same thing in *Middles* with Nicholas Kahnweiler."

"Come now." Marx seemed totally at ease now, even a bit pompous. "Nobody has a copyright on that—it's a common enough event in everyday life. I'm sure you have trouble with your name."

Sabine started to blush, remembering the receptionist at Mann's publisher. "All right then," she said, trying to regain her composure. "Both your Kahnweiler and Marx's Cohen were scientists and Jewish. I know, I know," Sabine raised her hand, "another coincidence. But what about the names Cohen and Kahn?"

"It's the standard question I get every time I introduce myself: 'What kind of name is this?' 'Where are you from?' and frequently, 'What kind of accent do you have?' Depending on my mood, I give different answers. Usually I just reply, 'It's of German origin but I don't really know what it means.'

"The real story is more complicated, and you may be interested in it. My family is Jewish and comes from Germany. You'll find immediately that for German Jews 'Kahn' is simply a germanicized—a laundered—version of Cohen. When the emancipation of the Jews began in Germany in the eighteenth century, they were ordered to assume last names, preferably German ones. Remember, Jews traditionally had no last names. The rich ones picked allusions to wealth—gold, silver—and others names of flowers, like roses. No wonder you now find many names like Goldberg, Silberstein, Rosenkranz. But the Cohens, the priestly class, were more subtle and found names that retained a phonetic connection with Hebrew but would still 'pass.' As I mentioned earlier, the ending 'weiler' is fairly common in German; hence 'Kahnweiler' sounded plausible, in that it might be derived from some hypothetical place like 'Kahnweil' and did not even sound Jewish. A more honest translation ought to be something like 'Cohenburg.'

"To the second question, 'Where are you from?' I frequently say 'I live in San Francisco,' even though I know perfectly well that this is not what they mean. If the questioner is persistent, he'll say, 'You don't have an American accent, where were you born?' and I'll reply that where I was born won't tell him anything: I was born in Bucharest, but that doesn't make me, or my name, or my accent, Romanian. I was two months old when my parents moved back to Munich, where they were originally from.

"The most common question is, 'How do you spell your name?' The very first time I was asked this, shortly after my arrival in the United States, I, the sixteen-year-old Nicholas, got flustered. When I tried to spell out my name the way I had heard others in

America spell theirs with reference to geographical or personal names, all the words starting with a 'K' in my native tongue that came quickly to mind were 'Kalifornien' and 'Kairo,' which in English start with a 'C.' Kalamazoo was as yet unknown to me—I, the Central European urban kid, would probably not have believed that a place could be called Kalamazoo—and neither Kansas nor Kentucky was as yet part of my spelling subconscious. Offhand, I couldn't think of a single English word starting with 'K,' so in desperation I came up with 'Kitsch,' and I have used this ever since. I got again stuck with 'W,' which of course I pronounced as a 'V.' The damn German confusion between 'V' and 'W' got in my way, until I found an all-American word, 'Washington,' which even though I pronounced 'Vashington,' everyone knew what I meant. Kitsch and Washington stuck with me for the next forty years. A psychologist would probably have a field day with the combination Kahnweiler-Kitsch-Washington."

"And does that spelling business bother you?" asked Marx.

"No, of course not. I rather liked it. Because you're right: it happens to me all the time. The other day someone actually called me Dildo."

"Dildo?" Marx broke out laughing. "Sabine Dildo? May I borrow that name for my next novel?" He snickered, then grew sober again. "So what else did you find, aside from that Marx also used a Jewish scientist for his main character?"

Sabine was surprised to find how readily her answers came: she hadn't been aware of preparing in this way, but she realized now that for days she had been drawing parallel columns in her head, one headed "Mann," the other "Marx," and drawing lines between them. "Well, take the manner in which your Nicholas Kahnweiler describes the writing style of scientists, not unlike the way Marx does in *Cohen*."

Marx leaned forward, clearly intrigued. "Give me an example."

"I know practically nothing about you other than that you are a scientist. Why don't you tell me something about yourself?"

"All right," replied Nicholas. "I'm a scientist, divorced, no children; but what is occupying me right now is a novel."

"What's it called? By whom?" asked Gerald Bogen.

"I haven't yet picked a title."

"You mean you're writing a novel?"

Nicholas wasn't sure whether admiration or amazement was behind Gerald's question. He was hoping for both.

"It's my first attempt."

Gerald had turned completely towards Nicholas, who could almost feel the searching, speculative—and, yes, admiring— look. "What made you do it?"

Nicholas decided this was the time to be honest. Not completely open, but honest. He would tell him why he wanted to publish it, not why he had written it. "It's the competitive scientist in me. I don't know a serious scientist who doesn't want to publish his work. This is one of the major differences between us and the literati. Take a poet like Emily Dickinson. She hardly saw a single poem published in her lifetime. Yet she wrote superb poetry and got better all the time. It's unlikely that this could have happened to a scientist, who must be nourished by peer-approved publication. A male Emily Dickinson in physics or chemistry is inconceivable."

Bogen continued to look at him. "Sounds to me like baloney, Nick. It's too simple. There must be more to it."

Nicholas felt himself bridling slightly under the charge—until he remembered it was true. "Of course there is. It's the pleasure associated with literary writing: that's what I'm after. It's different from the pleasure of scientific publishing. I'm quite well known in my field, primarily through my papers. But style in scientific publications really doesn't count; all the reader cares for is content, and all the editor looks for is concision. Most scientific papers are read only once, whereupon they either become part of the reader's data base or are discarded as excess baggage.

"Now that I'm writing a novel, I've started to read in a new way. I'm rereading books by authors who are real craftsmen. I already know the story, so I can focus on the hidden linguistic gems. They aren't really hidden; they are right there in front of us, but by attending primarily to the plot one misses a lot. These gems are exquisite candy; when I find one of them, I don't bite into it: I let it dissolve slowly on my tongue. I test it to see how long I can detect the aftertaste. Take Saul Bellow's *Herzog*. Have you read it?"

"No."

"Bellow is a real craftsman. It's strange—as I reread *Herzog* I read slower and slower, until it took me several minutes to complete one page. I stopped at each sentence; I tested it; I asked myself, 'How did the man think of this phrase? How can I do it without copying him?' At one point, Bellow describes the look in Herzog's wife as 'terrifying menstrual ice.' Not bad, eh?"

"I doubt whether a woman would find it very apt."

Nicholas snorted. "I was rather taken by it. The trouble with Bellow's metaphors is that when I find one I fancy, I want to produce one myself. I got so enamored of his endocrinological simile, all I could think of was some glandular equivalent like 'dripping adrenals.'"

"That's as bad as 'menstrual ice.'"

Nicholas looked annoyed. "I think you're being too literal, but I was unhappy with it for a different reason. It sounded too much like 'adrenal rage,' which I'm sure has been used lots of times, but I'd never heard of 'menstrual ice.' The beauty of such a combination is that, even though you've never encountered it, it makes immediate sense."

Suddenly Marx switched topics. "So why did you decide to interview me? There is nothing very special about writers of first novels, is there?"

It was one question Sabine knew she had considered. She was prepared. "I thought it would be interesting to interview the writer of a successful first book."

"Sure," interrupted Marx, "but why me? They're a dime a dozen—or even a gross."

"Frankly, Berg's review of *Middles* intrigued me. Your anonymity struck me as an interesting angle. So I got in touch with your publisher, and they claimed not to know anything about you. Even more intriguing, your agent said he'd never met you. Is that true, or was he fooling me?"

"Was that all?"

"Initially it was," said Sabine. "But then, as I started preparing myself for this story and rereading your book I recalled Berg's last comment—"

"The one about Stephen Marx?"

Sabine hesitated. "Yes. I was wondering whether he meant it in a generic sense, just using Stephen Marx as an example of a popular and highly successful writer, or did he have something more specific in mind."

"Such as?"

This is getting too close, Sabine thought. I'm not ready. "I thought maybe he'd detected some stylistic resemblance; that you might have been influenced by Marx. After all, you might have been an acquaintance or a student of his."

"Was Marx a teacher?"

"According to *Who's Who*, he's lectured at some colleges. Does that make him a teacher? It's one of the things I'll have to check."

Marx looked puzzled. "How come?"

A wonderful idea had just occurred to Sabine, so suddenly it was out before she had time to consider it. "I'm going to work on Stephen Marx's biography," she said.

It had the desired effect. Marx almost rose to his feet in surprise. "*You?*" he exclaimed. "Why do you want to write his biography?"

"Well, for one thing, no one has written one as yet."

"That's hardly enough reason to write a biography."

"I don't know about that," replied Sabine. "He's certainly an interesting writer, he's very well known, his death was mysterious—so why not be the first to write his biography?"

Marx kept looking at her without saying anything. Sabine continued.

"As I just told you, there is a bit of a connection between you and him." She didn't take her eyes of him as she spoke but Marx displayed no emotion. He just kept staring at her.

"When I gave serious thought to working on Marx's biography, I started to look at some of the other Marx books. Before I knew it, I'd read all thirteen of them. After I'd gone through Marx's novels, especially *Cohen's Dilemma*, I became curious about the stylistic resemblance between the two of you."

"And what did you conclude?" Marx's tone seemed devoid of emotion, but she noticed that his every limb seemed tightly held.

"Let me ask you," Sabine countered. She had decided that she was enjoying herself very much. "To what extent were you influenced by Marx, and did you know him?"

This time Marx did rise, though slowly. He walked over to the window, his back to Sabine. Until now, she thought, I'd always left him room to duck. But now he'll either have to tell the truth or lie.

Without turning to face Sabine, Marx spoke. "I've read many of his books. And I do admire him as a writer."

Well, thought Sabine, he's good at this game. "Were you influenced by his writings?"

"Who knows?" Marx returned to his chair, but kept looking out the window rather than at Sabine. "If I was influenced by him, it was probably unconsciously. You know how that is. You'll find similarities between many writers if you really dig for them. Maybe you've read too much Marx in too short a period." He gave a brief laugh. "Thirteen books is a lot. Especially if you read them all in a few months."

Sabine pretended to consider this. "Maybe you're right. Enough about Marx, anyway; what about Mann? Can we talk about you?"

Marx shrugged his shoulders. "You can ask."

"Why all the secrecy? Do you have something to hide?"

Marx let out an exasperated breath. "Don't tell me you've never heard of a writer who wanted to remain anonymous."

"Sure," nodded Sabine, "but offhand I cannot think of any who actually achieved it." She remembered Gumelkian's comments. "Take Salinger or Pynchon—they are very private authors but one does know something about them: at least we know they're men; we even know when and where they were born and a few other biographical tidbits."

"Oh, but there are authors who've remained completely anonymous. Take B. Traven—he didn't even disclose his first name. Or Robert Heinlein, who published under his own name and four others. When you publish under a pseudonym and don't broadcast the fact, you're anonymous."

Marx was very good at this. Sabine decided to push him a little. "But Mann isn't a pseudonym, is it? Or have you written other books under another name? Is this really your first novel?"

Marx was up to the challenge. He only smiled mysteriously. "What do you think?"

"Even before I met you, I was convinced you'd written quite a bit before *Middles*."

"What made you think so?"

"Initially it was your very polished prose. Even Berg remarked on it. And now, having met you, I'm even more certain."

Marx raised his eyebrows in mock surprise.

"What I mean," said Sabine, "is your age."

"My age?" Marx pretended outrage. "Come, Ms. Diehlsdorf, I'm not that old!"

"Call me Sabine."

"Are you sure you'd want to be that chummy? A serious journalist should keep a professional distance."

Something in his tone made Sabine decide to play it safe. "I didn't mean *ancient*," she said. "But you are . . . I don't know . . . middle-aged? You're surely in your late forties. Wouldn't it be surprising to find someone at that age who's never written fiction and right away comes up with a first-class novel?"

Marx shrugged his shoulders. "Oh, I don't know. To me it sounds plausible, but that's because it applies to me. It just depends when one starts writing."

"Well then, when did you start? And what did you do before then?"

Sabine waited for more but Marx said nothing. His eyes had again started to drift toward the window before he continued, "I think this is enough. In fact, more than enough. I didn't expect you and we've now talked for well over an hour. I have things to do—namely my writing—and I've got to leave for work by 5:30."

"What kind of job do you have?" asked Sabine.

"If you don't mind, I'd just as soon not continue the conversation."

Sabine felt it best not to push her luck; she rose and reached for her raincoat. "I hope we can continue this conversation some time."

Marx gave her a long look: speculative? scared? She couldn't tell. "Sure," he said finally. "Some time."

"Could I come tomorrow?"

Marx looked exasperated. "I said 'some time,' but frankly I didn't mean that soon."

"I don't mean to be pushy," said Sabine, "it's just that I can only afford to stay a few days; I've got to go back to New York by the end of this week at the latest."

Marx grunted. "Tomorrow is Wednesday," he said, as if that should mean something to her. "I can't do it then; every other day I also go swimming at the Y. I'm a creature of habit: I do regular exercise, I do regular writing, I'm really not very interesting."

"Look, Mr. Mann—"

"Why don't you call me Donald?" interrupted Marx. "Or do you think I'm too old for you to call me Donald?"

"No, of course not," Sabine added hastily. "Let me propose something. I'm a habitual jogger. Instead of your swim, why don't you jog with me tomorrow and we can talk while we run?"

"I don't like to run. I've never run in San Francisco."

"Have you run anywhere else?"

Marx seemed oblivious to the purpose of her question. "No. It seems rather dull, particularly running in a city."

"What's so interesting about swimming laps? You can't even talk while you do that."

Marx grinned. "That's precisely why I like to swim. I get some of my best ideas while swimming."

She looked him up and down. "You look in good shape. Don't you think it will be possible for you to run a few miles with me? If it turns out to be too much, we can always stop and sit somewhere."

They had been standing by the door, Marx leaning against it. His hand was on the door handle. Now he opened it and said: "Tomorrow morning at ten. Where do you want to meet?"

That was almost too easy, Sabine thought. She hoped she didn't sound smug when she said, "Would you be willing to come to my hotel? Of course, if you prefer," she added quickly, "I can come here and pick you up."

"I'll pick you up." The door was now wide open. "Where are you staying?"

"The Beresford, on Sutter near Mason."

He extended his hand. "All right, I'll see you tomorrow."

12

From the hotel elevator she saw Stephen leaning against the front desk. Oh my goodness, Sabine thought: is this how he's going running? Marx was wearing tennis shoes, blue jeans, and a turtleneck. She greeted him with a skeptical smile. "I've done all the necessary exploring. Are you game for a real run or just a modest jog?"

"What's a real run?"

"What I did yesterday. I ran from here to the Marina and then on to the Golden Gate bridge. It was so beautiful, I kept right on running to the other side and then back."

It was Marx's turn to look skeptical. "How far was that?"

"About fourteen miles. But we can take the bus to the Marina and start from there. That's only eight."

"Eight miles?"

"Is that OK?" she asked. Against her will, a touch of concern crept into her voice.

Marx responded, a little stiffly. "Eight is OK."

As they walked toward the bus, Sabine pointed to his feet. "Are those the best shoes you have?"

"What's wrong with my shoes?" retorted Marx. "They're perfectly decent tennis shoes."

Sabine broke out laughing. "So they are. But I'm taking you jogging, not to a tennis match. Never mind, you'll survive. But you should get some decent running shoes."

"I'm a swimmer, not a jogger."

"Is that the only exercise you do?"

"No, I go cross-country skiing in the winter. What about you?"

"I love cross-country skiing. I haven't had much opportunity since I moved to New York."

The bus was approaching the yacht basin near Fort Mason, in plain sight of the Golden Gate Bridge. Marx stood up, clutching a handrail for balance. Sabine rose as well, and as they stepped off the bus, said, "Stephen, would you mind if I ask some questions while we're running?"

Marx just shrugged. He had given no indication that she had called him Stephen. The lack of response had made her curious: was he not listening or was he still accustomed to thinking of himself as Stephen?

It was one of those great San Francisco early spring days: breezy, middle fifties, gin-clear blue sky. Sabine started on some quick limbering-up exercises. Marx just stood by, watching.

"Come on, Stephen, you need to stretch those tendons."

Somewhat self-consciously, he mimicked her movements.

"All right, let's go." Sabine started at a modest clip. Within a couple of minutes she noticed perspiration on Marx's face and stopped.

"I'm getting warm, how about you?" She took off her windbreaker, deftly tied it around her waist, and then stepped out of her sweatpants, draping them around her shoulders.

Marx had started to remove his turtleneck; by the time his face reappeared he saw a very different Sabine in front of him. God, what legs, he thought: hard muscular thighs and calves, recently shaved or naturally hairless. If he hadn't known she was a runner he would've assumed she was a dancer. As they resumed their run, Marx deliberately fell behind. Yesterday's physical impression of Sabine had been confined to her face, hands, and seemingly firm buttocks. Now he could see how firm they really were. There was nothing skinny about her, but also no excess. It was all smooth muscle. A spreading feeling in his groin warned him to be careful.

"Come on, Stephen," Sabine called as she slowed down to let him catch up. "You've got to run next to me if we're going to talk."

This time, *Stephen* had registered. "What did you call me?" he asked, stopping abruptly.

Sabine feigned innocence. "Why, what did I call you?"

"You called me Stephen. How come?"

"Did I really? I guess I've been thinking too much about Stephen Marx." She turned, as if about to run again.

Marx took her by the crook of an arm. "What really brought you here?"

"I already told you, I wanted to interview you," said Sabine.

"Where are you going to publish it?"

"I haven't decided yet. It depends on the story."

"You aren't serious, are you?"

"Dead-serious. It will make a real difference to my career."

"As what?"

"As a journalist."

For a long time, Marx simply looked at her. He was searching for something in her face, or just for something to say, she couldn't tell. The breeze from the water felt chill on her skin. Sabine was about to tell him that a steady rhythm was all-important in running, but he gave her no chance. When he spoke again, it was obvious he was in no mood for jokes. "What about my life?" he asked quietly. "Has it occurred to you what your article could do to me?"

Sabine answered truthfully. "I hadn't given it much thought—"

"You have the nerve to barge into my place, to intrude on my privacy, and then to tell me you haven't even thought about the consequences?"

Sabine didn't mind his anger—she felt strangely calm. She waved him on. "Come on," she said. "Let's run while I answer you. I didn't mean to sound thoughtless." She glanced at him to see if he was going to follow her, but he was rooted to the walk, arms crossed. "I just don't understand why you're committed to such total anonymity. How long do you plan to keep it up? If it's only temporary, then I'm prepared to wait."

"And if it's permanent?"

"Then I won't wait." Her voice was low but firm.

Marx shook his head several times. "You are so monumentally impertinent that I don't know whether I should laugh or just walk away."

"Donald." Sabine spoke rapidly so as to stop any interruptions. "You'll do neither. You won't laugh, because I'm serious. And you won't walk away, because then you won't get the answer to the question you asked earlier."

Marx looked blank.

"Don't you want to know how I found you? Of course you do. So why don't you keep running and let me talk."

Marx remained standing. "Why is writing about me important to you? Nobody wants to know about Donald Mann."

"Lots of people will be interested. Especially when they learn the reasons behind your compulsion to hide your identity. See?—I won't give away your address; I just want to delve into the reasons behind your decision. I want to be a good journalist—I'm in my final year at Columbia and such a story is bound to get some attention. Maybe even land me a good job. Don't you understand that?"

Marx was getting chilled. They were close to the Golden Gate and the wind was picking up. He was almost grateful when Sabine resumed running. He followed. In their brief rest, the muscles in his legs seemed to have congealed. This is getting absurd, he thought. Not talking to her won't get me anywhere—she's right about that. "Who else knows that you've found me?" he puffed aloud as they turned onto the walkway of the bridge.

Sabine was about to reply "nobody," but something kept her from saying so. She glanced back at him, but there was nothing in his face but annoyance. "What difference does that make?" she asked.

"Plenty. Have you talked to anybody else?"

"Donald, let's make a deal. First, answer some of my questions. Then I'll answer yours. After all, you don't have to answer any questions you don't want to."

Marx tried to give a wry laugh. It came out more as a wheeze. "You're extraordinarily generous, Ms. Diehlsdorf."

"Thank you, Mr. Mann," she said with mock courtesy. "Tell me, is Donald Mann your real name?"

For a long moment she only heard his labored breathing. "Can't you think of any reasons?" he panted.

"I can think of many," replied Sabine, "depending on whether they are personal or professional. Which were they with you?"

Coherent thought seemed to have abandoned Marx. He struggled, feeling as though every idea was as heavy as his leaden feet. It was simply unbelievable that all of his carefully laid plans were about to be destroyed by this hard-headed, hard-assed young woman. They reached the midpoint of the Golden Gate. The roadbed seemed to turn, just barely, down. Inspiration struck him.

"Tell me, Sabine, do you really think that a single story would launch your professional career? How would you prove it wasn't a cock-and-bull story? What if I disappeared as soon as you return to New York? Who'd believe you then?"

He is a smart man, Sabine thought, but he doesn't know all I know, and now I'm sure I won't tell him all. "I suppose that will depend on how well I do my job," was all she said.

Marx would not be put off. "You know," he puffed, "a newspaper article, however sensational, is very ephemeral. In a couple of days people will have forgotten it."

"How do you know I'll write a newspaper article?" replied Sabine. "How about a magazine article? Or maybe two?"

"The same—only slightly less ephemeral. Why don't you write a novel?"

Sabine was caught by surprise. "What do you mean?"

"Write a roman à clef—the story of a writer who decides to hide his identity. Then you can speculate about his motives to your heart's content. I might even help you—that is, if you're interested."

It was Sabine's turn to stop suddenly. "You must be kidding."

"No, I'm not."

Marx had expected this offer to confound her, but he hadn't been prepared for her response. Without a word, Sabine turned and took off. She set a blistering pace down the bridge, leaving Marx behind. He is very good at this, she told herself as the distance between them widened. She needed a minute to think, to calculate her next move. Maybe I'm out of my league.

Try as he might, Marx could not catch up with Sabine's new pace. By the time he had reached the Marin end of the bridge, Sabine had stopped and put on her running suit. She was breathing normally while Marx's chest was heaving, perspiration stinging in his eyes.

"Better put on your turtleneck or you'll get chilled." She pointed to a stone wall. "I sat there yesterday. It's out of the wind."

Marx sat next to her in the sun. They were both looking at the San Francisco skyline across the water; a few sailboats were darting back and forth among the whitecaps; a container ship was passing through the Golden Gate, outward bound.

"What a city," sighed Sabine. "I wish I could get a job here." Suddenly she turned toward Marx. "How long have you been living here?"

"Quite some time."

"That's what I call an informative answer. Look, Donald, this is not part of the interview, it's off the record. Does that sound official enough?" Marx made no response. "What kind of job do you have here? You mentioned you worked evenings. Remember, off the record—or if I use it, it will only be in my novel." Her tone was teasing.

Marx seemed oblivious. He was looking across the water in the direction of Alcatraz; suddenly he turned to her. "I'm a waiter."

Sabine was startled. "A waiter?"

Marx saw her surprise, and it pleased him. "What did you think I did at night? Bank president? Brain surgeon? What's wrong with being a waiter? All you have to do is exchange one letter—replace the *A* by an *R*—and you turn into a writer."

"I thought you were a teacher," Sabine confessed. "I thought you taught night school."

"And what would I be teaching?"

"Creative writing, of course. Besides," she added, recovering a little of her self-possession, "a waiter your age would look sallow and be flat-footed. With a belly. You don't look the part at all." She thought a bit of flattery would do no harm. She was right: Marx smiled and dropped the subject.

But he had presented her with an opening. "How long have you been a waiter?"

Marx grinned. "You don't give up, do you?"

A little shyly, Sabine grinned back. "No," she said.

"About a year."

"And what did you do before?"

"On or off the record?"

"Off. This is the novelist asking." Sabine tried to be offhand and joking at the same time. For a change it worked.

"I wrote full-time. And then I left my wife. . . ."

Deliberately, Sabine looked away from Marx, across the water, feigning a casualness she did not feel. Was he going to tell her about Marx? He was certainly getting closer to the truth.

Marx moved beside her at the rail, looking in the same direction. "I didn't want anyone to know where I'd moved to," he said. "Think about it: a forty-nine-year-old man, needing employment quickly, no references? He doesn't have many options open. Novelist Diehlsdorf—think about that one when you construct your hero."

"OK," replied Sabine slowly, "but whatever job you got, you needed a Social Security card, didn't you? How did you get one under a new name? Or did you just use your old number?"

Marx looked impressed. She's thought about this, he told himself. Why? "You're right," he said. "It didn't take me long to find that out. You can't even open a bank account without a Social Security number."

"Then how did you do it?"

"Off the record?"

"Off the record. Cross my heart."

"I went to the Death Records office here in San Francisco and looked for death certificates of men born around 1974. Can you guess why I picked that year?"

"Why '74?"

"Most young men of that age would already have a Social Security number, but would have accumulated so few benefits that the death would not even have been reported to the Social Security office. I copied the relevant information from the death certificate—all I needed was a name, date, and place of birth. I looked for somebody who died in San Francisco but was born elsewhere, in a large city. Donald Spencer Mann was born on July 5, 1974 in Seattle and died in San Francisco. I wrote to the Seattle Department of Vital Statistics for a new birth certificate and sent them a money order for $3.50. Once I got it, I mailed a copy of it to the Social Security office asking for a new Social Security card which Donald Mann had supposedly lost. If you're below eighteen years of age, you can order a card by mail, provided you enclose a birth certificate. If you're older, you've got to do it in person. Simple, isn't it?"

There was something boyishly triumphant about Stephen Marx as he concluded his explanation. Sabine listened with almost motherly pleasure, but as the look of triumph faded, something else that had been hidden beneath it persisted, until the boy before her eyes turned into a shrewd adult. She'd been on the verge of congratulations, but now she caught herself.

"That was clever," she said approvingly. "But," she continued innocently, "weren't you hoist with your own petard?" She'd always considered this phrase a terrible cliché. She always winced when she saw it in print. But now, it suddenly seemed apt: Donald Mann riding off into literary combat in supposed anonymity with one explosion of his petard—the success of his first novel—suddenly making him highly visible.

"How so?"

"Once Mann's first novel is out and a success, surely sooner or later somebody will put two and two together."

"What do you mean?"

"Your fellow waiters, the bank cashiers, the people in the coffeehouse where you have breakfast, the attendant at the Y where you swim—don't any of them read? One day, won't one of them ask whether you're the D. Mann whose book they'd just read?"

"I could always deny it. Mann is not that rare a name," he said.

"I doubt it," she said. "It's simply not in character."

Marx snorted. "You've got a good reporter's nose, Sabine. You're right. But let's see what kind of novelist you'll make. How would you've gotten your character out of such a fix?"

Sabine furrowed her brow, wondering if she wasn't laying it on a bit thick: she had already puzzled over this one, and after hearing Marx's story she knew she'd been on the right track. But she let her answer come out hesitantly.

"I would've gotten two social security cards—one for everyday use: the waiter persona. The other for the writer: for his royalties, income tax returns, that kind of thing."

Marx was torn between admiration and wariness. How does she know all this?

"Is that what you did?"

Marx just nodded.

"What is your other name?"

"Oh, come on, Sabine. You've got to leave a man some privacy. You won't need that second name, not as a journalist nor as a novelist. You do agree, don't you?"

It wasn't clear whether the last sentence was supplication, threat, question, or a mixture of all three. Sabine let it pass. "How did you figure out all this?"

Marx's grin was all-encompassing. "You probably won't believe it, but it's true: I needed such a scenario for an earlier novel—"

"Ah, so *Middles* is not your first book?"

"Off the record?"

"Yes, off the record. But if I promise this too often, I'll have no story left."

"Oh yes you will—you can use it in your novel. No, you were right earlier when you guessed that I'd written something before *Middles*. But enough of that—on or off the record. It's getting late. Let's head back. And this time, no talking."

In spite of his aching calf muscles, as they headed back Marx felt strangely exhilarated. For the first time in a year he felt some kind of contact with his former life; he could almost—though not quite—talk about it. And then there were the other attractions of the situation: the element of risk, the challenge of brinkmanship with a clever, attractive, young woman. His life in San Francisco had been virtually monastic. His choice; he hadn't wanted to be questioned by a lover about his past. But while he had come to the point of congratulating himself over how well he'd adapted to a celibate life style, there were times when he had missed not just sex but female company, with its hidden and overt sexual overtones. At least once the temptation had been too great to resist; he'd yielded on his first cross-country skiing trip in the Sierras shortly after Thanksgiving.

He had joined a mixed group, organized by the Sierra Club, that stayed overnight in the club's lodge near Donner Pass. One of the skiers was a high school teacher, Sibyl, in her early to middle thirties: no beauty, but a first-class athlete; well read; a cheerful conversationalist. Saturday night, after skiing, several members of the group walked to the sauna house in the woods. To Marx's surprise, he and one of the women were the only persons wearing a towel. The rest were naked. After a few minutes in the searing heat, Sibyl, nude and glistening with perspiration, approached him. "You haven't been in a sauna before, have you?" she said. Marx, distracted, had only shaken his head. "Come out into the snow," she called over her shoulder as she turned, giving him (on purpose? he wondered) a full 360-degree view of her taut body. "You'll feel wonderful," she promised as she opened the door.

Outside, she grabbed some snow, running it slowly over her arms and breasts. It made her nipples stand straight out. "Let me give you a snow rub." Without waiting for a reply, she rubbed snow over his shoulders, chest, and belly. The shock made Stephen drop his towel. Before he knew what was happening, Sibyl had laughingly reached down and given him two quick, expert, ice-cold strokes.

Stephen still remembered that night in the lodge. Was it Sibyl's expertise, or the fact that he had been celibate for months? Whatever the reason, it had seemed superb sex to him. He never learned Sibyl's last name. On the next Sierra Club trip, he looked for her, but she wasn't there.

At the Marina bus stop Sabine quickly slipped into her clothing. "Not bad, was it? Why don't you buy yourself some decent shoes and start running?"

"We'll see how I feel later." Marx answered as if his thoughts were elsewhere. On the run back, watching Sabine's bare legs pumping rhythmically before him, he had been hatching a plan. "But I think I ought to return the favor."

Sabine was fumbling with the cord at the hem of her wind-breaker. She looked up. "What do you mean?"

"How about going cross-country skiing with me? I've got the next few days off. You said you hadn't had much chance to ski lately. And there are professional advantages as well."

She looked at him with narrowed eyes. "Professional advantages?"

"Talking on skis is easier and quieter. It's also more private."

"I'd love to!" exclaimed Sabine, "but I didn't bring anything to wear in the snow."

"Don't you have jeans and a sweater?"

"That's the only thing I have, that and my windbreaker. That's not enough."

"Never mind, you can rent the boots, skis, and poles in the same place where I always get my gear. I'm sure they'll rent you a parka. I have an extra pair of gloves and I'll treat you to some wool socks. What more do you need? Wait till you see what spring skiing can be like in California." Marx sounded boyishly enthusiastic and Sabine liked seeing him in that mood. Why not? she thought.

13

Considering the intensity with which Noah Berg was scraping the recesses of his soufflé dish, it seemed to Miriam that his fork was on a never-ending search. For what, exactly, wasn't clear, but it had seemed to her for some time that Berg's passion for soufflé was one of the few clues to an inner life that he kept otherwise well under wraps. This reticence of Berg's had come to occupy more and more of Miriam's thoughts in recent days, enough to prompt her to extraordinary measures. She invited him to dinner at her apartment, breaking a social isolation that had been intact since Stephen's death. They had been seeing each other off and on for several months, but the venue had always been public, the subject ostensibly research for Berg's retrospective review. This was different; though from Berg's composure when she had extended the invitation it had been hard to tell if he felt anything similar. So she had planned the menu with an eye toward spoiling him, and perhaps something more: creation of a double-soufflé meal.

After melon and microtome-cut prosciutto, which he had brought, together with a bottle of 1984 Ridge Montebello Cabernet, as evidence of his desire for participation, she'd served the main dish: a cauliflower-leek-ginger soufflé with a Parmesan base—a composition, Berg volunteered, he'd never encountered before—followed by a black currant dessert soufflé, which had become the cause for the fussy scraping of his fork. She'd refused to volunteer any other cutlery.

"Only amateurs or pessimists offer spoons. The test of a perfect soufflé is whether you can eat it with a fork!"

Miriam knew at least why she had decided to spoil Berg so shamelessly. In contrast to Stephen, who had been utterly dismissive of her desire to produce a cookbook, Noah had been fascinated when she told him her plan. He had been especially taken with her explanation of the title *Can You Do It Backward?*

"What an all-encompassing title! You know, I think the principle would apply even in my business. Take the difference between reviewers and critics: a reviewer must first read the book before starting on the review. He can't do it backward. But not so with the critic: he or she," he gave a slight, deferential bow in Miriam's direction, "frequently starts with a position, an interpretation, an intellectual bias, that doesn't require reading of the book as the initial step. Any critic worth the salt can do it backward."

"So you admit to total bias?"

"Absolutely not," he said firmly. "The word 'bias' has no operational meaning in my critical vocabulary. Everybody is biased. Fame causes just as much bias as obscurity; wealth as much as poverty; brilliance as much as dimness—"

"Stop! I get the point. You know, Noah," she threw him an affectionate glance, "you're part wise man, yet also part wise guy. I've come to like that combination. But it's a tricky balance to maintain." She wagged her finger warningly.

"I promise to be careful," he answered in the same vein. "I'll balance each wise crack with at least one bon mot."

"It's a deal. And while I get the coffee, think of one."

"I'm not sure whether this counts as a true bon mot," Berg announced when Miriam returned with the cafetière and carefully pushed the plunger. "But this meal reminds me of something Francis Bacon wrote nearly four hundred years ago: 'Some books are to be tasted, others to be swallowed, and some few to be chewed and digested.' That was a meal that deserves plenty of digesting! I can barely move!"

"Don't then," Miriam said. "Relax and sip your coffee."

Berg sighed and settled back in his seat. "That's one of the tricks of the trade, you know."

"What?"

"Sentences like Bacon's. Or this one: 'a vexing potpourri of the laughable, the biting, and the wrenching.' A reviewer can use them for almost any purpose. It even fits into your 'can you do it backward?' category. You can begin or end with it."

"So where have you used them?" she asked.

"So far, nowhere. I've kept them in reserve. I may well use one or the other for my piece on Stephen."

Miriam had noticed over the course of the last couple of months how 'your husband' had become 'Stephen.' It was another sign of increasing comfort and familiarity between the two of them.

Berg picked up the thread of the conversation. "I've been skimming some of his earlier novels. There are a number that deserve digesting. Maybe that was Stephen's strength."

"Be generous in your critique," Miriam said.

Berg recalled that she had used that phrase when they first met. "Quoting Bacon with reference to Stephen's oeuvre surely falls within the definition of generosity."

"It all depends, Noah. Remember, you're talking to a chef. Chewing and digesting doesn't mean that it tastes wonderful. Better reread some of the books rather than just skim them."

In fact, Berg had not even skimmed the early books. He'd focused on the early book reviews, notably his own.

(1) *The Academy of Spite* (1962)

Stephen Marx, a young Yale man, has written a story of university life, apparently from the inside. Marx's exploration of the ins and outs of the academic profession—in a university whose reputation and hermetic atmosphere resemble those of Yale—is both rich in detail and suspenseful in unexpected ways. To accomplish this, Marx must delineate the particular dramas of academia clearly enough to make them universal. And he does.

(2) *Oxen of the Sun* (1964)

Marx's second novel, whose title comes from Homer via James Joyce, is slightly less crisply delineated than his first, *The Academy of Spite*. And yet it works remarkably well. The story is set on the vast plains of Africa, and once again we feel that Marx has *been there* and we are privileged to go there, too, on the strength of his considerable lyric and descriptive skill. The influence of

Joyce is perhaps too strong here, but Marx's final product is wholly original.

(3) *Flying from Rio* (1968)

In his latest novel, Marx has infiltrated the steamy world of tropical drug smugglers, and once again we are blessed with a richly rendered atmosphere. The hero of *Flying from Rio*, Christopher Braden, is a personality recognizable from Marx's earlier novels—a sort of Superman in skill and sensitivity, and intellectually aware of his own superiority. If drug smuggling is the frontier of the late 20th century—the last stage set from larger-than-life good guys and bad guys, then Marx has us convinced.

Everyone would agree that his early reviews fell into the "generous" category, Berg thought. The situation had become tricky with Marx's National Book Award winner, the one about nuns, and his Pulitzer Prize novel, *Gasps of Delight*. It's not easy to damn books covered with accolades, but all these had been after Monica. Berg had not shown these reviews to Miriam. And the more time he spent with her, the less satisfied he was reading his own commentary, so clouded by revenge. Yet he had to accept the truism he himself had applied to all reviews: "What is said cannot be unsaid." How many reviewers have changed their published opinion of a given book? Ungenerous judgment cannot be transformed into generous praise.

(9) *Listen, Sister* (1980)

In *Listen, Sister*, Marx has made another attempt at plunging into an unfamiliar profession or situation and has tried to make us understand how it works. In this book it's nuns, and we're expected to follow once more the incredibly detailed routes of Marx's research. While the premise is interesting—a hero fitting the description of Marx's usual hero finds himself in a position to tell his life story to a formerly married nun—the impact is lost in the wash of mere information.

(12) *Gasps of Delight* (1985)

Gasps of Delight, whose very title is a cheap shot at romance literature, turns out to be not about the medieval-maiden-taken-by-brutish-but-sensitive-knight, but about the pleasures of an art dealer in the works he handles. Marx's presentation is as off-kilter as the title, for as we wade through the mass of detail and trade jargon, we've forgotten why we started.

(13) *Cohen's Dilemma* (1988)

Steven Marx has once again immersed himself for months (we're told) in an unfamiliar milieu and has produced another over-developed exposé of its workings. One wonders about these abbreviated ventures into the jargon, etiquette, protocol and re-wards of a particular occupation (in this case, research scien-tists)—are they mere showcases for Marx's vaunted research abilities? Are we supposed to generalize these people's problems to our own lives? Or is the point merely educational? If we are supposed to relate to these people, then the novel is mired too deeply in the intricacies of the scientific world to do us much good. Perhaps after thirteen novels, Marx should abandon the genre altogether and take up writing the sort of journalistic his-tory turned out by Tom Wolfe and Norman Mailer.

"Let's stop talking about my profession," Berg said. "I'm tired of literature tonight. All we've talked about is Stephen's work, the kind of sense it makes, all that. What about him? Surely he didn't make sense all the time. What were his idiosyncrasies?"

"Let me think," she said reflectively. "It's hard to think of a good story about him without being. . . ." She didn't finish the sentence, even though *disloyal* was about to slip off her tongue. Did loyalty even matter now? she wondered.

"How about this one? Steve hated book schnorrers: the people who heard about his latest novel and immediately asked, 'why don't you send me a copy?' What pissed him off was that the most persistent schnorrers were invariably the most affluent ones. 'Can you imagine them going to an artist and asking for the gift of a painting?' And then he ran across the text of a letter written over one hundred fifty years ago by Michael Faraday. He had it framed and hung it in his closet so he'd see it every morning and eve-ning. You know Noah, I've still not touched his closet . . . it's still hanging there."

Miriam returned with a plainly framed page, evidently generated by a laser printer, and handed it to Berg.

Dear Sir,

I am much flattered by your enquiry after my book. I have no copies of it in my own hand but if you wish it, I will send word to the Publisher to send you a copy but I thought before doing so I would ascertain whether you might not rather like to order it of your own bookstore.

I am Sir

Your very obliged servant

Michael Faraday

"May I copy this?" asked Berg, laughing.

Miriam shrugged. "Sure, why not?"

It got her thinking what other tidbits she could offer Noah. There used to be a time when living with an author was great fun. Steve was like a sponge, soaking up daily every kind of oddity that might prove useful for his next novel. He'd pick them up in newspapers, books, conversations, jotting them down in the small notebooks he always carried with him. She wondered what he had done with them. He used to keep them around the house. Had they also gone to his study?

"He was very observant," she said, half-aloud, "and particularly interested in idiosyncrasies of ethnic or professional groups. He used them to authenticate his characters. For instance, did you know that Russians and Americans count differently with their hands?" She looked at him expectantly.

"I thought so," she said, seeing him shake his head. "Neither did I. Steve used it in *Gasps of Delight* with the Russian émigré collector. I've never forgotten the scene. Russians start with an open hand, closing each finger as they count, finally ending up in a fist at count five. We do it just the other way around. My God, Noah," she exclaimed. "Another illustration of how to tell apart two cultures with 'can you do it backward?'" She leaned back with a pleased expression.

"Steve's conclusion was an interesting one: is that a reflection of their closed and our open society? Is that a Lamarckian trait which will disappear in a generation or two once glasnost has become ingrained?"

They were sitting on the sofa now, Berg at one end, Miriam not quite at the far end. She sank back in the cushions and looked at him over her cup of coffee. Berg's gaze, abstracted, did not meet hers. They were silent a minute or two.

"What about you, Noah?"

He looked up.

"You sometimes seem something of a closed society yourself. You keep asking questions without disclosing your progress or when you'll be finished. What have you been finding?"

Berg hesitated, wondering whether he should disclose some of his more picayune activities. Why *was* he moving so slowly on this project? It wasn't simply the old truism about the dish best eaten cold—although that certainly was part of it. He wanted this piece to be perfect, his masterwork as a critic to coincide with his masterstrike of revenge. But his growing interest in Miriam was complicating things. Romancing the widow of the man who had taken away his woman had seemed a fine addition to his plot at first. But such plots, he was finding, were easier to plan than to carry out. As the years had passed since that infamous National Book Award festivity at the Plaza, Berg had acknowledged to himself that he had been a generic rather than deliberately specific victim of Marx's roving eye. Time, of course, is a great healer. Would he and Monica still have been together, even if she and Marx had never crossed paths?

He was about to relate to Miriam his sporadic current efforts at cataloging some of Marx's stylistic quirks, like the tendency to make lists of participles: instead of finding a woman "fussing," in Marx's text she would be "fretting, stewing, groping, and flittering." But he had to come up with something more than alerting her to his pedantic streak; he needed topics that would move the widow into the critic's camp.

"You know," he said slowly, as if reflecting, "books are edifices constructed out of abstractions, meaning words, but the builders are human. I like to focus on the human builders and their foibles. Novels generally don't use the present indicative unless they're written in the first person. Stephen never wrote a novel in the first person—maybe he didn't want to be accused of autobiographical mining—but he has written no less than two novels in the present tense."

"Which ones?" she asked curiously.

"The ones without sex."

She nodded slowly. The whole conversation seemed for her to have gone into slow motion. She had plenty of time to consider her response. "I thought about that question," she said hesitatingly. "Ever since you brought it up that first time."

"And?" Berg reclined in his corner of the couch, gazing at her.

"I don't know . . . but it did seem to coincide with writing in his other place."

"Miriam." He sat up suddenly, glancing at his watch. "It's not even 10 o'clock. Do you have to get up early tomorrow?"

No," she replied. "Why do you ask?"

"Let's take a cab over to Stephen's studio. We haven't been there since the time I picked up the book jackets."

If Miriam had read anything in Berg's question or facial expression, she didn't let on. She agreed without further hesitation.

"Why not?" she said, and got her coat.

Their first sexual coupling, that night on Stephen Marx's sofa had not been superb. Instead of concentrating on each other's bodies and pleasure, each was visualizing someone else. Miriam could not help but wonder what other women had spread their thighs on this very spot. Was the chasteness of Steve's last novels some form of denial? Or was that getting it backward? Had he been getting so much sex here that he had no further need to fantasize in his fiction?

Noah Berg's fixation was much more specific. When he had first sat on this couch, his fingers tracing the upholstery texture, his nerves had transmitted the imprint of Monica's naked ass to his brain. Now, he was imagining making love to her, even though it was Miriam's legs that encircled him.

Their lovemaking was nothing to trumpet about. Only partly undressed, the hurry with which Noah penetrated her when he found her wet and open, the absence of any words, just sexual panting: it had seemed almost furtive, as if they were afraid of being caught in the act. Even though it was hasty and almost adolescent, it was not so wanting that each had not decoded the significance of that act of sexual communion. Now that each had taken revenge on the dead man's sofa, their respective slates seemed to have been wiped clean.

"Let's walk back," Miriam had suggested as soon as she'd emerged from the bathroom. It was the towel hanging on the bar that had made her feel queasy. How long had it been dangling there? Who else had used it last? Her dead husband or some living lover?

They walked hand-in-hand down Central Park West to Columbus Circle and along 59th Street to the East Side.

"Stay with me tonight, Noah," she said when they arrived, well after midnight, at her apartment house. This time, they made attentive love to each other—naked and unhurriedly.

"We're doing it backward," she murmured, just before dozing off. "We should have started this way."

14

The borrowed car was a beaten-up, unwashed '81 Ford station wagon. Marx had never felt very possessive about cars—his years in Manhattan had converted him into a habitual taxi rider. The owner's assurance that the motor had recently been overhauled was good enough for him. He threw all the rental gear into the back.

"We'll stop at the neighborhood Safeway," said Marx. "We need to get something for the next couple of days. OK with you?"

Sabine nodded absentmindedly. She'd been reflecting on the drive ahead, the advantages of a captive conversational partner, one whose attention was necessarily focused elsewhere. The idea appealed to her. For once, her wandering eyes would not have to look for excuses on the floor or beyond her partner; she could study him in detail.

"Any preferences?" Marx sounded friendly. "I just realized I know nothing about your eating habits."

Sabine shrugged. "They won't teach you much. I'm a pretty simple eater. You pick the food; I'll just exercise my veto."

Marx took his backpack into the supermarket. "I don't want to be tempted to buy more than we can take with us while skiing." He selected several small cans of fruit juice, some hard apples, a couple of tangelos, trail mix, crackers, and hard cheese—all of it without eliciting commentary from his companion. But then he stopped to buy two tins of smoked oysters.

"Oysters? With trail mix? What kind of combination is that?"

Marx had expected such a comment. "You don't have to eat them together. But smoked oysters and crackers give a touch of elegance usually absent in cross-country ski snacks."

They'd been walking along one of the aisles. Suddenly, Marx stopped to pick up a bottle of TANG.

Sabine pointed to the container with amazement. "You talk of elegance and then buy TANG? I can't think of anything less elegant than mixing TANG with water. You've already bought several fruit juices."

"You're right about the elegance, but wrong about the water," replied Marx. "Wait and see."

Traffic across the Bay Bridge moved rapidly. In less than an hour they were past Livermore and well on their way to Manteca. "This is the first time I've gone skiing in the middle of the week," remarked Marx. "This traffic is a breeze. We'll be in Kirkwood before it gets dark."

Sabine had been gazing at the passing landscape; the winter hills were an unaccountably luscious green—an unexpected winter color for an Easterner—but otherwise she found the scenery bland. She turned toward Marx.

"What *did* you do before you became a waiter?"

The car covered perhaps three hundred yards in silence. "A writer."

"What kind?"

"Fiction; primarily novels, a few short stories."

"And before you became a writer?"

"I've always been a writer. Even as a kid I made up stories."

We're getting warm, thought Sabine. "Did you publish much?"

"A fair amount."

"Under what name?"

Marx looked at her sidelong. His glance was humorous, but it seemed to Sabine there was a little strain showing there. "This is for your novel, isn't it? Just make it up."

"I can't make it up for my article."

"Sabine, why do you want to be a journalist?" He said the word as if it referred to some lower order of life. "Think about your novel. You've got a good topic: a grown-up man, middle-aged, wants to start a new life without reference to his earlier one. Think of all the problems—simple ones—"

"Like a Social Security card?" interrupted Sabine.

"Yes, for instance that. Put yourself into the man's shoes: making new contacts in a city where he knows no one; learning how not to give away anything about his earlier life; training himself to turn around every time someone calls him by his new name; always being prepared with a plausible answer for sudden questions, which, precisely because of their sudden-ness, become dangerous. 'Where were you born, where—'"

"Where were you born, Donald?"

To her surprise, Marx replied: "New York."

"Is that the truth? Or one of your prepared responses?"

"It's both. I decided right away to make up as few things as possible. New York is such a big place, having been born there gives away nothing. It's not like Craig, Missouri, or York, Nebraska, where everybody knows everyone's family."

"Now why did you pick Craig and York?"

Marx threw her a quick glance. "You never give up, do you? That's precisely the type of question one might get and not antici-pate. Most people, of course, mean nothing by such questions—

they're just making conversation—but with you, I have to watch myself all the time."

"So why did you pick Craig and York? I've never heard of either one."

"I have, but I won't tell you how, because that would tell you something about me I'm not prepared to divulge at this time."

"But you'll tell me later?"

"God, you're persistent. I don't know whether I'll tell you later, but I certainly won't tell you now. At least not until I know whether I'm talking to a novelist or a journalist. Judging from your questions, you're still a nosy journalist."

A few miles slid by as silence settled between them. If I don't think of something soon, she thought, I won't be able to speak.

"What kind of men appeal to you?"

The question startled Sabine almost as much as the sound of Marx's voice. She looked carefully at him before answering slowly: "Kind ones."

"That's a strange answer."

"It's a strange question. What did you expect? Dark and tall ones? Kindness wears well, even better than humor. Kind and intelligent ones, affectionate too."

Another long stretch of silence descended on both of them. It was as if they had touched an unexpectedly sensitive nerve.

Eventually, it was Sabine who spoke. "What do you have against journalists?"

"I? I have nothing against journalists."

"You don't seem to like them."

"Nothing of the sort. I just think there are . . . higher aspirations."

"Oh? What's so high about novels? What's the difference?"

"It's a matter of style."

"Journalists have style."

"I don't mean journalists have *no* style—of course they do. Just take *TIME* magazine as an example—but the stylistic possibilities open to a journalist are much more limited. Not only can't you invent words; you must pitch your work at a very broad audience. Unless, of course, you write for the elite, like the occasional journalist writing in the *New Yorker*. Let me ask you a question. In your journalism course at Columbia, have they ever asked you to look at Empson's *Seven Types of Ambiguity*?"

"Never," replied Sabine. "He sounds like one of those typical 'how-to' writers: *Thirteen Ways to Avoid Paying Taxes, Eighteen Ways of Overcoming Shyness*."

"You're dead wrong," laughed Marx. "It's exactly Empson's type of insight that a good journalist ought to acquire, but rarely does."

"So why are there only seven?"

Marx had drawn a sudden blank. It had been years ago, at Yale, when he'd read Empson. "Sabine, you're a born journalist."

"Ouch. No style, too, I'll bet."

"Oh, you've got style," he said generously. "But style is only one difference—not even the most important one. The crucial difference between a journalist and a fiction writer is the latter's preoccupation with plot. An author is in total command of the plot, while the plot invariably governs the journalist. She has no leeway whatsoever—the moment she departs only slightly from the plot she becomes a lousy journalist. Just think about it—if you write a novel about D. Mann, you could even make him a woman."

Sabine regarded him with a skeptical eye. "Somehow," she said slowly, "I just can't see that."

Marx did not reply. The remark hung between them until it had acquired more significance than Sabine had intended. She could feel herself starting to blush.

Marx didn't notice. For the first time in weeks, he was thinking of Miriam, and this troubled him. Why now? he wondered. Why had it been so long?

Once they reached Highway 88, a two-lane road in the Sierra foothills, traffic became very light: no commuters traveled on this section of the foothills, and in the middle of the week, few skiers were heading for the mountains. In Jackson, Marx stopped for gas and a toilet break. As they passed the four thousand-feet altitude marker, he turned to his companion.

"This is the Mother Lode area, rather peaceful foothill scenery, but pretty soon it will change," he remarked. "Yesterday, when I called about reservations, I was told they'd had quite a snow storm a couple of days ago. I just hope we won't need chains." He grimaced, as if in pain. "I've never learned how to put them on without getting filthy."

Soon patches of dirty snow appeared on the side of the road and then a sign, reading *Road Clear. No Chain Requirement.* Marx let out a sigh of relief.

"I guess we're lucky; it's certainly clear now. Tomorrow is a full moon. Maybe we can try some night skiing on the lake."

Sabine looked impressed. "Have you ever skied at night?"

"Last Thanksgiving. It was spectacular—I don't think I'll forget that trip."

Sabine didn't know it had been the non-skiing component Marx had remembered so vividly. Nor could she have understood the subsequent thought association.

"We're making such good time, we may get to Kirkwood before six. Are you game about driving on for another half hour across Carson Pass to Markleeville? They've got a couple of funky Western restaurants where we could have dinner."

The establishment was really more of a bar than a restaurant. Marx hadn't chosen it for its food. As they studied the menu, he turned to Sabine.

"Sabine, what kind of underwear are you wearing?"

For a moment, Sabine looked startled, but then she broke into laughter. "That's the damnedest question I've ever heard. I presume—no, I hope—you're asking because you're worried I'll be cold."

Marx persisted. "You didn't bring a bathing suit, did you?"

"A bathing suit? Are you kidding? At this time of year?"

"It just occurred to me, because we're only a few minutes away from the Grover Hot Springs." Marx was not telling the truth: the hot springs had already occurred to him in Jackson, where his train of thoughts had careened from full moon to Thanksgiving-skiing to sauna to Sybil and his first as well as last sexual encounter in California. "It's like a giant hot tub. You've been in a hot tub, haven't you?"

The last comment was disingenuous, to say the least. Marx himself had been in a hot tub only twice—a northern California custom that had hardly spread to Manhattan.

"No, I haven't."

Marx didn't know whether the blandness of her answer was owing to ignorance or suspicion.

"The hot springs pool is over one hundred degrees—it's outdoors, right in the snow. It's fabulously relaxing and we've almost got a full moon."

"I've got a leotard in my bag—"

"That'll do," exclaimed Marx.

"What about you?" asked Sabine. "Did you bring a bathing suit?"

"I'm a swimmer." Marx tried to sound nonchalant. "I'm always prepared."

"Do we really want to do this?" For a moment, Sabine looked and sounded like the suspicious provincial she was.

"Sure. Let's try it. It's even better after a day of skiing, but you might as well experience it the first night out."

The hot springs pool could hold forty to fifty people; weekends, especially in the last hour before closing, it usually did. This evening, however, there were only a handful soaking in the steaming pool.

"See you in the pool," Marx called as he entered the men's changing room.

Marx ran carefully along the ice-cold cement, his breath forming clouds in the frigid night air. He plunged into the pool. The heat of the water was startling, almost painful, but in a minute it felt tolerable; a little longer and it felt good: he could sense the stress of the day's drive starting to slacken.

Sabine appeared, wearing a tight black leotard. Like Marx, she ran quickly toward the pool, but at the edge she stopped, teetering, and cautiously stuck one foot into the water.

"My God!" she exclaimed, "this is boiling!" She stood shivering on the side of the pool, her nipples standing out against the tight leotard. For the first time, Marx could clearly see the outline of her breasts, unencumbered by a jogger's bra. In the moonlight, they looked almost as tempting as Monica's.

"Come on in," he called, stretching out his arms. "It's fabulous, once you get over the initial shock." As she headed slowly into the water, he could see a luxurious growth of pubic hair escaping from black nylon.

As they drove through a steep canyon on the two-lane mountain highway, the dark trees were etched sharply against the snow, but once the road entered open country, the moon threw light over the snow-covered meadows, turning them into silvery skin crossed occasionally by dark veins—blemishes which proved to be merely cattle fences.

For once, neither of them spoke. Sabine lay relaxed in the passenger seat. She was dozing, her mind luxuriously empty. Not Stephen. He knew how much caution was indicated tonight. Sabine had not given any sign of physical availability. The entire relationship still rested on very thin ice. He couldn't risk offending her—neither Stephen Marx nor Donald Mann could afford to do so. He intended to let events develop by themselves. But in the meantime, there was little of Sabine's body he couldn't visualize—silvery skin, hollowed by luxuriant darkness.

As they pulled up in front of the rental office, a half mile or so from the condominium complex, he found Sabine soundly asleep. Gently, he touched her cheek. Except for a single handshake, this was the first physical contact between the two of them. He wanted Sabine to decide whether it was a caress or a wake-up gesture. She didn't help; stirring slightly, she snuggled up toward his hand, whereupon he ever so lightly shook her head. As her eyes opened slowly, still retaining the blank look of a sleeper who hadn't yet completed the transition to the waking world, her cheeks had remained between his hands. He sensed that if she'd permit this touch for another moment, it would, for both of them, turn into a caress. But before those critical seconds had elapsed, Sabine's eyes had recognized Stephen. With one move forward, she had transformed his touch into a wake-up call.

"Where are we?" she asked, looking out of the car. "I must have been sound asleep."

"I didn't want to wake you. Wait here while I get the key to our place; it won't get cold if I leave the engine running."

Sabine saw no sign of life. A few cars were parked in front of the low, dimly lit building. Somehow, she had visualized a typical motel: neon, traffic, people. Instead there was only moon-bathed silence without a soul.

"Where are we?" she repeated as Marx entered the car. By now she was wide awake; an element of caution had prompted the question.

"This is just the office. Weeknights, the manager just leaves the key in an envelope with the number of the apartment. Tomorrow, this place will be jammed. But tonight we've got it all to ourselves."

As Marx drove slowly away from the office, Sabine's unconscious radar started to sweep. What am I getting into, spending the night alone with Marx out in the middle of nowhere, not a single person in sight?

The condominium complex was huge, or so it seemed, with softly lit entranceways and an occasional lighted window. A few cars were parked here and there, but still Sabine saw no one.

Sabine shivered as she stepped out of the car. After the warmth of the vehicle, the night air brought her fully awake. Quickly, she zippered up the rented parka, grabbed her bag and boots, and ran into the building. The entrance was unheated. By the time Marx had arrived, knapsack on his back, with a bag in each hand, Sabine was distinctly unhappy.

"God, it's cold," she exclaimed. "Don't they heat these places? I wish we were back at the hot springs." Or preferably San Francisco, she added to herself.

"Don't worry," replied Stephen, searching the dimly lit corridor for the door to number 27. "The apartments are heated. They're probably saving money during the week. Here we are."

Inside, the temperature was nearly seventy degrees: not high enough for Sabine, who found the thermostat and raised the setting. The sound of the hot, forced air reassured her. While Marx unloaded the food in the kitchen, Sabine, still wearing the parka, explored.

The place was fully carpeted, probably in deference to the skiers who, once out of their heavy boots, usually were shoeless. The bedroom was standard American motel-style, circa 1970 or thereabout, dominated by a huge king-sized bed. One wall, opposite the bed, was floor-to-ceiling mirrors. On closer inspection, Sabine found that they slid aside to reveal a walk-in closet. She had just slid back one of the mirrored doors when she looked up to see, reflected in the glass, Stephen Marx standing in the doorway. How long had he been observing her?

"Is the bedroom OK?"

"Yes," she mumbled, "yes, of course." But meanwhile she was wondering: are we both supposed to sleep in this bed? It seemed large enough for five adults. With only two persons in it, the open space between them, if respected, might be acceptable. But the mirrors? Why are they always placed so the bed is reflected? Is this All-American design of all American vacation rentals supposed to cater to the All-American voyeur? Out loud she said, "But where . . ."

Stephen Marx was not crude. Writing had made him an acute observer of people and of their responses. On this particular night, his antennae were even finer tuned. He could tell that a certain wariness had surfaced.

He finished the sentence for her. ". . . will we sleep? You use the bedroom, I'll sleep on the couch in the living room. There's only one shower," he nodded toward a closed door next to the closet, "but there's a half-bath off the living room. We'll manage."

Sabine felt relieved. "Are you sure you don't want to use this bed? It's so huge. I can cope with the sofa."

"You stay here. It's been a long day and you must be tired. Just tell me what you want for breakfast—remember, I'm good at serving meals." Marx grinned.

"Let's see," she mused. "Blueberry pancakes, sausage, fresh—"

"Sorry," interrupted Stephen, pretending to scan a waiter's notepad. "We're all out of pancake mix, and blueberries, and sausages—"

"How about dry toast and Nescafé?" Sabine felt like her usual self. The vague discomfort, the unconscious suspicion had all disappeared.

"Nescafé we've got—or tea—but we're out of toast. English muffins, we've got; trail mix, cereal, and low-fat milk, we've got. Oh yes, and grapefruit juice. But don't order all of it or we won't have enough on the trail tomorrow."

"In that case, I'll take tea and whatever else you have. Good night, Donald."

"Good night, Sabine."

15

"I've made breakfast." Stephen's voice boomed through the bedroom door. "It's a fabulous day: clear sky, cold but not much wind—it couldn't be better." She heard his voice receding. "There's a meadow behind the condo; we can warm up there before taking off in the car."

The bedroom was comfortably warm—Stephen seemed to have turned up the thermostat for her benefit—but Sabine put on all the clothes she'd brought along. When she emerged from the bedroom, the only sign of Stephen's presence was a cup of tea steaming beside a pair of English muffins, a glass of grapefruit juice to one side; a few dishes stacked beside the sink suggested that he had eaten without her. From outside the entrance came muffled thuds. As she sat down, the door opened. He stood outside the entrance, both pairs of skis in his arms. Sunlight poured in around him.

"Damn," Sabine exclaimed as she squinted into the sun. "I didn't bring any sunglasses."

"You can use mine."

"I can't. What will you wear?"

"I've got a pair of goggles. Take the glasses, Sabie."

"Nobody calls me 'Sabie.'"

"Don't you have a nickname?"

"No. Do you?"

"Sure. It's 'Saint.'" He'd said it aloud before realizing what he had done.

"'Saint'? I don't see anything saintly about you. Is it some variation on your real name? You didn't tell me in San Francisco—"

"I know I didn't," replied Marx. "Let's put on the skis and run once around the meadow. There will be plenty of time to talk when we are out on the trail."

Saint. She had heard it before, Sabine realized as she carried her dishes to the sink. Ambrose MacPhearson had used it at Rocco's. She wondered what it meant that Marx had let that slip. Had it been a slip?

It was getting too complicated, she decided. It would keep. She emerged from the apartment into the brilliant sun, and for a moment she was blind.

Stephen was the first to take off, heading around the perimeter of the meadow; quickly, he reached a steady clip—not fast but in good style. Sabine stayed behind, following in his newly made tracks. About half-way around the meadow she switched from a steady glide to a fast skate—the stride she'd learned at Nordic races at college. Breaking out of Stephen's tracks, in no time she had left him behind. She continued at that speed back to the condominium.

What Stephen loved about cross-country skiing was the steady rhythm, not unlike swimming laps, coupled with the fresh cold air entering his lungs, his eyes focused on the pattern of the old track ahead. His mind was nearly blank, blissfully so. He hadn't thought of Sabine until she passed him on his left. He misunderstood her passing, taking it as a challenge. Good form, he admitted grudgingly to himself, as he picked up speed. But no matter how much he extended himself, Sabine's taut ass maintained its insurmountable distance. She was no longer gaining on him, but he couldn't close the gap. By the time they had returned to the parking lot of the condominium he was panting and perspiring heavily. She had already undone her bindings.

"This is great, Saint." She called to him as he labored up to her side. She didn't seem winded at all. "Do you mind if I call you Saint?"

"It's OK." He knew he sounded like a beached whale, but he didn't care.

"I can't wait until we really get moving. Is the trailhead far?"

Really get moving: he'd barely survived the warm-up. Marx squinted at her sidelong as he bent to release a balky binding. Was she playing with him?

Marx had decided on Silver Lake rather than the mountain meadows near Carson Pass. He parked near the spillway, at one end of the elongated lake. All along the shore, side trails led into the woods and up to fairly steep terrain. For the moment, however, Marx's competitive drive had left him. For now, they could ski side-by-side along the lakeshore and talk. Later on, they could take off in the direction of the surrounding mountains and climb.

Sabine concurred with his plans. For the first time in California she felt sufficiently relaxed to look at Saint as a social companion rather than as a journalist's prey. At ten o'clock, the temperature was just above freezing. Both skiers had established a comfortable stride: not so fast as to preclude conversation, but fast enough to stay warm without sweaters. He had offered to stuff the extra clothing into his backpack. Sabine felt light in body weight and mental baggage.

Stephen was the first to speak. "Remember this morning when you wouldn't let me call you 'Sabie'? What do people call you? Or is it just plain Sabine?"

"Not 'just plain Sabine,' simply Sabine. But that isn't completely accurate. My father's family were German immigrants who settled in central Pennsylvania. My favorite uncle still spoke a lot of German at home—he was the first to call me 'Bienchen.'"

"Little bee?" Stephen exclaimed. "I should have guessed. *Ich spreche doch Deutsch.*"

She nodded. "Bienchen stuck, but nobody in New York calls me that."

"I like stories about names."

"I know," replied Sabine. "That's what you did in *Middles.*"

"True enough. I collect names and stories of names. You see? One more novelist's pleasure denied to a journalist."

Sabine let out a mock groan. "Not that again."

"Seriously. Why not write a novel about a writer who disappears and then writes under another name? Even the genderless author, who seems to bother you, isn't really a problem. When people discovered Doris Lessing had written two novels under the name of Jane Somers, she admitted in one of her interviews that if she were to do it again, it would be a man's name."

"Like George Eliot?"

"No. Most people in the end knew Eliot was a woman. I think Lessing really meant to hide her identity."

"That's not my problem," interjected Sabine. "The story has a fatal flaw."

"Yes?"

"A well-known writer can't just disappear. There'd be pub-licity; a search; sooner or later he'd be traced. Unless," she added slowly, as if considering the possibility for the first time, "he faked his death. That part of the story stumps me. How do you fake a plausible death? Any suggestions, Saint?"

Perhaps it was the way she said his nickname. Or the certainty that had grown on him as she raised the question of his staged death. She was playing with him, had been playing with him, from the start: and he had known it, from the moment she had appeared outside his door. He hadn't been able to admit it—he, Stephen Marx, the object of someone else's game—but now there seemed no more possibility of evasion.

Still, how to stop? How do you call a halt to something like this?

For a minute the two of them skied side by side, each concentrating on the track ahead.

"You told me about your nickname," he said finally. "Aren't you curious about mine?"

"Of course I am," she said quickly.

"I got it in Switzerland," he said.

Sabine was silent for a moment. "But 'Saint' isn't a German word."

"Of course not. It's *Sankt*. But the German abbreviation for Stefan is 'St.'"

"So?" Sabine reacted before she realized what he had said. Then, slowly, she asked, still not believing. "Was your name Stefan?"

"No," he replied, as the same deceleration seemed to overtake his mental processes. "My name was Stephen . . . Stephen Marx."

The actual enunciation of the name came to Sabine as not so much a revelation but a door opening onto the unknown. Everything is different now, she told herself. But how, she could not say. She realized she was unable to look at the man beside her. Unconsciously, the steady motion of her arms and legs diminished, until she came to a halt in the snow.

And at her side, Marx, seemingly stunned by his own mouth, came to the same sleepwalking halt.

It was some time before either spoke.

"Was it really a surprise?" Marx asked in a low voice. He was looking off over the frozen lake.

He might have been talking to himself, Sabine thought. "No," she said. Caution kept her back for another long moment. "I suspected it. For literary reasons. I already told you that in San Francisco." Sabine was tempted to admit to their first meeting at Rocco's, but then repressed the thought. "Still, it came as a surprise to hear it so suddenly. To hear you say it."

"What will you do now?" His voice had turned flat and slightly ominous.

"What do you mean?"

"Are you going to tell anyone?" he persisted.

"I don't really know," replied Sabine. "To be quite honest, Saint, I haven't had time to digest it."

"All right, Sabine. . . ." No Bienchen. "Digest."

They skied for nearly an hour on the frozen snow-covered lake bed, quite close to the shoreline, without exchanging a further word. Marx increased his speed, Sabine following in his tracks. It made the absence of conversation less clumsy. Suddenly he stopped.

"Let's head to the shore for a bite to eat. But watch out for streams entering the lake. You don't want to break through a snow bridge."

He sidestepped up the steep embankment, moving cautiously parallel to the lake. "See what I mean?" He gestured to a deep hole in the snow. "A stream falls into the lake here." He gestured up the slope, where Sabine could make out a steeply falling watercourse. "The bank is steep here, so the stream cuts a little gorge for itself; when the snow is heavy, it can make a bridge from bank to bank. But it's hollow, see?" He struck with his pole into the hole. Its interior was lost in a deep green shade, the water down below so deep, so clear, it seemed to chill the surrounding air. "It won't hold any weight. Eventually it collapses. The water down there's probably twenty feet deep. Steer clear."

The snow underfoot seemed suddenly unstable to Sabine. She gave the hollow a wide berth.

"How about there?" He pointed to a flat spot with a view of the rushing stream with the natural snow bridge.

Sabine nodded while taking in the scenery. Marx opened the backpack and removed the extra clothing which both now put on. Next, he extracted two huge green plastic garbage bags which he placed on the spot in the snow he had trampled down with his skis. After releasing his bindings, he turned the skis over and sat on them.

"You may get a cold ass, but at least it'll be dry. Let me empty the backpack—you can sit on it; that way you won't even feel the cold."

While Marx spread out the food, Sabine let her eyes fall over the expansive landscape. She scanned the path of the mountain stream, until it disappeared under the snow, her gaze then jumping to the trees on the other shore. The lake was just below the timberline; except for occasional rocky outcroppings, the mountains were a solid mass of white, their peaks sharply outlined against the blue sky.

She was still in her bindings, leaning slightly forward, supported by her poles. Marx's brief question "want some?" with the proffered open can of smoked oysters suddenly reminded her how hungry she'd become. As soon as she'd stepped off her skis and sat on the empty backpack, she reached for a cracker and an oyster, still dripping with oil.

"My God, you were right. These are the best oysters I've ever had. I wonder how they taste at sea level?"

Marx ignored her comment. He opened the thermos.

"Here, take a sip."

Sabine eyed the thermos cup suspiciously. The color looked unfamiliar. "What is it?"

Marx drank with an exaggerated slurp before passing the cup. "See, it's not poison. But be careful: it's hot."

Sabine took a dainty sip, followed by a fuller one. "It's delicious." She examined the cup skeptically. "But I'm still not sure what it is."

"It's tea with TANG," Marx announced, watching for her reaction.

"TANG?" Sabine made a face. "I don't believe it." She took another sip. "It's too good."

Marx nodded proudly. "It's good in the snow in the mountains, but I wouldn't recommend it at sea level."

Conversation faltered while they ate. Sabine continued her visual sweep of the surroundings, occasionally glancing at Marx. He seemed deeply lost in thought, his eyes focusing on the streambed and snow bridge just below them.

Sabine rose, and put on her skies. "I'm skiing over there behind those trees."

Marx made no comment as she left, and he paid no attention upon her return. His eyes seemed glued on the stream bed.

"What's the matter, Saint? You're awfully quiet." Sabine looked down on him.

"I'm thinking," he mumbled.

"Is this Mann or Marx thinking?" Her question was meant playfully but the effect was unexpected. Marx looked annoyed, as if he'd been interrupted.

"I've never written a thriller before—unless you count my drug story in Rio." His voice trailed off.

"So?" Sabine was surprised by his non sequitur, by the non-conversational, offhandish manner of his reply. He looked up; a sharp, almost cruel, expression crossed his face.

"Sabine, you ask too damned many questions. It's always Marx or Mann. So let me give you an answer that applies simply to me. I'm a writer. I keep thinking about the events of this morning. Suddenly, the outline of a good story has started to appear. Maybe I'll make it my first detective story, although the detective can't be the hero because it will describe a perfect, unsolved murder."

"In the snow?"

"In the snow, and on skis. What's wrong with that?" He broke off, lost in thought again. "I'll have to see if anybody's used skis before. Anyway, all I've thought of is the bare outline."

"Can I hear it?"

Marx looked up. He couldn't see through her sunglasses. "I'm not sure you'd like it," he said slowly.

"Try me."

"OK, why don't you take off your skis and sit down?"

"I'm comfortable standing up," she said quickly. "It's easier keeping warm by sliding back and forth. Just tell me the outline."

Marx had put his arms around his bent knees. He leaned forward, staring down at the stream. "Suppose we had a man who had reason to kill this woman. Not for money, not for revenge, just some very private motive. He hardly knows her; nobody is aware they've met."

Sabine, anchored on her ski poles, was sliding slowly back and forth. "Sounds damn implausible."

"Really?" The word came out sharply, with a quick look in her direction. "Just think of us."

"What do you mean?" She responded automatically, before the significance of his words could sink in. The movement of her legs stopped.

"He persuaded her to go skiing with him, not downhill, where there are crowds, but cross-country, like you and me. On a week-day, like today, when there are few people; in a place like this, where there are none. Do you know we haven't met a single skier?" Again he turned to Sabine's hidden eyes.

"Yes." Her voice was low.

"They weren't registered in a hotel; they stayed in a condo. Remember, nobody saw us enter the place last night when I picked up the keys. Sometime that morning, the idea occurred to my hero—"

"Hero?"

"All right then: my protagonist. He realized if events moved the right way, he might solve his problem—"

"What problem?"

"Stop interrupting." He made no attempt to hide his annoyance. "I haven't figured out the details."

Sabine felt as if her skis had frozen to the ground.

"They were skiing in an area like this one. My man skied ahead, when, suddenly, one of his poles opened up a deep hole: he had crossed a hidden snow bridge. He called out a warning to the woman. Occasional streams, like this one," Marx pointed straight ahead, "ran into the lake. That's when he realized the scenario for a very plausible accident: she could have fallen through the snow, down some ten feet or more, become unconscious, and drowned or froze to death. A snowstorm developed that night. The snowfalls from a Pacific storm can drop whole feet of snow here. The tracks, her body, the stream, all got covered. Her body was only found months later, after the spring thaws. No identification, probably not even any recognizable physical features. Perfect teeth."

Marx had stopped, still staring at the stream. Sabine tried to break the silence, to bring them back to reality.

"What do you mean, 'no identification'? What about a driver's license?"

"Right now, do you have one on you?" The question was posed without emotion, the voice matter-of-fact.

"No . . . but . . ."

"Listen, Sabine, I'm working on a murder, not an accident. The couple had lunch in a place like this. While they're sitting— the way you and I did earlier—the man gets up on some pretext. He has to take a leak, or something. He takes a big garbage bag, like the one I'm sitting on, and suddenly pulls it over her and smothers her. There are no strangulation marks, no evidence of a fight. When she's dead, he goes through her pockets and removes driver's license, credit cards, and the like. He then throws her body down into the stream—"

"What about her skis?"

"I thought of that. First I wanted to have him put them on her before throwing her down the embankment. He'd be simulating an accident while on the trail. But then I realized there's a problem. Look at your skis."

Sabine peered down as Marx, leaning over, brushed the snow off her skis just ahead of her bindings. Sabine felt violated; she stared at her exposed ski.

"See?" He pointed to the name of the ski-rental store painted on the skis. "They might identify her that way. So instead, my protagonist skis out, carrying her skis and poles. He returns them with his own to the store two hundred miles away in San Francisco. Before leaving, he sidesteps down the embankment to cover her completely with snow, then picks up all the items from their picnic and skis off. Of course, he needs some luck: a snow storm to cover his tracks and the trampled-down spot where they'd eaten—"

"And where he'd killed her." Sabine's interruption surprised both of them.

"Fortunately, the weather can change quite quickly in the Sierras," Marx continued. "Just look behind you to the west. We're still in the sun; to the east the sky is blue. But take those clouds behind us. That's where the winter storms come from. Even today, we could be caught in a storm; a real one, not just one for the story."

"There's no such thing as a perfect crime. The murderer always overlooks something. It's his fate to outsmart himself."

"That's a convention, Sabine. Good fiction is like life: it breaks the rules. Except for the snowstorm, which I need for covering the tracks, what else have I overlooked?" Suddenly Marx recalled his first meeting with MacPhearson at Rocco's; how his friend had asked the same question. In the end, he had forgotten something. . . .

Sabine's voice interrupted his thoughts. "Surely she has a family, friends . . . they'd be looking for her."

"Sure," replied Marx, "but take your own example: who knows you went to California to look for me?"

Sabine remained silent.

"You mean, nobody? Not one person? I'm amazed." Marx had swung around, still sitting on the garbage bag, but now facing her directly.

"Your agent Merryfield."

"How much did you tell him?"

"Well . . . he gave me your post office box number when I told him that I would look for you."

"Does he know you actually left for California?"

I'm not on trial and I won't let him treat me like he's a district attorney, she thought. "Yes," she said. "I told him."

Sabine was a lousy liar and one look at Marx told her that she hadn't convinced him.

"Anybody else?" The question was peremptory.

"The travel agency. I bought my plane ticket and hotel reservation through them."

"Have you ever used them before?"

"No." The answer had slipped out before she realized what she'd said.

"So?" He just looked at her. "How would they miss you if you never returned? Of course, your parents would, but what would make them look in California?"

A deep chill had descended on Sabine. Is he serious? The possibility was starting to cut through the surreal air that had surrounded the conversation, starting to pose itself as a series of extremely practical questions—but Marx's voice intervened.

"Of course, one would have to think of all eventualities. For instance, taking you as an example, I just overlooked one important fact: your three rings. Somebody may have noticed them. Wearing rings on one thumb and two index fingers is too unusual."

Yes, thought Sabine, thank God for the rings. Even the old lady on the plane noticed them.

Marx continued. "The cashier at the hotel may have noticed them when you checked out. I'll have to make my man think of that. You know, it would make a good twist. He's about to throw her body down into the water when he remembers the rings. He tears off her gloves in order to remove the rings, but has some trouble getting the one off her thumb. By the way, Bienchen. . . ."

The unexpected use of the diminutive felt like a slap. At that instant, Marx's facial expression appeared positively lupine to her.

"How easy is it to get that ring off?"

Sabine stared speechlessly at her left hand which was covered by a glove.

"Never mind. In my story, the man gets anxious, he pulls and pulls, and suddenly the ring slips off her finger and flies in an arch into the deep snow. My hero . . ."

Hero? she wanted to exclaim. The guy is a murderer!

". . . panics, he steps over to the spot where he saw the ring disappear, not realizing he has left the security of the garbage bag. That's when his left leg sinks into the deep snow and before he knows it, he's fallen all together. By the time he manages to reach his poles, or maybe hers, he's made a mess of the area." He shrugged his shoulders dismissively. "Obviously, he can't find the ring. So you see? He does leave a clue. If her skeleton is encountered when all the snow has melted—"

"Why should she have turned to a skeleton?" Sabine was relieved to have found something in the plot to pull at, to make it all fall apart. "Wouldn't the snow preserve her body? Certainly some of her clothing, her boots—"

Marx banished the interruption with a wave of his hand. "Those are trivia. I haven't worked on all aspects of the story. Maybe I'll bring in some predators—feral dogs or coyotes—who consume the body. Anyway, the person finding her somehow stumbles on the ring. Here I'll bring in the first element of doubt: why would a woman, who ostensibly just died in an accident, have taken off her ring? Tell me, is your thumb ring a distinctive one? Could one trace . . . Hey, Bienchen, where are you going?"

Before Marx could move, she'd pushed with her ski poles toward the tracks they'd made less than an hour ago. She vanished in the direction of the lake.

Marx jumped up.

"Sabine, Sabine . . . wait!" In his haste to grab his skis, he stepped off the garbage bag into the deep snow.

16

In the weeks after they spent the night together, Miriam had two distractions from her catering business. There was her cookbook, which she finally had started to write. And there was sex. Miriam had been celibate for well over a year. She hadn't realized how much she had missed a sexual partner. There were nights when Noah came over and they didn't even discuss the cookbook. And Noah's questions about Stephen dwindled away without Miriam seeming to notice. They still met with sufficient infrequency that each date, each get-together—alone or in company—was spiced by sexual overtones that tended to make Miriam focus on today or tomorrow, rather than on yesterday.

For his part, as the weeks had passed since the episode on Stephen's couch, Noah Berg had come to appreciate that his growing interest in Miriam would make it difficult, if not altogether impossible, to pursue his plan about a critical *pièce de revanche* on Marx. For all his concern about his critical objectivity, it had never occurred to him that one could lose one's neutrality by sleeping with the widow of one's subject; or that lusty sex effectively quenched any remaining lust for revenge.

This weekend, things were clearly heading toward some new level: Miriam had freed herself from all catering commitments; she had invited Noah to spend the weekend. It was her proposal that they spend the entire sixty-hour stretch in the Marx residence without leaving it once. Noah had agreed readily. He arrived with a few bottles of special California vintages—his newest oenological preoccupation—some videocassettes, and an armful of books.

Seeing the books, Miriam pretended shock. "If you have to read all that this weekend, there won't be any time for . . ." Her arms opened up in an all-encompassing greeting.

"You're wrong," he said, dropping the books on the floor and unbuttoning Miriam's blouse. "Critics also have their right priorities. First things first."

That was Friday night. Now it was past eleven o'clock on Sunday morning, and Miriam had spent the intervening hours spoiling him shamelessly. This morning she had announced "brunch in bed," wrapped herself loosely in a robe, and disappeared into the kitchen, reappearing—after a tantalizing interval—with a chestnut soufflé, a side dish of Canadian bacon, and a compote of mixed berries topped with a dollop of crème fraîche.

"My God!" exclaimed Noah. "Is this the standard breakfast Mrs. Marx serves in this bed?"

She ruffled his hair affectionately. "*Mrs.* Marx has *never* served soufflé in this bed, and if you use that word once more in combination with 'Marx' this will be the last soufflé you'll ever see here."

"A terrible faux pas," he admitted with a quick laugh. But it had not been: he'd used the matrimonial appellation deliberately. The idea of making love to Stephen Marx's wife in his bed; eating breakfast in his bed—a breakfast made lovingly by *Mrs.* Marx for her lover; the posthumous cuckolding of Stephen Marx: sex and food were all very well, but *this* was something special. He kept these thoughts to himself. He didn't think Miriam would understand.

The brunch was fabulous; yet Noah couldn't help that in this bed his thoughts kept returning to its former occupant.

"I've been unable to trace a single book review by Stephen," said Noah. "Surely he must have written some. Most authors do."

"He didn't," replied Miriam. "Although over the years he received many requests. And his answer? 'Action causes more trouble than thoughts.' His motive, I'm now sure, was a bit more devious: he didn't want to insult potential tattooists. As you, Noah, once told me: what's written and published can't be unwritten."

"But Stephen wrote all the time. And published a great deal!"

"Sure, but it all dealt with *his* fantasies, not someone else's."

Noah, propped up by two big pillows while lying supine on the bed, had been looking pensively out the window. Now he turned sideways to face Miriam. For a while he played absentmindedly with her hair before running his index and middle fingers gently down her forehead, then separating them as they slid down on each side of her nose, to finally meet again by her lips. Miriam started to kiss his middle finger—her favorite foreplay finger, she'd called it earlier—but he didn't seem to notice.

"There is nothing wrong with an active fantasy life," he mused. "But in my reading, I'm always interested to see whether I can detect when the author's fantasy turns into roman-à-cleffery and ever so often into straight autobiography." He resumed his absentminded caressing of her hair. "That's why I keep returning to the absence of sex in Stephen's last novels. That is hardly fantasy." He shook his head, as if he had just woken up. "What a subject to discuss in *this* bed after we have—"

She put her hand over his mouth. "Stop talking about it." She pulled off the blanket and swung over to straddle him. "Do something about it."

"Noah," she murmured, cradled in his arms, "I haven't made love like that for a long time."

He nuzzled her. "Tell me what 'like that' means."

"Oh you know . . . urgently. . . . And at this time of the day!" She sat up, her arms folded across her naked breasts.

"You know Miriam," he said lazily, "someone, some artist I think, maybe Jenny Holzer, said that romantic love was invented to manipulate women."

"So?"

"So perhaps it follows that sexual love does not."

Miriam returned to his arms before whispering. "I don't feel manipulated. But Noah, it's strange, lying with another man in my connubial bed."

"Have you ever done it before?" he asked softly. "In this bed?"

"Before?"

"Before he died. Now, it's not a connubial bed any more."

"No, never before. Or since."

"Never before?" he persisted. "Not even elsewhere?"

Miriam's head moved backward so that she could catch his eyes in focus. "Why those questions?"

"I'm interested in faithfulness."

"Are you faithful?"

"Basically, yes. And I certainly would be if I were married. And you? Were you faithful during your marriage to Stephen Marx?" He tried to make it sound like a biographical inquiry.

"Yes and no."

It was his time to move back in order to see her face more clearly. "But that's a meaningless answer. Like—"

"I know," she said quickly. "Like pregnancy: it's yes *or* no. 'Yes' meant I was faithful as long as I *felt* married."

"Did you stop feeling married when your husband got his writing studio?"

She squinted at him again. "What's that have to do with faithfulness?"

Noah levered himself up on an elbow so that his face was close to hers. He stared into her eyes for a long moment. "Was your husband faithful?"

There was something intense about his gaze that made Miriam lean back. "Does it turn you on, having me speak about Stephen while we lie naked here, on this bed?"

Noah's eyes, though narrowing perceptibly, did not shift from hers.

"Well?" she repeated.

"Yes," he finally said. "As a matter of fact, it does."

"So you want me to continue?"

"Yes."

"All right. What do you want me to talk about?"

"You once told me that what seemed to have kept you together at the end was tact."

"I said, 'tact in public.'" Miriam turned on her back to look straight up at the ceiling. "He never humiliated me. Not once."

Noah expected more, but nothing more was said. Out of the corner of his eye, he inspected her, only to find her face unreadable.

"And in private?" he finally asked.

"I wonder."

Noah and Miriam were standing by the door, exchanging last-minute chitchat, as if they'd just met. Monday morning had arrived. They had been putting off the moment of Noah's departure for five, ten minutes, until finally the inevitable long silence occurred. They looked at each other helplessly. But then Noah took her by surprise. He closed the door and stepped back into the foyer.

"Miriam, why don't you live with me?" he said excitedly. "You write your book, and I will cook for you and do the laundry. It's an offer I never made before. I mean the cooking and laundry," he added with a sheepish grin.

"*You*? Cook for *me*? You're a darling, Noah, but—"

"All right, I'll rephrase my proposal. You don't want to cook for yourself, you want to *write* about cooking. What if I *feed* you and do the laundry? That should give you time to write."

Miriam embraced him. "No one has ever made me such an offer. But what about my business? I am supposed to be a successful caterer, which means that I must cater—"

"Delegate!" he interrupted. "The sign of a successful entrepreneur is to know when to delegate. What about your Thomasina?"

"I can't Noah." Miriam still had her arms around him. But she muffled the words in his chest, and they lacked all conviction.

"Try it. One month only, during which time you'll write at least five pages a day. After 150 pages, you can reconsider. And Thomasina with her crew won't wreck the business in just a few weeks. Think about it: an author being fed by a reviewer-critic. Isn't that the ultimate way of doing it backward?"

17

Sabine was a small dark figure well out on the lake bed. Rather than following their original tracks, she'd headed diagonally across the lake, toward the highway on the other shore. Marx plunged down the steep bank, losing both his footing and another minute as he struggled to rise to his skis. He made a rough estimate of Sabine's speed and set a course to cut her off.

It took him nearly an hour to catch up. As he neared her, panting and drenched in sweat, he yelled: "Stop! Goddammit, Sabine, stop!"

By now she was skiing leisurely within eyesight of the highway and occasional car traffic. She stopped without turning.

"What the hell got into you?" he snarled. "Are you nuts?"

Sabine had long since regained her composure. She had prepared herself for this scene: no looking down into the snow; only a cool, measured response.

"I was getting cold," she said calmly.

"Come on, something was bugging you."

She spoke in measured tones. "I didn't want to hear any more of your story. I didn't like your murderer or your victim."

"Listen, Sabine, I was just thinking out loud, I was kidding. Surely . . ."

"Come on, let's ski to the car," interrupted Sabine, "I'm getting cold."

They ended up having early dinner at a western steak and pizza place. The atmosphere was strained. Sabine had retreated into a completely professional demeanor: throughout the meal, she attempted to interview Marx.

"Tell me how you staged your accident."

Marx found himself in a disadvantageous position. If he was to recover from this afternoon's debacle, he would have to make Sabine some sort of peace offering. But how much could he afford to give? How much was this young woman going to demand? Since telling her his name, everything seemed to have changed. He seemed to have surrendered all control.

Out of habit, he hedged. "I spent a lot of time getting ready."

"What did you do?"

"I went sailing three weeks in a row on a Wednesday or Thursday afternoon. I wanted the harbor master to get used to seeing me mid-week. I made it a point to talk to him each time—about how less crowded it was on the water as well as on the highway. I planned carefully what to put into my duffel bag. It was going to be found in my boat, and I wanted it to be distinctive: I chose English saltwater biscuits from Fortnum and Mason, and a bottle of Brown's celery soda."

Sabine broke out laughing. "Celery soda? Not TANG?"

Stephen continued as if she'd asked a serious question. "No, celery soda seemed completely out of the ordinary. I needed distinctive items. I offered the harbormaster some of the biscuits. I told him they were my new fancy survival ration. I showed him one of the celery soda bottles and told him it was my new sailing drink. I picked an old windbreaker and wrote 'St. Marx' in it with indelible ink."

"'St. Marx'? Are you serious?"

This time, Marx snickered. "I know, it was a theatrical gesture, but I felt one was OK. You think I overdid it?"

Sabine shook her head. "Go on."

"I spent so much time on each detail I finally got worried I'd be overdoing it; that I would leave too many clues. Just listen to this one. Years ago, as a high school kid, I took water survival lessons at the Y. Do you know how to make a substitute life vest out of pants?"

"Pants? You mean, take them apart and sew them into a life vest?"

Marx let out a short guffaw—the sailor laughing at the land lubber. "No, I mean swimming in your pants and then converting them in the water into a life vest."

"Come on, Saint. Are you kidding?"

"No, I'm serious. I still remember what they taught us at the Y: if you have to abandon ship, take your pants off while treading water, tightly tie each end of the pant legs, then grab them at the waistband, swing the pants through the air and quickly pull them down on the water. Enough air is caught in each pant leg to make it possible for you to lie in the crotch with the two new air bags supporting you. You see? You just learned something: you can now float in your pants."

"Does that really work? Have you ever tried it?"

Marx grinned. "Well, yes. Once, in the Y swimming pool."

"How long can you float that way?"

"I don't really know—it depends how firmly you tied the knots. The instructor told us to repeat the process if we lost buoyancy."

"What's that got to do with your accident?"

"Good point," replied Marx. "I was toying with the idea of taking along an extra pair of sailing pants and writing my name on the inside waistband—"

"St. Marx, I presume?"

Marx ignored the mocking interruption. "I never got that far. I just toyed with the idea of throwing them into the water before jumping into the other boat. If the pants were found, it might look as if I tried to survive in the water by using them."

"And why didn't you?"

"I felt I was getting too cute. How do I know the people who'd find the pants would understand why the ends of the pant legs were tied? They might actually have suspected foul play. Besides, surviving with or without pants in cold November water for more than a few minutes seemed unlikely. So I decided to forget about fancy nuances and to keep it plain and simple: the abandoned ship, the life vest, and the duffel bag with the salt water cookies, celery soda, and St. Marx jacket in the boat. And, of course, the broken safety line."

"What happened on the real day?"

"Almost an anti-climax," responded Marx. "Everything happened exactly as I'd planned—"

He explained the plot, leaving out only MacPhearson's name.

Hearing Marx tell the truth—knowing that he could not know she'd heard it before—reassured Sabine. He repeated the conversation from Rocco's Restaurant almost verbatim. "Tell me . . ." she said.

Marx could feel himself tense up. I know what's coming, he thought. She wants to know how I'd planned to stage my return. Consumed with his apprehension, Marx missed the beginning of Sabine's question.

". . . had you given any thought how your wife would respond to your death? Disappearing in a sailing accident is hardly a joking matter."

Marx frowned. I'll be damned, he thought, it's the same question Boz asked.

"I'm not sure I can give you an honest answer." He stalled; he didn't want to come across as a heartless bastard.

"Then make one up!" Sabine said curtly.

"I don't have to," he replied, trying to get up on his dignity. "Maybe 'honest' is not the right word."

"If it isn't, what's the problem? You're the expert with words."

My god, Marx thought, the realization striking him with sudden force. I'm not talking to some piece of ass any more, I'm not even talking to a reporter. It's all for the record, each word a potential ingredient for the biographer's soup pot.

"What I meant," he said warily, "is that my response is bound to be colored by everything that's happened since. To be honest, I can't remember what I did and didn't think about."

Sabine wasn't having any of it. "Come on, Saint. You can't have forgotten how you felt at that time. You claim to have thought of every eventuality: you must have thought how your wife would take it. Or, for that matter, other people: your agent, your publisher, your relatives, your friends—unless you didn't have any," she added.

Again, Stephen was struck by the resemblance to MacPhearson's questions. "During the last few years," he said tentatively, as if probing the terrain ahead for hidden snow bridges, "my marriage to Miriam wasn't . . . a roaring success."

"Why?"

"Now look." He didn't even try to hide his irritation. "You're not the prosecutor and I'm not the defendant. You've got to let me answer one question at a time."

"I'll try not to interrupt. At least not all the time," she added with a forced laugh.

"Our marriage was going to pot because each of us was changing. I'm not blaming Miriam, certainly not now. It wasn't her fault, it wasn't anybody's. We should've talked about it. Instead, I found a separate studio to write in and basically cut her out of my work day. I simply felt too circumscribed writing at home."

Marx laughed sarcastically. "There's a good word for a writer: 'circumscribed.' I felt I was becoming a circular scribe and simply had to break out of the circle. The mistake I made—at least as far as our marriage was concerned—was not to talk openly to Miriam about my reasons for getting a separate work space. I just went out and bought the place. Cash. No mortgage. It was to be my private island."

"Was that your only reason for getting the place?"

This time, Stephen didn't seem to mind the interruption. "Then it was." Actually, it wasn't the sole reason; he was also getting bored by monogamy. But that insight had no place in the public record.

"And later?"

"Our mistake was that we focused on avoiding conflict rather than examining the root of our problem. Pretty soon, Miriam got . . . other interests. When her catering business took off, many of her evenings were also taken up. Frankly, by then I didn't mind. I don't think she did either. To answer your original question: what did I think my wife would feel when she learned about my disappearance? I thought, deep down, it wouldn't hit her very hard. Sure, she'd be shocked, but also relieved. Anyway, I had decided to file for a divorce after my reappearance. If she didn't beat me to it."

Dammit, he thought, why do I keep talking about reappearing? It's as if I want her to ask about it.

But Sabine didn't. "But you didn't come back. Did she have anything to do with that decision?"

"In a way," he replied. "I thought it would be better for her."

"Better?" she asked. "How?"

"In two ways. If I returned in a couple of months she would have felt used. She would have gotten over it; but it would have made the divorce even more unpleasant. This way, I didn't have to hurt her pride. But even more important, I'd had time to reflect on our marriage, especially the earlier years. As is so common, the irritations and the faults recede, and the good me-mories remain. I thought she'd feel the same way about me. Instead of turning into the bitter, divorced wife of Stephen Marx, she'd end up as the widow without divorce hassles about dividing our property."

Sabine wondered whether he really meant that. "You mean you didn't mind giving up everything in return for a new life as Donald Mann?"

"Not *a* new life. I could have done that with a divorce. But a new literary life as D. Mann—that's something else. You're just focusing on my apparent sacrifice of material possessions. But these can be replaced. Now I can try experiments I probably never would have undertaken."

"Experiments?"

"Literary ones."

"Why couldn't you do this as Marx?" she asked.

"Well, of course, I could have, but I probably wouldn't have done so. It would have been too autobiographical. As D. Mann, known by no one, I can write just about anything."

Sabine persisted. "What sort of things?"

"Oh, whodunits, thrillers—"

"I know all about your thriller plots," she interjected wryly. "Be serious."

"You're right, I was joking."

"Then be serious," she repeated.

"I decline to answer, your honor. I'm taking the Fifth."

"Oh, come on, Saint." Sabine wanted to coax the answer out of him but he didn't budge.

"Not now. Maybe some other time."

"In that case, I'm going to sleep," said Sabine. "I'm taking the red-eye tomorrow. I'd just as soon get a good night's rest."

Sabine woke up first. On her way to the bathroom, she pulled aside the drapes to find a completely altered landscape. It was snowing: steady, vertical snowfall. Judging from the accumulation on the car roofs, it had been falling that way for hours. Opening the bedroom door, she called out, "Stephen, are you awake?" Not hearing any response, she walked over to the sofa. Marx was sound asleep.

She stood beside the sofa for a minute, watching him sleep. It was easier to look at him—and as she studied his face it was with the feeling that she'd never really had a chance to do this: simply look at him. When he was awake it was all lunge and parry, attack and defend: the game. He had a good, strong face, she decided, almost in spite of herself. But in repose it was harder to miss: whatever doubts she had about the waking Marx, the sleeper before her was something different. The past year seemed to have changed him. He looked grayer and older, or perhaps just wiser, than in his beardless photographs. Already at Rocco's she'd noticed his bushy eyebrows; so prominent she'd overlooked his eyelashes. They were long, almost feminine: D. Mann, the sleeping androgyne.

Gently she pulled his beard. "Saint, wake up. I've got a surprise for you."

Marx opened his eyes. "What time is it?"

"I don't know," smiled Sabine, "I don't think it matters. Come look out the window!"

Marx groaned, but made no move.

"Come on, Saint, get up and look." She grabbed his blanket and pulled it off, only to jump back. He was naked and his penis erect.

Sabine blushed and dropped the blanket, stammering. Marx, now fully awake, gathered it slowly around him as he sat up.

"Get dressed, Saint," Sabine finally managed. "But then look what's waiting for us out there. Your detective story is coming true."

Marx jumped up and ran to the window. "Dammit. I just hope the chains fit."

The trip back promised to be long, and the driving hazardous. Nevertheless, as the borrowed Ford wallowed down the road, yesterday's tension had been broken.

"Tell me, Bienchen, what do you plan to do? You aren't still thinking about some damned article on Mann for the *Columbia Journalism Review?*"

Sabine's eyes followed the sweep of the windshield wipers as if she were watching a ping-pong game. "Last night you told me about your sailing accident, but I didn't ask you the key question: who else knows you're alive?"

"Nobody."

"Come on, Saint, how can you say nobody? What about your friend with the motorboat?"

"He died in a car accident; three weeks after I arrived in San Francisco. One morning I opened the *Times* and there, among the obituaries, was Ambrose MacPhearson's. Of course, I was shocked; yet at the same time I felt a peculiar elation. I know this sounds cold-blooded—much of my disappearance does—but I just took it as a sign. As I told you, I'd been toying with the idea of not returning, but I hadn't figured out how to convince Ambrose never to tell anybody I was still alive. I don't think he'd have kept it indefinitely from Miriam. When I read about his death, I decided right then to start a new career."

"How had you planned to return? You must have had a plan."

"Who's asking the question?" he stalled. "The budding journalist?"

Sabine didn't answer. For a long time she sat staring at Marx's profile. He could feel her look but couldn't afford to turn toward her; the visibility was too poor to take his eyes off the road for an instant.

"No," she said slowly. "Not the budding journalist. Stephen Marx's biographer."

Marx stepped on the brakes, carefully, deliberately. The car started a slow skid; he caught it, brought the car to a stop, and turned toward her.

"Are you serious?"

"Yes," replied Sabine, "I'm serious. If you help me, that is. If you give me the proper information, I'll write a book about Marx rather than an article about Mann. I've decided I wouldn't mind being your first biographer."

"And where will you end the biography?"

"That depends on you," she said quickly.

"What does that mean?"

Now Sabine seemed to be calculating.

"If you make life as a biographer easy for me," she said slowly, "I'll stop with the *Times* article about your death."

Another silence fell between them. Sabine was struck, suddenly, how quiet the world had become. Outside, the snow fell heavily, without a sound.

"And if I don't?" Marx said at last.

"Then you'll have to wait till you see my book in a bookstore." She laughed nervously. "Come on, Saint, don't just stare at me. Get going so we get out of the snow."

Marx released the brakes; the rear wheels spun for a moment, and then they were moving again.

"Bienchen, let's stop fencing. If I help you with the Marx biography, will you show me your first draft?"

A set of intriguing consequences had suddenly occurred to him: how many persons *ever* have read their own obituaries and then their posthumous biography? Reading his own obituaries had been a heady experience, but it had worn off unexpectedly quickly. The newspaper obituaries were too factual to satisfy his obsession. To learn what people really thought of him he needed the reflective literary ones, and these were fewer in number than he had expected. Berg, for instance, had so far written nothing. So why not look forward to the reviews of a quasi-posthumous biography? A personal history, where he would still know what had appeared and, even more important, what had *not*. It could be done, he mused. If I do this right. . . .

"Is that a bargain?" he asked.

Sabine felt strangely elated and powerful. After all, she had the ultimate weapon: disclosure of his existence. She wouldn't rub it in, but she wouldn't let him forget it.

"It's a bargain. Let's start right now. First question: how had you intended to return to New York?"

Marx broke into laughter. "You don't waste time, do you? No, you don't need that information. At least not now. Remember? The biography ends with Marx's death. If you're going to write a biography, you're supposed to write about what *did* happen, not what *will* happen. Biography is not prophecy. No, let's start at the beginning: Stephen Marx was born in New York on March 20, 1937, the son of Harold J. and Anna S. Marx—"

"Saint, cut it out. I'm serious about wanting help and starting now. But not this way. I hate biographies beginning with 'he was born in. . . .' I want you to point me to sources. I'll check the material myself, I'll write the first draft, and then I'll verify it with you." Marx couldn't know that Sabine had just promoted herself in terms of the *Sports Illustrated* hierarchy. "I want to be accurate, but I don't want to follow your schedule. It's going to be *my* book."

He raised one calming hand from the steering wheel. "OK, OK. So what do you plan to do first?"

"I want this to be a critical biography. I want to get some insight into how you write, how you first get ideas about plots. For instance, was this ghastly skiing story an example of how your mind works?"

"Not always."

"Do you keep earlier drafts? Do you keep clippings of reviews? A clipping book would simplify life tremendously."

"And what will you do with the reviews?" he asked suspiciously.

"Compare them with the books; ask you which were important to you; did any of them influence you? Then, I'll interview some of them."

"Them?"

"Some of the more serious reviewers."

"I suppose Noah Berg will be one?" he asked sarcastically.

"Of course. Why not?"

Marx gave more attention to the road than it actually demanded at that moment. "No reason," he said casually. Marx had to admit that. At least he'd have a chance for a vicarious rebuttal, something editors of book reviews rarely offer. And how many objects of biographies can do that, he consoled himself; especially dead ones?

"I do have a book of clippings," he added. "But I don't know whether you'll be able to get it."

"Oh?"

"Surely you don't think I took it with me to San Francisco? It's in my studio apartment where I worked. You'd have to get access to it. My God!"

"What's the matter?" Sabine looked startled.

My God, thought Marx, if she gets into my studio she could tell me what Miriam has done with my papers. And what happened to the computer and the damn disks. It was the one oversight, he could never forgive himself for committing. He was reminded of it every time he booted his computer. MacPhearson had been right: something is bound to be overlooked. But why did it have to be the memory of his word processor; the hard disk with millions of bytes; the backup floppies? None had been erased when he went on his one-way sailing excursion, because Marx had simply over-looked their existence.

He improvised. "I just realized most of what you'll need is in my studio. The only way you could get the stuff would be through my wife. I don't even know what she's done with it. Maybe she's thrown everything away and sold the apartment."

Sabine studied Marx curiously. "Tell me something about your wife. Tell me how I should approach her so she'll talk to me. So she'll give me access to your files."

"I wish I knew."

18

In the end, Miriam split the difference between yes and no: she decided on an alternating regime of two weeks with Noah and two alone back at home. The fourteen days alone she dedicated to her SoHo business. But the rest of the time, Miriam, who had never delegated, started to learn that indispensable tool of successful management without much risk: no major damage could possibly be wreaked through supervisory absence in just two weeks.

The days with Noah were dedicated to Miriam's psychic and physical well-being: cooking, eating, sex, and daily work on her cookbook. That last had been Noah's idea. "If you can't write under these conditions," he told her, "forget about turning into an author."

The arrangement had worked out well. In the time with Noah, Miriam made great progress on her book; soon, sitting down to write had come to seem as natural to her—as essential to her identity—as Noah's companionship had also come to seem. And in the weeks away from Noah, away from her book, desire for both grew sharp.

One problem from which Miriam Marx never suffered was sleeplessness. It used to irritate her husband to no end. "How the hell can you fall asleep just like that?" he would accuse her. "The moment your head hits the pillow, you're out like a light." He, who always tossed and turned, who always "wrote" in his mind before falling asleep, took it as a personal affront whenever his bed-companions didn't suffer along with him. During their premarital cohabitation and early years of married life, Stephen Marx bore the insomniac's resentment silently. But later, when overt affection and sexual intimacy had become dully conventional, his pique had turned into pillow pounding, violent turning, and loud groaning—all to no avail. At most, they caused Miriam in her sleep to turn her warm, plump ass toward Stephen. All night long, Miriam slept soundly. When the alarm on the headboard went off, invariably it was Stephen who shut it off.

But that was many months ago. Now, when the alarm sounded at 7:45 A.M., Miriam, alone in her apartment, leapt out of the warm bed. She had moved the alarm across the room; by the time she had silenced it, she was up, she was moving: she let the momentum carry her, still semiconscious, through the routine she had taught herself since Stephen's death.

Miriam never wore pajamas or nightgowns; naked she groped her way to the kitchen to turn the stove on "high." Only then did she fill the kettle, thereby gaining a few seconds in heating the water. The machine gun rattle of the coffee grinder completed her climb to wakefulness. After dumping the ground coffee into her Chemex, she headed for the bathroom. By the time she had retraced her path to the kitchen, the still-naked Miriam was shivering, but now the water was boiling. As soon as the first cup of water had passed through the coffee grounds, she filled her mug, poured more water into the funnel and headed, still naked, to the shower.

Miriam had been drying herself when the telephone rang. She took it in the kitchen, within replenishing distance of the coffeepot.

"Is this Mrs. Marx?" a clear female voice asked.

Mrs. Marx? Nobody has called me that for the last year, thought Miriam. What is she trying to sell?

"Who's calling?" It left her with the option of claiming to be the housecleaner.

"Sabine Diehlsdorf."

"Who?"

Sabine was accustomed to such questions. "Dee—that's capital dee—eye, eee, aych, ell, esss, dee, oh, aar, eff: Diehlsdorf."

Surely, she wouldn't use such a name for phone selling, thought Miriam. "I'm Miriam Marx."

"Mrs. Marx." The voice had turned anxious, but Miriam had missed the change. She had been called "Mrs. Marx" twice now, and she definitely didn't like it. But how does one tell a stranger to cut it out—politely, that is?

While Miriam was pondering this, the voice continued. "I know this may sound like a terrible imposition, since you don't know me. But would you grant me an interview?"

"Interview?" Miriam's pique vanished. Occasional articles had started to appear here and there in food magazines; one of them had gone so far as to call her dishes "edible art." Was this a reporter for a kitchen or society column? No publicity is bad publicity, she reminded herself, and started rummaging in her inner files for some clever culinary soundbite. Not surprisingly, Miriam was unprepared for what followed; for a few seconds, the words didn't even register.

"I'm working on a biography of your husband. . . ."

The voice went on. Miriam remained silent, a bouillabaisse of thoughts racing through her head. Turn her off? See her briefly? Or—the thought occurred to her with a start—tell her to help herself to all of Saint's papers and finally get rid of that albatross? Victor Sedgwick, Stephen's agent, had been bugging her, in her capacity of literary executor-by-default, to do something about his files. Even Noah had advised her to face the inevitable chores of a literary executor; either that, or to assign that function to someone else.

The first and even second time Sedgwick had called, she'd managed to turn him down easily: Stephen's death was too recent, she didn't have it in her to go as yet through her dead husband's papers . . . the list of excuses was easily expandable. To Noah, she gave a more honest explanation.

"The dead are in no hurry. I want to finish my own book first."

But as time passed, Miriam's feelings toward Stephen mellowed markedly—not the least because of the conversations she'd had about him with Noah. And then there had been the obituaries and the subsequent critical retrospectives, summarizing Marx's literary career. That career had spanned their lives together. In that mood she had reread *Listen, Sister*, her favorite. To the extent that every novel has autobiographical components, this one had shed a new light on Stephen. It had even occurred to her that it might have represented a discreet rebuke to his male shrink, since in the novel the hero turned to a total stranger, a nun, for a kind of therapy. She remembered when Stephen first hit on the subject of a nun—at a time when he still talked to her about the birth pangs of a novelist. The childless Miriam almost envied him. Whenever he thought of a new character or a new plot, his boyish enthusiasm, which initially had attracted her so much, always returned.

The birth of the nun had occurred practically in front of Miriam. It was the sort of story she could tell a biographer. Stephen had thought of the character the weekend she had spent with him in a hotel in Saratoga Springs, near Yaddo. Two weeks of sexual abstinence (in Stephen's vocabulary, masturbation was still abstinence) had prompted him to invite Miriam for a weekend. Both had basked in their mutual pleasure—in as well as out of bed.

It had been Stephen's first stay at an artists' colony. On several occasions Stephen had been courted to spend time at McDowell or Yaddo, but he'd always turned them down. He was a city person, he had his own study with all the privacy he required—so why go to an artists' colony in the sticks? One of his writer-friends had finally convinced him to give it a try by pointing out that there are other people at artists' colonies—often interesting ones. Stephen, the ever curious, people-collecting novelist, went, and promptly bumped into his first nun—not a hundred-percent nun, he explained to Miriam that weekend, but close to it. Sister Sharon (maybe she wasn't called that yet, but Stephen Marx, the storyteller, had so anointed her) taught creative writing at Maryville, a Catholic women's college; she had published several volumes of poetry and one collection of short stories; and at age thirty-one, she had started to think seriously of entering a Carmelite monastery.

One evening at dinner—the best time at artists' colonies, when self-imposed privacy is broken by professional one-upmanship, social grace, and amazingly high-level raconteurship—Stephen Marx had found himself next to Sharon O'Grady. Etiquette never allows artists in the same discipline to admit that they haven't heard of a fellow colonist. Consequently, the initial probing is diplomatic; its aim to learn as much as possible about one's partner without giving away one's ignorance, and at the same time providing useful autobiographical details oneself.

After learning that Sharon O'Grady had been teaching for several years at a small women's college, Stephen had asked, "Tell me, are you ready to move, or are you content in your place?"

Sharon O'Grady gave him a long, thoughtful look before replying. "Yes, I've thought about it for the last couple of years. I'll be leaving Maryville at the end of this academic year."

"Where to?" asked Marx, wondering whether she was moving up or sideways on the academic ladder.

This time, her glance was short and amused. "I'm joining the Carmelite order—I'm going to a monastery in Brooklyn."

Within seconds—barely sufficient for recovery from total astonishment—Stephen Marx, who had never met a nun, had turned into the novelist-inquisitor. After three and one-half hours of nonstop questioning, the outline of *Listen, Sister* had been drawn in his head. By the end of the week, the first draft of chapter one had been typed on his Olivetti Lettera 22—his faithful pre-computer writing companion. In his usual manner, he found it necessary to amuse as well as instruct the reader. After all, how many people know about Carmelite nuns and their lifestyles?

"Sister Olivia Fitzsimmons?"

"Yes?"

"Did you order the special vegetarian dinner?"

"Yes, I did, thank you."

"Would you like anything to drink before dinner?"

"Do you have any white wine?"

"Yes, a California Riesling and white Zinfandel."

"No Chardonnay?"

"I'm afraid not."

"In that case, just some Perrier with lime."

"I'm sorry, we have no Perrier; will soda water do?"

"Yes, of course."

Michael finally looked sideways at his neighbor. "Sister?" British nurses are called sister, he thought, but the accent was east-coast USA with a slight southern touch. A nun? I've never met a nun, certainly not in first class. How come she's so choosy about the wine? Is that what they drink in their cloistered cells?

Michael had turned to the woman to study her more carefully. She was dressed in a brown wrap-around skirt, her legs out of sight, a light-brown, high-buttoned long-sleeved blouse covering most of her torso. She wore no jewelry except for a necklace with a silver cross. No make-up. He focused on her face: short but professionally cut hair, excellent complexion, full lips ("What do they taste like?" thought the womanizer in him), warm brown eyes and a slightly amused smile. She had obviously read his mind.

"You look as if you are about to ask me a question."

Michael looked slightly embarrassed. "When the stewardess addressed you as 'Sister,' I first thought of an English nurse, but as soon as you spoke—"

"You mean my accent?"

"Yes, your accent, and also something in your tone. I concluded you must be a nun, but you don't look like one."

"You don't know much about nuns, do you?"

A moment of silence passed as Michael looked past the woman's face out the plane window, and then added quietly:

"Why don't you tell me about a nun's life—I mean your present life, what brought you there?"

"Like most outsiders, you probably think only of the dictionary definition of a nun: a woman belonging to a religious order, living in a convent under vows of obedience, poverty and chastity. You'd be surprised what a range of behavior, lifestyle, and even appearance is possible within this definition, especially now. I belong to the Order of the Carmelites. Have you heard of us?"

"Can you meet me at my downtown office?" The words sounded fancier than the converted loft in the former sweatshop building in SoHo.

Sabine bubbled over with gratitude. "When would you like me to come?"

"Wednesday at eleven." It was the same hour she'd picked for her first appointment with Noah Berg, and for the same reason: potential contrivance of a phantom lunch appointment.

Stepping into the freight elevator, Sabine didn't know what or whom to expect. The elevator opened directly into a large loft in which at least half a dozen women and a couple of men moved around in organized chaos. Unless they're filthy, food establishments, and especially kitchens, are inherently cheerful. This one was impeccably clean—white walls, white ceiling, stainless steel reflecting the light from the fluorescent overhead lamps—as well as tempting. The all-pervasive aroma of the freshly baked bread immediately gave Sabine hunger pangs. No one paid her the slightest attention. Finally, she approached a man in blue jeans and a white apron, who was busily kneading dough.

"Excuse me. I have an appointment with Mrs. Marx."

The man looked up, momentarily bewildered. "*Mrs.* Marx? Miriam is over there," he gestured with his head. "Behind the glass partition."

Sabine, in her nervousness, hadn't noticed Miriam's own wariness while introducing herself. She had rehearsed plausible answers to likely questions—for instance her reasons for wanting to write a biography of Stephen Marx. But Miriam surprised her.

"Whom have you seen so far?" she started.

"Whom have I seen so far?" Sabine repeated the question to stall for time. "Actually, you're the first person . . . in New York," she added quickly. "I wanted to ask about your husband's literary executor—"

"Because?"

"I'd like to get access to his files. Nothing personal right now," Sabine hurried on. "Just his literary papers. I thought they might be in your possession."

"Possession?" A wan smile crossed Miriam's face. "I do know where they are, but I haven't had it in me to go over them. Not yet, at any rate."

"I understand," said Sabine. "It must be painful."

The two women exchanged glances, each waiting for the other to continue. Sabine was the first to break the silence.

"I realize you know nothing about me. Here," she reached into her bag, "is a list of references you could contact. My boss at *Sports Illustrated*, a couple of my professors at the Columbia School of Journalism—"

"So you're a journalist?"

"I'm trying to become one," said Sabine. "I'm pretty good at checking facts and researching. The *New Yorker* and *S.I.* are two of the best places to learn those skills. If you think about it, that's exactly what a biographer must do: dig out facts, verify them, organize—"

"How good are you at this?" Miriam looked at the typed sheet with the names.

"I think I'm very good, but why don't you check with my references."

"I may do that." Miriam liked the young woman's confidence. She leaned back in her chair, ready to listen. "Tell me something about you. How familiar are you with my husband's work? And why do you want to write his biography? How old are you? Where. . . ."

By the time noon had arrived Miriam had invited Sabine to lunch at her favorite local trattoria Arleccino. The Italian restaurant connection among the Marxes did not escape Sabine, who considered it a propitious omen. She sensed that Miriam had been satisfied with her answers, which, in turn, had spurred Sabine to pose questions of her own, mostly literary ones dealing with Stephen Marx.

"Sabine, I could've hugged you after you finished with your list of questions." Miriam was almost gushing. "You know why?"

Sabine shook her head, her face beaming with pleasure.

"It's been well over a year since Stephen's accident, yet this is the first time somebody has approached me as a resource about his literary work, rather than as a repository of anecdotes to be used as fillers in literary obituaries."

Of course, this statement was not fair to Noah Berg, but in Miriam's mind Noah didn't count anymore as a seeker of Marxian memorabilia; he had been elevated to the status of significant other. Nor was it the complete truth with respect to Sabine. This young woman—so eager, so bright—might be the ideal person to relieve her of a burden she would otherwise have to shoulder herself. Not so long ago, her lawyer had said, almost prophetically, "Just wait when the first biographer knocks on your door. You can't just tell them to help themselves to the files if you don't even know what's in them."

Why not? Miriam wondered now, as they left the restaurant to take a cab to Stephen's West 68th Street pad. It struck her as a splendid deal: in return for organizing all of Stephen's papers, Sabine would get access to them. After all, allowing access did not mean granting permission to quote. That might come later, after she had seen how Sabine performed with the organizational aspects of the job—the crappy part, as Stephen would have called it.

"My niece stayed in the place for a couple of weeks. I doubt she's a great housekeeper." Miriam held out the key. "Here, Sabine, you open it."

Sabine's heart was pounding as she placed the key into the lock. Not in her wildest imagination had she imagined she would be entering Marx's inner sanctum after one meeting with Miriam. Sabine had wondered about the wife whom she couldn't visualize for want of any physical description. She hadn't had it in her to ask, "What does she look like?" and Marx had offered not one iota of useful information—only the distinct impression that the marriage was well over, as far as he was concerned. And given the means he had used to end it, Sabine could hardly disbelieve. Was she so awful that Stephen willingly handed over all his material possessions, including the entire Marx literary oeuvre, just to get rid of her? It seemed too simple. Or was Marx a man to whom material belongings meant nothing? Who lived only for the next book and thus was willing to leave behind everything he had earned and written before? There would have to be more complicated motives; how else could such sacrifices jibe with his obsessive preoccupation with his own reputation? She had come to realize that by studying and ultimately understanding what drove Marx, she might learn to decode and eventually articulate her own ambitions.

Prior to laying eyes on Miriam, Sabine had considered her an adversary. As Marx's biographer, it was only natural for her to commence with a vested interest in the central character of her book. Nevertheless, she didn't fall into all of the mistakes of a novice biographer. Her journalistic training at *Sports Illustrated* had already taught her that information provided by the subject should always be confirmed through other sources. Otherwise one is likely to author the worst kind of biography: an autobiography written by a surrogate. By definition, all autobiographies are automythology, and to that extent either incomplete or partly incorrect. Not necessarily by design, but because each word passes through a fine filter with a mesh made out of narcissism, conceit, pride, or even shame. In the absence of such filters, few autobiographies would ever see the light of day.

And Sabine knew as well that, in taking on the Marx biography, she was starting out with a major handicap: a subtle indebtedness to the biographee, supposedly dead, who would feed her private information, in return for showing him the manuscript and not bringing him back to life. She had accepted the deal, thinking she was getting a bargain: a free editor, who would simply check the manuscript for accuracy. It hadn't taken her long to realize that the deal had strings attached. Marx still wanted to fill the role of censor. How to cut those strings?

These questions were uppermost in Sabine's mind as she turned the key, but as she preceded Miriam into the dim and musty apartment an entirely new quandary arose. Her new and generous friend thought herself a widow—seemingly a contented, self-assured widow. Had Sabine the right to demolish that supposition? Or did she have the obligation to tell her that Stephen Marx was D. Mann? At this stage of their acquaintance, she knew, either decision would have been wrong: she simply didn't know enough to decide. But how long could she wait?

Miriam was moved by the combination of awed pleasure and keen curiosity displayed by the young woman as she wandered around the studio. Sabine behaved like a museum visitor, even to the first question she asked.

"Why isn't the Pulitzer Prize or the National Book Award hanging on the wall? Or do you keep them at home?" Sabine was thinking of the framed certificates she had seen in the publisher's office when she first searched for Mann.

"Saint actually did have them framed. 'Saint' was my husband's nickname. . . ."

Sabine, about to say "I know," caught herself in time. She reminded herself henceforth to count to five in the company of Miriam before responding to any comment about Stephen Marx.

"He had them hanging on the wall until he worked on *Cohen's Dilemma*."

"I remember," exclaimed Sabine. "In the book, Cohen makes some snide remarks about physicians hanging even the most trivial certificates on their office walls and padding their CVs, while he, the Nobel Prize winner, takes it for granted that people know about his kudos."

"Precisely. And if they don't know about his achievements, they simply don't count." Miriam enjoyed these recollections. "When Saint returned from interviewing that Nobelist, he stripped his wall. I gave him this Paul Klee poster so it wouldn't look so bare." She pointed to the fairy-like figure with wings, a red heart on its chest, bearing a tray with a teapot and other accoutrement. "It's one of my favorites: 'An Angel Bringing a Continental Breakfast.' I got it around the time I started my business."

Miriam looked at her watch. "My God," she exclaimed, "do you realize that it's past three o'clock? I was going to show you around Stephen's apartment—'showing' is actually the wrong word. I was going to look around in your company, but I don't even have time for that. I'll have to call my office to tell them I'll be late. I nearly forgot the phone here," she pointed to the telephone at the desk. "It's still connected. Don't ask me why. I suppose it's tangled up with my inability to do anything about the apartment or Stephen's belongings. The only things I removed were his clothing. It was simply too bizarre to have his clothes hanging around. I packed them all, the ones here and those at home, and gave them to Goodwill." She laughed nervously. "They asked whether I wanted a receipt, but I declined. It seemed terribly cheap and disloyal, giving away a dead man's belongings and taking a tax deduction.

"Sabine, I've got to run. You can stay here and look around. When you leave, just lock the door behind you. Call me tomorrow and we'll take it from there."

Sabine sat motionless, her eyes traveling over the space accessible from the sofa. She felt surprisingly ambivalent. Matters had progressed at a spectacular rate; as biographer, she should have been on cloud nine. Yet at the same time she couldn't shed the feeling of an intruder, who'd conspired with Marx's wife to spy on his private space. But was looking around an intrusion? To ease her conscience, Sabine started in neutral space: the kitchen and the bathroom. The kitchen, clearly no active cook's headquarters, looked like an afterthought, added while carving the apartment space out of some larger unit. The refrigerator fitted under the two-burner stove; a small microwave oven was mounted over the minute work space. The sink was empty but stained, as if it hadn't been cleaned for a long time.

Sabine opened the refrigerator to find age-hardened mustard, a half-filled bottle of mayonnaise, three eggs, two Diet Pepsis, and a jar containing strawberry jam covered with a crust of crystallized sugar. For a moment Sabine shuddered, thinking she was looking at one-year-old eggs. Then she remembered that the apartment had been used by Miriam's niece. But where had she slept? She returned to the study to examine the couch. It was solid, of one piece, and certainly no sofa bed. It was only then that she discovered the cleverly disguised Murphy bed, which must have been built specially for the space near the kitchen door.

Sabine's next stop was the bathroom. Unlike the kitchen, it must have been part of the original construction. There was something charmingly solid and old-fashioned—middle thirties, she guessed—about the fixtures, the deep-purple tiles, and especially the medicine cabinet. Sabine had a surprisingly rude habit, one she had formed one evening as an adolescent, when she'd opened a medicine cabinet in a friend's house, searching for aspirin, and discovered instead a diaphragm container and a huge tube of spermicidal jelly. Ever since that day, Sabine always opened medicine cabinets in private bathrooms for evidence of contraceptives.

This time, the contents were uninformative. There were no contraceptives. The bottle of aspirin without top, the dried out deodorant stick, the small can of Band-Aids, the Mercurochrome bottle, and the nail scissors could have belonged to anybody. The only tube was a maltreated toothpaste, squeezed in the middle, with the bottom end partly rolled up. Sabine was a meticulous toothpaste-squeezer; in her secret inspections of medicine cabinets, the shape and state of the toothpaste was her version of a Rorschach test.

Back in the study, Sabine sat down behind the L-shaped desk, an IBM XT model personal computer by her left side on the lower desktop of the L—the former home of Stephen's Olivetti Lettera 22. Sabine, whose work at *Sports Illustrated* had accustomed her to more up-to-date electronic gear, looked for a long moment at Marx's computer. Going through the files on its hard disk would probably be a time-consuming process. She decided to leave it for later. Sliding open the narrow desk drawer in front of her, she found pencils, paper clips, rubber bands, a roll of one-cent stamps—the usual paraphernalia of a writer, all in immaculate order.

Next on her inspection was the right-hand lower drawer. Before she could see its contents, the weight of the drawer told her she had struck gold: a nearly full file drawer, all folders bearing handwritten headings. Sabine picked one at random: *Listen, Sister.* Inside were photocopies and clippings of book reviews. There they were, all thirteen titles of Marx's books, each file filled with clippings. Exactly what she had asked of Stephen in California.

She carefully returned the files to their places and slid the drawer back in. This, too, could wait for another day. It was good to know they were there, but today she was hoping for something more. Something she had not expected. Something she didn't already know about Marx. She looked up from the desk, and found herself facing her own reflection in the sliding mirror doors of the wide closet. The mirrors reminded her of the room at Kirkwood, but here her reflection looked back from a desk, rather than a bed. She rose and slid open one mirrored panel, expecting to find a closet devoid of clothes. Instead, she was staring at two four-drawer file cabinets. On top of one stood an indexed file box of floppy disks. Each cabinet had a single lock on the upper right-hand corner. Both were locked.

19

By the end of the second week Sabine had mapped out her exploration of Stephen Marx. Actually, it was Marx who had done the mapping: for each book, there were background notes, manuscript drafts, business correspondence and, of course, the reviews. Every mention, long or trivial, of each book was there. Marx, the author, had thrown away nothing—a real pack rat when it came to paper. All that was left for Sabine was to follow the trail. Although she had read all thirteen Marx novels—fourteen, if she counted *Middles*—she started all over again. Each time she completed a chapter, she would look at the corresponding notes and drafts. For the earlier work, this was a significant undertaking: Marx's typewritten drafts were palimpsests, recording early intentions and their gradual evolution toward the finished work. With the later novels, however, Sabine came to understand why literary biographers regret the advent of the word processor. Here, the files were thinner, the pages uncontaminated by inked embellishments or corrections. She, who had always reveled in the undefiled hygiene of a laser-printed page, now wished for the occasional slovenliness of a typed paragraph. Count your blessings, she consoled herself: at least Marx had been a latecomer to the computer age.

As Sabine dug deeper into the Marx archive, and her own notes stacked correspondingly high, she quickly came to begrudge hours spent away from Marx's desk or hers. She found herself confused, at times, with a sensation almost like vertigo, when she would look up from her work and see herself peering back at her in the closet mirror: whose desk was she sitting at? Her's or Marx's? Whose notes were these? Whose life was she writing? At times like these she would pull herself away from the desk, leave the not-quite-familiar confines of the apartment for a walk or jog to clear her head. A master's degree in journalism now seemed trivial—part of someone else's life, not hers. She dropped out of Columbia, keeping only her part-time job with *Sports Illustrated* as a link with her old life. The income was necessary, no matter how much she regretted the time away from her biographical trawling and dredging. Within weeks, even that limited income came to seem almost dispensable: at Miriam's suggestion, Sabine moved out of her apartment into Stephen's; rent-free, including utilities. If she hadn't needed to stock the small refrigerator, she might have given up her job entirely. But the *S.I.* job fit her perfectly: it honed her research skills; it provided unlimited photocopying facilities as well as access to a first-class reference library; and the income could now be used for luxuries ranging from spur-of-the-moment purchases of impractical shoes to membership in an upscale fitness club.

Other than *S.I.*, only one fixed obligation interrupted her progress on the manuscript that was starting to take form. Every other Monday at 8:30 P.M., the telephone would ring: Stephen Marx, checking in for the biweekly inquisition or consultation as circumstances might demand.

"What's it like to read thirteen novels, not once, but twice?" he asked.

"I'm starting on my third pass," she reminded him.

"Well, what's it like?" he repeated.

"It's like peeling an onion, looking for layers the author wasn't aware of."

"Let's hear an example," he challenged her.

"Not yet. I'm still peeling."

Sabine would switch to her list of accumulated questions, and Marx would answer or critique them. He had insisted there be no written correspondence, but since he had not specifically excluded taping, Sabine recorded all conversations. He didn't trust her—he didn't even volunteer his unlisted telephone number—so there was no reason for her not to broaden the rules of the game. Sabine was good at such rationalizations. Any residual feeling of guilt she might have had disappeared when Donald Mann announced that he had a new post office box. He had left the Castro district, he said uninformatively, "for a less intrusive place."

The week Sabine moved into Marx's old studio she was careful to be at her old apartment to intercept Marx's call. The place was nearly empty: it held only the phone, on the floor in a corner, and a few cardboard boxes. When the phone rang, the sound off the bare walls was harsh.

Back in San Francisco, Sabine had decided never to volunteer information to Marx. Although his interest in her seemed focused almost entirely on her project—on himself, as she often reminded herself—keeping her own secrets helped her hold onto a sense that she was in control. That Marx was often oblivious to this aspect of their relationship—as he was now—added to this sense.

"I'll call you in two weeks," Marx had started to end the call.

"I nearly forgot," Sabine responded, not entirely truthfully. "I'm moving. The new number is 873–2719. Good night."

The number did not register in Marx's mind until two weeks later. It had struck him as amusing, for the moment or two he had thought of it, that Sabine would match his change of address with her own. It was not until he actually punched the keys on his telephone that he suddenly realized what the 87 in Sabine's new number stood for: TRafalgar! Marx belonged to the rapidly disappearing number of New York snobs who still used—or even knew—the old names of their exchanges. TRafalgar 3-2719 still existed? For a moment the coincidence pleased him: the phone company, in its inscrutable wisdom, had seen fit to give Sabine his old number.

Then the truth was on him in a rush.

Marx's voice came out of the receiver like a panther out of a crouch. "What the hell are you doing in my place? Who let you in?"

Sabine had to hold the phone away from her ear. It fulminated for another minute, panther snarl reduced to a more manageable, mechanical, buzzing. Sabine took the time to review: she had prepared herself for all eventualities, including this one.

"What do you mean 'my place,' Donald?" She couldn't resist using the name. "You've reached Stephen Marx's apartment. Stephen isn't around anymore. This is his biographer. I'm sitting at his desk, by the way."

Marx was not amused. "How did you get in?"

"His wife gave me the key."

"Miriam?" Marx was stunned.

Sabine wished she could have seen his face. "Who else?" she teased. "After all, she is Marx's widow. Who, but she, should have the key? Hey, it even rhymes," she added, laughing.

Marx fell silent at last. The silence stretched out so long she finally asked, "Saint, are you there?"

"Yes."

There was something in his tone that made her drop the playfulness. "Sorry," she said, a little contritely. "I couldn't help kidding you. I was going to tell you how I got to sit in your chair . . ." she waited out a theatrical pause, "and sleep in your clever Murphy bed. Who made it for you?"

"What?"

In a soothing voice, Sabine related what had happened during the past weeks. Not everything, but enough to allay any suspicion that she might have told Miriam that her husband was still alive. As the story unraveled, Marx calmed down.

"Miriam is a marvelously generous woman," Sabine continued. Marx's low snort was lost over the telephone. "She's been so occupied with her catering business, she hadn't touched your papers or belongings." Sabine didn't deem it necessary to tell about his clothes having ended up at Goodwill. "Miriam felt no time pressure, because legally you aren't dead. Did you know that?"

His response was curt. "Yes, I guessed so. But go on."

"In return for giving me full access to your study, I'm supposed to prepare a complete inventory of your literary papers. Your agent has been pestering her about it, and she hasn't had time to go near them. You know, Saint, you're God's gift to biographers the way you kept your files."

Marx was no longer listening. Nobody had removed his papers, and if they hadn't inspected his files, then his hard disk and backup floppies must have been left untouched as well. The relief flooding through him left him momentarily uninterested in anything else Sabine had to say. Now all he had to do was to convince Sabine to send them to San Francisco—unread. The material had no place in Marx's biography—at least not in his version.

He could do that, he told himself. He just needed an angle. While Sabine chattered on about the relatively untouched state of his studio, making what seemed to Marx impertinent comments about his housekeeping, he did a furious survey of the possible lines of approach.

What Marx might have deduced, had he been paying closer attention, was that Sabine had already surveyed the entire apartment: every drawer, every file, even the box of floppy disks. The few spot checks she'd permitted herself had provided more than an inkling that the right-hand bottom file drawer contained material pertinent to another side of Stephen Marx. But once having surveyed the scene, Sabine stuck to her schedule: first the author, because she wanted to complete her obligations to Miriam; then the person. She left the bottom drawer unread—for now. She was confident she would have a use for it before her work was done, but for now she had a plan, and she intended to stick to it. The disciplined biographer, Sabine started with the file labeled "The Academy of Spite," Marx's first book—the one he'd started while still in Switzerland.

"Why are you volunteering all that to a virtual stranger?"

"Stop fussing, Noah, and sit down," Miriam said good-naturedly. "You're interfering with my creative process."

Noah sat, shifted his position three times, and then was on his feet again. "But why go so far as to have her move into your dead husband's pied-à-terre? Or is it lit-à-terre?"

"What's that supposed to mean?" She frowned—he couldn't tell whether it was prompted by confusion or suspicion.

"I was trying to be cute. . . ." he explained lamely. "'Lit-à-terre'—'lit-ra-ture'?" Why explain that instead of literature, he'd meant the French word for bed, with reference to Marx's extracurricular bedding of Monica. "You treat this woman like a long-lost daughter," he continued.

"And why not?" Miriam stopped slicing nectarines. She was working on a low-calorie sorbet. "I like her. If I'd started early enough," she mused, "I could have had a daughter in her twenties—"

"Exceptionally early," he interrupted.

"You're full of compliments today. Here, try one of these." She placed a slice of nectarine into his open mouth. "But what I'm trying to say is that Sabine is a young woman after my taste: smart and ambitious. So why not help her? And help myself at the same time. Even you've been bugging me to do something about Stephen's papers. Well," she said with a small, smug smile, "I have." Miriam steered Noah into a chair and pressed him down into it. "You stopped pretending long ago to be doing anything on Stephen. So let her do it. Don't be jealous."

Noah reached up and took her face into his hands. "I have no reason to be jealous. I am much too happy with you. But you know why I stopped working on anything even remotely dealing with Stephen. He brought us together, but he can't hold us together. That's our task, just yours and mine."

"Agreed," she whispered, and kissed him.

"I'd like to meet your vicarious daughter," he said with an air of decision. "Let's have her over for a meal at my place. I'll take care of the food."

"It's a deal," Miriam laughed, and kissed him again.

Sabine was curious to see Noah Berg in the flesh. Over the past several weeks, as she'd made her way through Stephen's collection of reviews, Berg's name surfaced time and again; more often than not, it was Berg's review that lay at the head of the file, as if Marx had assigned it that place—or taken it out to reread some time after the file had been filled. In Berg's work, too, she thought she could detect a similar—what? attraction? obsession? Berg's reviews came to read, over the years, as though there were something more at stake than a mere book review. In the later ones the tone was by turns hectoring, sarcastic, triumphant over Marx's perceived missteps, grudging in his praise. And now, she thought, I'm having dinner at Berg's apartment. She could hardly wait to tease Stephen about it during their next conversation.

Berg lived in the London Terrace complex in Manhattan's Chelsea district, between Ninth and Tenth Avenues. His apartment was on the fourth floor, overlooking a well-kempt interior garden, protected from most of the street noise. It was a warm May evening; Sabine, Miriam, and Berg were drinking white wine on the small balcony. Noah was working hard at making conversation with what struck him as an unusually reticent young woman.

"Miriam tells me you're in the journalism program at Columbia. What got you interested in a Marx biography?" Noah had learned long ago that the best way to get people talking was to ask them how they came to do whatever it was they did. It was a ploy that had never failed him yet.

To Sabine, however, the question was anything but innocuous. Worse yet, she hadn't expected to be questioned directly about her darkest secret: she had no plausible story in reserve. She remembered something Marx had told her when he was still Donald Mann. How he coped with unexpected questions: "Make up as little as possible."

She swirled her wineglass what seemed to Berg a long time before replying. "In a way, you did Mr. Berg."

"I?"

"I'd set out to write a story for our Columbia magazine about a new author, D. Mann. Do you remember? Nobody knew anything about him."

"Of course." Berg nodded emphatically. "What makes you so sure it's a 'him'?"

For a second, Sabine was flustered again, but then she recovered. "I suppose that's because of you." She hurried on. "Don't you remember? You ended your review with the statement that the unknown author was probably a man." She took a protective sip of wine. "I think you even said he was an early Stephen Marx."

Miriam had been glancing idly over the balcony railing. She looked up. "You never told me that, Noah."

Berg responded with a dismissive shrug. "I've reviewed a couple of hundred books since then." He turned to Sabine. "But how did that turn into a biography of Marx?"

Sabine shrugged. "I didn't have much luck with my Mann project. But along the way, I'd followed up on your Marx lead. I read some of his books and when I found out that he'd died in an accident. . . ." Sabine didn't wish to continue. What she had said so far was not a lie, but the chronological sequence was an untruth. She was anxious to change the subject. "Anyway, I'm not at Columbia anymore. I dropped out to work on this."

Noah's eyebrows went up. "That's quite a leap of faith, isn't it?"

"Probably. But I've got such a fabulous opportunity here. . . ." She gestured at Miriam. "And it seemed to me that a project like this would be as good training as I'd get at Columbia." She turned back to Noah. "Don't you think journalism and biography are pretty close, Mr. Berg?"

"Call him Noah, Sabine. You two are likely to see a fair amount of each other."

"Miriam is right," concurred Berg, "call me Noah. And I agree: journalistic inquisitiveness can be useful to a biographer. Just don't let it degenerate into muckraking."

"Noah, darling, don't lecture Sabine. You're supposed to be the host." Miriam cast a hungry glance in the direction of the kitchen. "And cook."

"Beg pardon, ma'am. Dinner is about to be served in the dining room." With exaggerated courtesy, he bowed them through the door.

"You cook, Noah?" Sabine asked as she passed him on the way inside.

"Just wait and see."

The first course, a mousse of white fish, was already on the table. Berg came from the kitchen with a plate of thinly sliced cucumbers, which he proceeded to arrange around the mousse. "A Viennese recipe," he murmured.

Miriam used her fork like a judge at a culinary competition: selecting a morsel, she held it for a moment before her open mouth, as if she wanted to taste any aroma, then placed it carefully on her tongue. "First class," she pronounced. "But how—"

Noah interrupted her, with an abruptness Sabine found difficult to understand. "The cucumber is cut it into very thin slices," he explained, a bit pedantically, Sabine thought. "Sprinkled with a bit of salt, allowed to sit, the excess moisture then pressed through cheesecloth. . . . Never mind, just enjoy the first course."

Both women cleaned their plates. "I'm glad to see you liked the mousse," remarked Noah. "And now the pièce de résistance."

He returned with a covered serving dish, placing it into the middle of the table. "Just one moment, before I serve you." He went out to bring a plate of potatoes, which he sprinkled ostentatiously with fresh parsley. "Steamed new potatoes, with just a bit of butter. And fresh parsley. I finished them just before you came. And now. . . ."

He lifted the cover and proceeded to serve, first Miriam, and then Sabine. "A blanquette de veau. It needs nothing but the potatoes. The carrots, onions, and, of course, *fresh* sage are already part of the base."

Sabine couldn't figure him out. The preciousness of his description went along with the cooking well enough, but there was a slightly mocking air about the whole performance that made her wonder. Miriam, however, did not wait nor did she taste this course in the reverential way she had done with the mousse. Before Noah had even finished serving himself, she quickly took a bite.

"Why, you fake," she exclaimed.

Noah stopped her with an admonishing finger. "One moment, please. Sabine, would you please taste this blanquette." After observing Sabine obediently follow his command, he asked. "Now what do you think of it?"

"Delicious," pronounced Sabine.

"You see?" he turned back to Miriam. "Our guest is pleased. How can you be so ungrateful—"

Miriam did not let him finish. She reached over and clamped one hand over his mouth. "You've never made me a mousse and the one you served us was nearly perfect." She turned to Sabine, hand still firmly over Noah's mouth. "Who knows? I thought, maybe Noah has been practicing. But this?" With her other hand she pointed to the dish containing the veal. "Fresh sage! Do you know where he must have gotten it from?" She dropped her hand and broke out laughing. "Noah, darling, did you really think you'd be able to fool me?"

Sabine looked from one to the other. They were behaving like lovebirds. But what was going on?

"I should explain, Sabine," said Miriam, wiping her tears. "Before you decide we're completely mad. Clearly, this man ordered the entire meal from the Marx Catering Service in SoHo. Or would you care to inform us where you buy your fresh sage?"

"My lips are sealed. But I did not order the *entire* meal from that fancy SoHo outfit. The cucumber salad and the potatoes are the exclusive products of Noah Berg's culinary skill. And later, you'll observe my personal touch with the dessert."

The two women broke into applause when the final course, a cold amaretto soufflé, was sprinkled by Noah with some ground Amaretti di Saronno, crushed grandiosely before their very eyes with a pestle and mortar. This time, Sabine judged Noah's performance as authentic preciousness, not fake. Like the literary posing she'd picked up here and there in his reviews.

They were sipping coffee when Noah returned to the subject he'd broached on the balcony. "Do you plan to do this biography completely on your own, or are you getting some expert advice?"

Sabine was struck by how quickly a seemingly innocuous question brought her to dangerous territory. "Advice?" she said, almost wincing as her voice went up to its higher registers. "You mean," she swallowed quickly, "like the help Miriam has given me?" She looked beseechingly toward Miriam, who simply nodded brightly. "Miriam's been so helpful, I feel as though I've had more help than any biographer could wish for."

Berg waved a dismissive hand. "I don't mean sources." He nodded graciously toward Miriam. "I'm sure Miriam's been able to give you all the help you need in that regard. I mean technically, my dear: in the art of the form. Biography. It's not as simple as it looks. Otherwise I wouldn't have to review so many wretched ones."

"Oh," exhaled Sabine, suddenly relieved. For a moment she had been sure Noah knew about her biweekly conversations with the greatest living expert on Marx. "Certainly, as I collect my material, I may look for advice."

"Be sure to find the right experts," Noah said, "or it won't do you any good. A beginning tennis player won't learn anything, playing with a Wimbledon champion. The ball will just whiz by. You'll never hit it once. You could do that for hours and not pick up a shtick."

"What about you, Noah? You could give her some advice. Did you know?" Miriam reached over and touched Sabine by the sleeve. "Noah had set out to write a major piece on Stephen's oeuvre—sort of a summation of his literary career. A rather generous one. That's how we met, Noah and I."

"And that's why I am not writing it," Noah added. "Because we met."

I'll be damned, thought Sabine, what would Stephen say to all that? "Do you have any suggestions, then?"

"Why not start with the discussions we had on style?" Miriam said to Noah. "Sabine might even find some of the notebooks I told you about."

"Good point," he said. "Quite early, I got interested in Marx's stylistic mannerisms: his antecedents, early influences. For instance, Miriam told me about his adoration of James Joyce. I found it rather entertaining searching for Joycean borrowings in Marx's opus."

Sabine wished she could take notes. Not only for Marxian literary traits, but also Berg's. "Can you give me some examples?"

"I'll give you a hint and then let you look for some. It will be good practice."

Miriam smiled, listening to his explanation with examples drawn from the *Dubliners* all the way to *Finnegans Wake*. She had grown familiar with Noah Berg's pedagogic streak, but it was amusing to see it practiced on others.

"Miriam also told me how her husband always carried a small notebook with him, where he jotted down interesting phrases, personality traits—"

"And idioms he found in other people's writings," Miriam interrupted. "I wonder whether any of those notes are still around."

"Yes," concurred Noah, "I wouldn't mind seeing them. I am always interested in the question of appropriation of other authors' phrases, the crossbreeding that occurs. In the case of Stephen Marx, there are times when he cultivated the flora of language so well he produced hybrids of unusual beauty."

The guy talks in prose, thought Sabine, quickly committing the phrase to memory.

"But one wonders," Noah went on musing. "When does one cross the line from literary window shopping into shoplifting? From crossbreeding to—ahem—rape?"

"Why Noah Berg!" Miriam interjected. "I would hardly call anything Stephen did *rape!*"

There was an awkward silence, while Noah looked at Miriam with a faintly embarrassed expression. For the second time that evening, Sabine was puzzled. There was something more to Noah's silence than the confusion of a man caught in an indelicate choice of words. The silence went on for what seemed a very long time.

"I'm sorry, my dear," he said finally. "Poor choice of metaphor."

"But following your horticultural analogy, Noah, what's wrong with swiping a plant or two to embellish your own flower bed?"

"Just so it's not too rare a rose. Then they might catch you. Microplagiarism is OK," he lifted his eyes and snickered good-naturedly, "it keeps the literary goodies in circulation. Go look through Marx's files, Sabine. Tell us what you find. But keep *both* eyes open." He wagged an admonishing finger. "That's the difference between a journalist and a biographer. A journalist is always out gunning for someone. But to aim a rifle, you have to close one eye. A biographer needs to keep both eyes open, looking for context, perspective. . . . Incidentally, that one is borrowed."

Sabine looked at him, both eyes wide open. Until now she had considered her biographical venture some sort of ménage à trois. Why not involve Berg in a ménage à quatre? she asked herself.

"Saint," Sabine said the moment they had exchanged standard greetings on their next phone call, "do you know what Noah Berg said about 'Marx's opus'?"

"What?" The suspicious tone came across the miles quite well.

"Marx cultivated the flora of language so well he produced hybrids of unusual beauty."

"Now where did he write that?" With the speed of sound, suspicion had been replaced by curiosity.

"He didn't write it, he *said* it."

"Who told you that?"

"Noah did."

"I don't understand."

"Noah told me, when I had dinner at his place."

"*You*? You had dinner with Berg? At *his* place?"

"Yes," Sabine replied in the coolest tone she could muster. "Miriam and I."

20

Miriam's schedule of two weeks for writing, sex, and pampering Noah, followed by two weeks devoted to her catering business, had a great deal of appeal: ostensibly still independent, she felt warmly connected to a man who adored her. Any time Noah's mood darkened—usually whenever a particularly heavy potboiler landed in his in-basket—a daring soufflé restored his humor. He had also prompted Miriam to start a can-you-do-it-backward soufflé chapter for her book: having the reader select a favorite fruit or even mixture of fruits or tastes, and then working its construction backward. In principle, it was the way Julia Child handled her recipes. But Miriam had raised the ante.

She paid only scant attention to the standard soufflés of the chocolate or Grand Marnier variety, other than pointing out that oiled soufflé dishes, cream or butter, or even egg yolk-enriched bases, were now all déclassé in this low-calorie, low-cholesterol nouvelle cuisine age. According to Miriam, only taste and gossamer appearance could not be sacrificed.

First, she taught a simple gimmick: the soufflé duet, a concept opening the way to interesting visual and gustatory combinations. She started out with the classical Harlequin: one-half Grand Marnier, the other chocolate—not letting them run together, but piling the two components gingerly in the baking dish in bicolored fashion like a harlequin's costume. The trick was the careful, last-minute removal of the baking paper separation, used to avoid inadvertent mixing of the two components, just before placement into the oven.

Having gotten the reader hooked on duets, Miriam proceeded to a more sophisticated level: the use of fruit not commonly used in dessert soufflés. Mango or banana, though uncommon, were not rare. But kiwi, mulberry, passion fruit . . . ? The list went on, much of it prompted by the wild soufflé experiments she had conducted as culinary homage to her current lover. (Noah spurred her on, claiming her creations passed the blood-brain barrier faster than crack with unexcelled highs even more addictive than pure cocaine.) Some components had never been used in American cookbooks, because they were difficult to get. Mulberries were not a standard item in Manhattan, let alone in Topeka or Peoria. But kiwis? Or fresh pineapple? According to conventional cookbookery, there were practical reasons why such fresh fruit would not rise when mixed with egg white and baked. And the taste: how could inherent tartness or acidity be mellowed by judicious choices of the right liqueur or even another fruit? Say mango and kiwi in duet form.

Miriam's clever gambit consisted of an ongoing consultation with an organic chemist, who happened to be something of a gourmet. He gave her technical hints—the occasional need for proteolytic enzymes, the import of pH coupled with the apposite choices of buffers—each tip constituting biochemical wizardry with which extraordinary leaps, way beyond the standard soufflé repertoire, could be achieved. During one postprandial analysis, he had explained to Miriam the "retrosynthetic" strategic approach of the organic chemist to synthesizing a complicated molecule: starting out with the desired product, the complete molecule, and then removing one structural feature at a time to arrive at the appropriate "synthon," the chemical building blocks required to assemble the required molecular framework.

Miriam decided to call the chapter "A Retrosynthetic Approach to Sassy Soufflés," sprinkling it with tongue-in-cheekish scientific jargon, including ingredients available only by mail order from biochemical supply houses, whose addresses she provided. Noah, admittedly a biased judge, pronounced the chapter bewitching.

During this phase, Noah's presence was never obstructive; if anything, it was supportive, even catalytic. Gradually, Miriam's two-on, two-off schedule slipped to a three-on, one-off calendar. Given some more time, it seemed to be heading toward an all-on arrangement.

"Miriam," Sabine said one day over coffee in SoHo, "of course, it's none of my business. . . ." She trailed off.

"But?" Miriam prompted.

"I couldn't help but notice during the last few days that the *New York Times* carried a legal—"

"I can't believe it," exclaimed Miriam. "Somebody actually *reads* the legal notices? I wonder whether Noah picked it up. But he couldn't have," she leaned over the small table for reassurance, "he would've said something."

"Why do it now?"

Miriam brushed some nonexistent crumbs off the table. She didn't want to appear defensive. "The only way you can get divorced from a legally undead person—"

"That's a strange word, 'undead.'"

"Well, what would you use?" Miriam sounded testy. "According to latest New York law, legal presumption of death requires no contact for five years. And, as my lawyer put it, 'demonstrating that a diligent search has been made for the missing person.'"

"I didn't mean it that way." The more Sabine thought about it, the more applicable the word seemed to Stephen's present status. She might even borrow it for the biography. Would "undead" be the kind of thing Noah might admire?

"I don't want to wait for the remaining three years," Miriam added. "I want to keep all my options open. And according to my lawyer, the only way to serve a summons and notice of divorce to an 'undead' husband is by publishing it in a newspaper."

"I understand that. But why now?"

Miriam raised her eyes to meet Sabine's. "Just in case."

Stephen Marx, of course, knew nothing about the legal notice, nor about Miriam's progress with *Can You Do It Backward?* If memory could have taste, a faintly bitter flavor may have lingered from Miriam's wacky plans to write a backward cookbook, but that would be all he remembered of it.

Not long ago, he'd settled on a title for his own "work in progress"—the cryptic description he had borrowed from Joyce, who had used "Work in Progress" as a cover for *Finnegans Wake*—whenever Marx had read from his Achilles Luftig episode in a bookstore or similar venue. At that time Achilles Luftig's sex life, indeed the character himself, had only been a distant, isolated star in Stephen Marx's psychic firmament. He'd used it purely as a lure for sex. But in his D. Mann reincarnation Achilles Luftig had become the main character in his next novel, *Doctor Amoroso.* And there lay the rub: writing as D. Mann he found he was still Stephen Marx, the meticulous researcher. He had spent years of research for such a novel—all of it now out of reach, locked away in his personal files back in New York.

He decided to be circumspect. "You seem to be making extraordinary progress," he remarked to Sabine when she told him the title she'd settled on: *The Resurrection of St. Marx.* She didn't volunteer the subtitle: *In My End Is My Beginning,* borrowed from T. S. Eliot's *Four Quartets.* She hadn't even given him a chance to worry about the potential ambiguity of the title.

"I'm talking about the resurrection of a literary life—"

"Surely you mean 'reconstruction,'" he interrupted.

"Never mind," she said quickly. "What I plan to do is to relate your life to each of your books, and to do it backward: I'll start with *Cohen* in the first chapter and end with *Academy.*"

Sabine didn't inform Marx of the original impetus for such a reverse chronological sequence, but she promptly confided it to Miriam, who had become hooked on retrosynthetic chemical analysis, accepting it as scientific validation of her can-you-do-it-backward approach to recipe construction. Miriam had found Sabine's "retrobiographical" angle charming, even provocative. Noah had just stroked his chin pensively. "It could be interesting, provided it doesn't seem forced."

Once again, Stephen wasn't paying much attention. "Don't you think it's time for us to get together—face to face—and recapitulate?" He made it sound as if the thought had just crossed his mind.

"Why not?" Sabine said.

"Would you mind bringing a couple of items I need for my current project?"

She had no problem when he described the "couple of items." On the contrary, it drew her attention to a part of Stephen Marx she had so far put off writing about. "Of course," was all she said. "I'll bring them."

Curiosity about his new address had been the chief reason why Sabine acceded so promptly to Stephen's request for a meeting in San Francisco. But when Stephen insisted on coming to her hotel or other neutral ground—"my new place is totally out of the question"—Sabine concluded that her second reason for coming to San Francisco was even more compelling. If he didn't trust her, why should she tell him everything? She suggested they meet at Salmagundi on Geary. She had eaten lunch there herself on her last visit, and the layout of the place—a self-service establishment, on two levels—struck her as potentially useful. But she didn't tell Marx that. Marx, pleased by the apparent ease with which his need for the *Amoroso* files had been answered, didn't say much more than "fine."

At Salmagundi, the food dispensing and cashier sections are located just inside the entrance, whereas the tables are in the back, spread over two levels within a generously wide space. Sabine appeared purposely early, selecting a ground-level table easily visible from all angles as well as from the mezzanine.

When Stephen arrived, he self-consciously pecked her on the cheek. "Here you are," she said. She shoved the tightly wrapped parcel across the table. She wanted to test him, to see whether he could refrain from ripping open the wrapping to assure himself that the contents were the real stuff.

"Thanks," he said, moving it to the right, and placing his elbow on it before resting his head in his hand. Silently, Sabine conceded him some points for the gesture: the studied diffidence with which he'd pushed the package aside, coupled with the proprietary manner in which part of his body rested on it, as if he dared her to reclaim it. "I'm impressed by your progress," he said. "And I like your approach, doing it backward. It's unusual, and anything unusual is worth considering, provided it doesn't look contrived."

My God, she thought, he sounds like Noah. What else do these two have in common?

"I might even use it in my next novel," he mused. "But you understand, of course, that I couldn't acknowledge the source."

"Help yourself." She dismissed the gift with a wave of her hand. "I borrowed it myself. But tell me about your new novel. Why do you need that stuff?" She nodded at the parcel under his elbow.

"Tsk, tsk, Bienchen!" He wagged a warning finger. "This," he thumped the parcel with his elbow, "is raw material for Mann's next masterpiece. *You* are working on Marx's biography."

Sabine enjoyed such fencing, especially since her opponent had no way of knowing the extent of her armor. "True, but since these goodies were born during Marx's life," she reached over and gently pulled on the string, which she herself had tied not so long ago, "am I not entitled to know something about their significance?"

So she's read it, he concluded—not that I'm surprised. Otherwise, why ask about *significance*, rather than *content*? "A biographer has no *entitlements*. It's all based on *sufferance*."

"That may apply when the subject is still alive," she countered. "Noah Berg advised me never to be tempted into doing the biography of a living person. 'With them, most of the time you end up as a one-eyed journalist. Only dead subjects deserve two-eyed biographers.' Clever, isn't it?"

"Too clever for me. What's a 'one-eyed' journalist? Or for that matter, a 'two-eyed biographer.' What other kind is there?"

Sabine leaned back, a smug expression on her face. Stephen was too taken up by the conversation, by Berg's seeming involvement, to note Sabine's visual sweep up to the mezzanine, to confirm that a photographer's telephoto lens was aimed in their direction.

"I think Noah used 'two-eyed' as a synonym for balanced, reflective, and fair," Sabine opined, after having explained the one-eyed muckraker.

"You certainly covered a lot of ground during that dinner at Berg's—or Noah's, as you so chummily call him. How did you become such good buddies?"

"I've been seeing a fair amount of Noah," she said airily. "You're a marvelous resource, Saint, but you aren't unbiased. I'm consulting as many sources as possible: your agent, publisher, other writers, Noah. . . ."

"You think *he*'s unbiased?"

"Of course not. All of them are biased—in their own ways. But your bias is of another type, and it's my job to uncover the difference."

"With one eye closed or both open?" His tone was facetious, the mien stern.

Sabine's eyes wandered to the mezzanine again, but the photographer was gone. She was curious about his current vantage point, but her search would have to be done in installments so as not to give him away. "It's a good question, because Stephen Marx is a very special case: an undead subject of a biography."

"'Undead'? You're getting clever with words, Bienchen. Or does that also come from Berg?"

"Noah?" She used the pause to let her eyes sweep the right side of their dining room. "Of course not."

"Where do you meet him?"

"Noah?" Berg's name had turned into Sabine's stalling device. A quick glance to the left located the photographer, not more than three tables away. His camera was pointed away from them, in the direction of the entrance.

"I can take close-ups without anyone ever noticing," he'd told her with a wink, when she'd commissioned him. She wasn't looking for a paparazzo, just someone quick and reasonably priced to take some candid shots in a restaurant and on the street. "I have a right angle mirror lens, the sort anthropologists use. You point the camera straight ahead, but you're taking pictures of the object to your right or left. No problem."

She turned back to Stephen. I hope the expression I'm about to produce on his face is caught on film, she thought. "Actually, mostly in your former place. I sit behind your desk and he's usually on your couch."

Marx responded like a piranha exposed to some bleeding flesh. "What the hell was he doing in *my* study?"

"I invited him. But calm down. When I met him the first time—at the dinner I told you about—I learned he'd been toying with the idea of writing a major critical piece on you, a sort of recapitulative literary obituary."

"Those were his words?"

Sabine couldn't repress a grin. "No, Noah doesn't talk like that. I just made it up. But you should be pleased—"

"Pleased? Maybe I should be worried." He sounded neither—only curious. "Any idea what he'll say?"

"He'll say nothing." She said it quickly, not wanting Marx to build some narcissistic castle in the air. "For some reason, he's given up the idea." She waved Berg's change of mind aside as if it were of no importance. "But he offered me advice."

"Advice? What kind?"

"Come on, Saint." His persistence started to irritate her. "You must leave some privacy to your biographer."

"Sure, sure. But you better check anything he says with me. You don't want to be sued for libel."

"'The dead can't be libeled. Furthermore, they can't sue.' That's another piece of advice from Noah. And Stephen Marx is dead, or at the very least undead." Sabine decided to move to a less confrontational subject. "I like that word. I've been wondering how I could use it in my book."

"Be careful. Words are like butterflies. They die when you catch one and try to impale it on a page." He gave her a long stare. "I'll give you a butterfly metaphor you can use, though not in reference to me; maybe to some reviewer. Call him an 'intellectual butterfly,' because it took him an inordinate time to reach some level of maturity, only to then lose it abruptly. Be sure to write, 'it wasn't due to death.'"

Marx withdrew into the silence of a still-active volcano, the flow of lava ready to discharge without alert.

"Saint, you worry too much about your critics. Do you know what Noah's real ambition is with his reviews? At least that's what he told me: to fight the publishing conglomerates, who claim to know the price of everything, but do so at the cost of knowing the value of nothing."

"Good luck," he murmured.

"He truly has been helpful, especially when I told him how I'm trying to relate your novels to your life as a novelist. I'll give you one example, something I'd overlooked until he'd called it to my attention: the virtual absence of any sex scenes in your last couple of novels."

"Berg said that?" Marx sat up, his elbow freeing the parcel.

"Yes. And that it was the sort of thing I shouldn't allow to cocoon in the vaults of your archives."

"Some vaults," he muttered, throwing a disdainful glance at the parcel by his side.

"But he does have a point," insisted Sabine. "In an analysis of a writer's work, one must pay attention to what the subject avoided telling, and to the corollary: what the author is saying without fully appreciating the message."

"We're being awfully presumptuous, aren't we? Still, since you seem to have analyzed all thirteen masterpieces of mine—"

"Fourteen of yours. Thirteen of Marx's."

He raised his hands in a pacifying, almost benedictory, manner. "Correction accepted. Whatever the number, I'd love to hear from you what I said in those novels without realizing it; and perhaps even more interestingly, what I neglected to say."

"Other than sex?"

"That was a deliberate omission. And you can send my compliments to your advisor for noticing it. I'll give you one hint— one only! The title of my next novel is *Doctor Amoroso.* And for your *private* information," he leaned forward, "it is a narrative based on the habits and habitats of persons I knew." He tapped the parcel. "Incidentally, a statement I will deny I made, if you should ever quote me."

"Habits and habitats?" she repeated. "You mean?" Unconsciously, she reached toward the parcel.

Marx snatched it away. "Enough!"

"You're right. Enough."

Sabine pushed back her chair, ready to rise. She'd learned more during the last few minutes than she'd ever expected. Even though she'd barely arrived in San Francisco, she was now itching to return to New York, to unravel any cocoons in Marx's archival vault. She was rather proud of those words, the way they'd just slipped out, and pleased how wordsmithing had started to move beyond avocation to vocation.

"Let's stop for a moment across the street at the Curran Theater."

The remark was addressed to Marx, but she meant it to be heard by the photographer whose table she was just passing. "I want to check what sort of plays you people get to see here in the sticks. Surely you must miss the Manhattan theater scene."

Sabine had chosen the spot for the last photographs with great care. She wanted Stephen next to her, either full face or at least in profile, while she was pointing to the placard listing the dates of the current play at the Curran. She needed at least one unambiguously dated photo.

The next day's meeting site was picked by Marx. Even though Nob Hill was only fifteen minutes' walk from her hotel, mostly up Taylor Street, the last block, one of the steepest in hilly San Francisco, made even Sabine breathe hard. At the top of the rise she found a small park, across from Grace Cathedral, and at that time of the morning primarily populated by Chinese elders practicing t'ai chi. In exchange for what he'd told her yesterday, she felt it appropriate to start with an offering of her own.

"Let me tell you the latest news about my first chapter, 'Cohen's Dilemma: Marx's Conundrum.' How do you like the title?"

Marx was half-reclining on the wooden bench, his face held out to the late November sun, eyes closed. "It has possibilities, depending upon what you're putting in it," he said, eyes still shut.

"I already told you, I'm relating each novel to your life. Not to trivial activities, but to your changing psychological perspectives: the messages delivered, the thoughts unsaid."

"Let's hear some of the unsaid thoughts." Marx had turned partly toward her, his eyes closed. "Aside from sexual ones."

"In a moment. First, a general point: what I've found so intriguing about your novels, right from the initial one—corresponding to *my* penultimate chapter—"

"Penultimate?" Sabine could tell he'd been paying attention to every word. "If you're talking about *The Academy of Spite,* and you're doing it backward, shouldn't that be your last chapter?"

"Not necessarily. I want to keep one for myself, for the biographer's distillation of the Marx essence."

"Marx's essence? I can hardly wait to smell it."

"At the rate I've been going, you may not have to wait all that long. But to return to what I set out to say: in each novel, you immersed yourself into the culture and behavior of a single tribe—shrinks, art dealers, nuns, scientists . . . until your writing almost acquired tribal characteristics. I found that fascinating: your transformation into a psychological chameleon."

"I'll take that as a compliment."

"I meant it as one," she said firmly. "And now, let's go to my first chapter: to *Cohen*'s message, and to Marx's conundrum. You expose us to the overwhelming desire of scientists for name recognition. In the guise of fiction, you smuggle their tribal behavior into the general reader's perception. You do it painlessly, and your message about their egocentric nature is very convincing. So far so good; in fact, brilliant. What you are also saying, but may not have completely realized, is that writers—top writers, the Marxes of this world—also crave such recognition."

"You think I don't realize that?"

"You mean you wrote *Cohen* in order to make *that* point?" She shook her head. "The novel has only scientists—except for one interior decorator."

Marx stroked his beard, a gesture Sabine hadn't noticed before. "You are right. It happened in reverse. I knew all about a writer's obsession with recognition. Only as I dipped into Cohen's persona did I realize that scientists are even worse because their fixation is concentrated only on their peers. Ours, at least, is diluted by inclusion of the public and the press."

"All right!" Sabine was ready to pounce. "So we agree on the content of the message, and on the part the author didn't quite realize he made. And now to the conundrum, at least as I see it. It's money."

"Money?" The question was posed dismissively. "Other than the Nobel Prize, the word is hardly mentioned in that novel."

"What about grantsmanship, which *Cohen* covers in such exquisite detail; which, in the final analysis, deals only with money? You point out that even name recognition among scientists has a great deal to do with getting grants, without which no research can be done. But what you seem to have failed to develop is the difference in economic motivation between your Professor Cohen and, for instance, Saint Marx." Sabine's tone had become fast and urgent. She wanted to demonstrate how many layers she had peeled from his fiction. "What scientists get through grants, which, according to your novel, are distributed by a very sophisticated audience—essentially their peers—you, the author, can only hope to get through wide, popular sales. So the Marxes and Manns of the world have to choose between economic viability and artistic integrity. The first can debase your art, whereas retaining your integrity may cost you a bundle."

"And you found that out all by yourself?"

If he was going to be indirect, so could Sabine. "That's why I need a last chapter all for myself. To describe how you are solving that problem."

"*Are* solving? Don't you mean *have* solved? How Marx solved it?"

"Are Marx's and Mann's solutions different?"

Marx shook his head; not in denial, but in irritation. "Why can't you stick to one subject: the biography of Stephen Marx? For you to do a proper job, Mann does not exist. Cannot exist."

"'Proper job'? Who is to say what's proper?"

Sabine stayed in San Francisco for three days. Much of it was spent on minutiae which they could have discussed on the telephone. Everything important, at least as far as Sabine was concerned, had been accomplished on their first day together, all but uncovering Marx's new address. He had become very cagey. He'd transferred his mailbox to the Main Post Office so that the zip code would not offer a clue to his residential neighborhood. He intimated having discontinued his waiter's career without indicating whether *Middles* or some royalty advance was now supporting him until his next novel was complete. Keeping mum had become the guiding principle for Stephen Marx, and Sabine saw no purpose in pushing her luck. On their last morning together, Sabine left a tacit warning about her view of her job.

"Noah suggested I look at other literary figures: how they responded to critics while alive; how some tried to cope with their biographers even from beyond the grave. The moment he suggested that, I thought of you, because you fall into both categories. *Avis rarissima*, wouldn't you say?"

"Very funny. And Latin too!"

"Actually, 'rare bird' is one of the few Latin phrases I ever learned. That and *abeunt studia in mores*." In fact, she'd picked it up only recently, while looking through a phrase book for a bon mot.

"Bienchen, you're overdoing it." Stephen was in an exceptionally good mood.

"You mean you know what it means?" She sounded disappointed.

"You tell me."

"'Practices zealously pursued pass into habits.'"

"Does that apply to me? My practices? Or is it the habits you're curious about?"

"Both, I think."

Marx grinned evilly. "And you want me to list some of them?"

Sabine gave a mock shudder. "Hardly. No, I need to find those myself. But when I do, I'll ask you for explanations."

"You may just get justifications instead."

"I'll take either. But let me tell you about the problem I foresee. The usual source for all biographers is archival material. And that's where I've become intrigued by what I've read about other famous writers. Take Thomas Hardy. He called biographers 'post-mortem exploiters,' and decided to preempt them by writing an expurgated pre-mortem biography himself. He left it to his second wife, much younger than he, with instructions to publish it under her own name after his death. In the process, he destroyed a lot of relevant documents and papers."

"Sounds positively inspiring. Go on."

"This is the part I thought might interest you, Saint," Sabine said. She paused a moment. "He made one mistake. His scenario depended on the reliability of his wife, Florence. But Florence was the second Mrs. Hardy, and she had agenda of her own. She doctored his version by removing any favorable mention of his first wife, Emma. Who knows what else she changed along the way? And did you know he was very sensitive about reviews of his novels, calling them 'biography in diguise'?"

Marx's amused expression had started to dissipate. "I have a feeling you're trying to tell me something."

"Am I? I thought I was building up to a question. How much of your personal archive—important material, not trivia—have you destroyed?"

He shrugged. "Everyone gets rid of something. I'm no exception. In fact, I wish I had done more. But enough of that." He started to get up from the bench. He had taken several steps before he stopped, and, a little dramatically, Sabine thought, turned.

"Here is a message for *you*. And your guru Berg. 'What every author hopes from posterity—a hope usually disappointed—is justice.' W. H. Auden said that. I happen to agree with him. But there is one difference between me and Auden: I plan to be around to see how posterity treats me."

21

Miriam had finally taken the step she had long postponed: she had asked the bank to open Stephen's safe deposit box. The divorce required an accounting of all their assets. To her surprise, it contained only floppy disks.

"Let me know what's in them, when you have a chance," she said, handing the lot over to Sabine. Miriam preferred to fill her own floppies rather than to rummage through Stephen's.

It had taken Sabine some weeks since that discovery to separate what was new—and valuable—from material she'd already picked up in the files at her disposal. Overall, she was pleased with the first small treasure chest she'd uncovered. She wasn't certain yet how much light it would shed on Marx, the person, but the contents seemed to contain some semiprecious jewels.

Considering the number of questions the find had raised in her mind, she was prepared for the length of her next phone conversation with Stephen, but not for the contentiousness with which it started.

"How did you find that out?" he challenged her. "Does that mean you're rummaging through *all* my files?"

"Stop whining, Saint. I'm a biographer, Stephen Marx's biographer. Files, letters, pictures, floppies are all fair game." She hoped light irony would dampen his irritation, not realizing the word "floppies" had acted like a blast of bellows on a flickering flame.

Floppies? Is she talking about backups I left around my study? Or the ones in the safe? Did Miriam have it opened as my widow?

"What would *you* use to commit suicide?" Sabine had been itching to ask that question ever since their last phone conversation.

"What are you talking about?" he asked, startled.

"You tell me, Saint. That's what it says here."

"Here?"

"On your screen."

"Jesus Christ!"

"Come on, Saint. Don't be childish. Tell me about this suicide business: it's not exactly a trivial question you posed. Or did someone else write it?" Noah Berg's occasional questions about evidence of "plagiaristic grazing" had made her sensitive to the issue of the origins of authors' notes. According to Noah, Rudyard Kipling's widow had destroyed his "notion book," containing her late husband's sketches and ideas. She had done it to protect him from biographical inquisitiveness, "higher cannibalism" Kipling had called it, and the damage had been irrevocable. As soon as Sabine had learned that, she'd started to look for evidences of Marx's notion books.

"Of course not," he sounded gruff, but normal. "It's a first sentence for one of my novels."

"What novel? I thought I'd read them all."

"I haven't written it yet," he replied. "That's how I get ideas: making up good beginning sentences."

"And 'May I ask Dr. Wisterman why he used goats'?"

"The same," he chuckled. "I thought it was a damn good first sentence—a teaser. I bet some people will think of sodomy after reading it."

"Very funny," Sabine said primly. "What was it supposed to mean?"

"It's too complicated to explain, and really beside the point. I told you, these are first sentences for as yet unwritten novels."

"Still, give me a hint." The presumed jewels in her treasure box had acquired a dull tarnish. She needed some polish to make them sparkle.

"OK. It dealt with animals for medical research."

"Goats? Who uses goats in medical research?"

"Bienchen, stop being a pest. I'm a novelist. I can damn well do as I please. *My* scientists use goats."

"And 'Hasta la Wiedersehen, Baby?'"

Perhaps it was the zany hodgepodge, but for a moment Sabine had him stumped. Then he remembered. "I saw it in some cartoon in the *Washington Post*."

"Does the *Post* carry cartoons?"

This is getting preposterous, Marx thought. She's like a snapping bulldog, her teeth biting at every object presented to her. I'll throw her one more morsel, he concluded, but then she's got to stop asking questions and answer my own.

"It's for another story—maybe a novella. It already has a title: 'The Dubber.'"

"Daba? What's that?"

"*DUBBER*. Get it? I thought of an actor who dubs movie dialogues from English into German—"

"Why German?"

"Can you listen to a sentence of more than half a dozen words without interrupting?"

"Sorry. Go on."

"First of all, it's German because that's the only foreign language I speak well. My dubber specializes in macho roles— Clint Eastwood, Jack Nicholson, maybe even Humphrey Bogart. 'Hasta la Wiedersehen, Baby' is supposed to sound funny, but my story is serious, probably even tragic. The second reason is that of all European countries Germany is virtually the only one that uses no subtitles for foreign films; all of them are dubbed. So dubbing is a real profession over there."

"Is that all?" Sabine's disappointment didn't escape him.

"My dubber is a dubber's dubber; he even writes the text. He finds the right idiosyncratic expressions; he manages to compress them within the all-too-brief span of the original English sentence; and, most important, he does that in sync with the American actor's mouth. All that, Bienchen, is not easy, considering how inherently more time-consuming German is compared to English. But *my* dubber," Marx's voice acquired an edge of intimacy, "over the years, has immersed himself so deeply into the macho personality of one particular American actor, he not only became his verbal doppelgänger, he even subsumed his private life to the American's film image."

Sabine remained silent as Marx's voice rose and fell during his elaboration of the dubber's private life. Just as he reached the climax, the first *mano a mano* encounter between the American actor and his German voice, Marx stopped. He realized that he hadn't yet worked out the culmination of his dubber's life.

Sabine felt that a veil, perhaps one of several, had just been lifted. Was Stephen a literary dubber? Dubbing from real life into fiction? As Marx unwound a tale he had never written, Sabine found herself unable to shake a strange sensation. She had no idea what it was, but it made the hairs on the back of her neck stir uncomfortably.

"It's an interesting metaphor," Noah said approvingly. As she started to write sections of her manuscript, Sabine had felt the need for an editorial and critical foil. Noah fitted that role superbly; without specifically being asked to act, he gradually assumed that task, with the consequence that Sabine had to be careful not to give away the existence of her conversations with Marx. In this instance, it was easy: "I just thought of an interesting simile for an author: a dubber of life into fiction."

Noah had continued with a warning. "It's probably only true of some authors, because dubbing, by definition, doesn't allow much departure from the original. I suspect such dubbing often turns into a high-wire act above the abyss of exploitation."

"Exploitation?"

"Yes." Berg's tone was stern. "Of human relationships. You better do some more research on Marx the Dubber."

"I'll remember that," she said, nodding slowly to herself.

But Berg wasn't finished. "There is another aspect of dubbing in fiction writing: the dubbing of words, but within the same language. Incidentally, Sylvester Stallone is reported to have used a dubber in English for some of his films. For all I know, there may be other famous film stars whose real voice we've never heard. But I'm now thinking of the musical meaning of the word: mixing recorded sounds from different sources into a single record. In the context of your literary dubber, it can become an important skill whereby incipient plagiarism is converted into originality."

"Saint," she started in the most innocuous tone she could muster, "did you know Sylvester Stallone sometimes uses a dubber?"

Marx had other things on his mind; the question seemed to him the height of triviality.

"Of course. Why shouldn't he? I doubt he speaks fluent German. Let's turn to something more important: the floppies—"

"No," she said quickly. "I'm talking about dubbing from English into English."

"You mean Rambo's voice is someone else's? Now where did you find that out?"

"I have my sources. When you started with the *Washington Post* and then kept spouting about dubbing, I wanted to check it out. The *Post* really did carry a cartoon with the legend 'Hasta la Wiedersehen, Baby' by one Richard Thompson."

"You mean you went to such extremes just to confirm I told the truth?" Marx's astonishment came through undiluted.

"I check everything. It's my *S.I.* training. It turns out Stallone's dubber is tall, handsome, curly blond—sort of the cerebral type. Just think of the possibilities for your novel! Your actor has only the muscles, but someone else has his voice. I don't even know whether the muscle has ever met the voice. How about giving the muscle man a hopeless lisp—"

"Bienchen. Are we exchanging roles? Are you now feeding me plots?"

"Look what I've found." Sabine inserted the disk into Marx's computer. She had invited Miriam and Noah over to Marx's studio for dinner, but the meal, although successful, had only been the pretext for this. With Miriam and Noah crouching over her, she slowly scrolled the text on the screen.

"I told you," exclaimed Miriam. "Stephen always jotted down ideas for his fiction. He said it was something he got from Henry James, who kept notebooks for decades—"

"These," muttered Noah, "can't be compared to Henry James. By the way, Miriam," he straightened up to face her, "didn't you say your husband used small notebooks? Why is this stuff on floppies? And where are the notebooks?"

"Maybe he transcribed them," offered Sabine.

"And why can't they be compared to the notebooks of Henry James?" Miriam found herself bristling.

"Henry James jotted down names of characters and of locations, literally dozens and dozens of them; plot ideas; more conventional journal entries. . . ." Noah paused for effect. "But essentially no quotations of other people. That's all you have here."

He started reading.

"He is so selfpropagated, he can afford no debts or attributions (Penelope Lively).

"Truth is different when told with sympathy (A. B. Yehoshua).

"The art of the quoter is to know when to stop (Robertson Davies).

"Unpublished writing is like masturbation or coitus interruptus, something shameful and unsatisfying (David Lodge).

"What a mixture," said Noah. "There doesn't seem to be any system or order to them."

"He probably never intended one," noted Sabine. "The file name on the disk was simply 'goodies.'"

"Like *Kinoielpyew*?" He spelled it. "Another one by Lodge. But what does it mean?"

Sabine grinned. "I think it's phonetic for a Cockney 'Can I help you.'" She reached over and tapped a couple of keys. "I'm prepared to use this one myself; it's credited to Freud: 'He whose lips are silent, chatters with his fingertips; betrayal oozes through every pore.'"

Noah turned from the computer. "Remember what I said about literary dubbing, using borrowed words or phrases to reform them into something supposedly brand new? In my opinion, that's what you have here," he motioned with his head to the computer screen behind him. "That's why I claim this is no Henry James journal. No offense meant," he said to Miriam. "Of course, I may be wrong. And we'll never find out."

Miriam gave a nervous laugh. "I might as well confess something. Now that I'm a writer myself, I've started to keep my own notebook—to keep track of what fiction writers have to say about food." She fumbled in her handbag. "My latest discovery about polenta from a story by Adam Mars-Jones: 'You have to stir and stir until your elbows ache with it, but in the end it sets into a delicious bland golden brick of friable starch.' I'm going to find some place to use it."

"Is there anything you don't consult him on?" Marx asked, almost plaintively. "Is he going to be a coauthor?" His sarcastic edge was sharper than usual.

"Don't be nasty, Saint. I have a reason for bringing this up. One of your floppy disks contained pages after pages of quotes from various writers. Some had changes in parentheses. All of them cited the sources. Why lock that up in a safe?"

Marx didn't answer, because now he knew she'd read them all. Miriam must have arranged for the safe deposit box to be opened. The weight descending on him wasn't literary quicksilver, but the much more trying one of a gnawing memory. Before his demise in New York he'd scanned his study for personally incriminating letters. He didn't think there were any—at least not on paper. What about the only letter he'd ever written to Noah Berg? He knew he'd kept no copy. But when he erased the text on the hard disk, had something in the back of his mind persuaded him to copy it first on a floppy?

Yes, I did learn of Monica's relationship with you, but only after the fact. When my friend bumped into you at the Updike reading at the Y, should I have come up to you to reveal when, precisely, she told me about you? I doubt it.

Am I sorry that I broke up your "engagement" or whatever it was you two had going between yourselves? Of course I am.

Do I feel guilty? Not really. Does my wife know of this affair? "Affair" is the wrong word, but I'll let it pass. I don't know—I don't think so unless you told her.

What do I plan to do? Nothing. I cannot undo what has happened. Why don't you call her? It was she who left you. Besides, Monica and I do not see each other any more.

"Have you gone through all the floppies?" His voice was low and flat.

"Yes."

"The hard disk?"

Sabine hesitated. "Most of it."

What she really meant was that she'd understood most of it, but not all. For instance, that intriguing letter about Monica: to whom had it been addressed?

"And the handwritten notes you gave me at Salmagundi?"

"Yes."

"Did you copy them?"

"Why should that be important?"

"You don't believe in privacy, do you?" His voice had risen, ominously so.

"Of course, I do," she said quickly. "I believe in the privacy of an individual."

"But?"

"But nothing."

"And you don't consider what you've done a monumental invasion into my privacy?"

"'The dead have no privacy.' Noah said that when I asked about his opinion on the permissible limits of a biographer's inquiry."

"Fuck Noah!"

22

Marx felt his control slipping. Henceforth, he decided, he would only respond to written questions. He would still answer them, of course, on the telephone. Written replies were out of the question—but he would no longer allow Sabine to pose questions over the phone. Their conversations seemed to be going all her way. Marx felt himself losing not only control, but somehow also his identity. He was becoming the subject of someone else's writing.

Sabine didn't mind; for some time, she, too, had been feeling oppressed by their conversations. For her, too, the nature of the oppression she felt was difficult to characterize. All she knew was, the less contact she had with Marx, the freer she felt.

She still recognized her need for an in-house critic, but at this stage, she preferred Noah's pedagogic touches, which felt like caresses compared to the bruises associated with Marx's combative style. But she did have a problem—her ever increasing qualms about having shielded Miriam from the truth about her very much undead husband. Initially, Sabine had rationalized her behavior as protecting Miriam's desire for a new life with all options open. But the longer she kept her secret from Miriam, the more devious and exploitative she feared she would appear—especially when her conduct was viewed in the light of Miriam's generosity toward her. Now that Miriam's divorce was final, Sabine's best excuse for procrastination had been removed. Her options rapidly narrowed to keeping the secret forever. Sabine's problem would then be at worst a load on her conscience.

But increasingly, as chapter after chapter of *The Resurrection of St. Marx* took form, she knew that such an option was not truly open to her. What if the first chapter of her manuscript were not the one she had completed several months ago, the one entitled "*Cohen's Dilemma:* Marx's Conundrum"? What if it were preceded by a *very* first chapter, numbered zero, that would be the exact counterpoint to the *very* last one, the idea of which she had already intimated to Marx—the one describing his essence? If she did that the literary biography might well metamorphose into a journalistic coup. Initially, she rejected the idea. In addition to the guilt associated with having to face Miriam with such a disclosure, she now had the additional complication of Noah Berg. How would her advisor, consultant, and critic feel when he learned she had never opened up to him? Still, she enjoyed playing with the notion of public disclosure the way one gets pleasure with scandalous sexual fantasies. Fantasies, sexual or otherwise, are harmless until the fantasizer begins to rationalize. With Sabine, the first rationalization commenced with names—women's names. Forty-seven of them.

It looked innocent enough, at first. Farida Latif, Kalman Tory, James Gnarra, Masahiro Yao, Fuh-Mei Duh, Lou Orcutt, Thomas Stackhouse, Igor Kuzmin, Laura Geil, Peter Choyke, Damjan Glavac, Berton Zbar, Craig Chinault, Yongkai Weng, McClellan Walther, Gladys Glenn. . . .

She couldn't resist writing Marx a note about this extraordinary ethnic and phonetic hodgepodge. On the face of it, his answer sounded preposterous. During his work on *Cohen's Dilemma*, one of his scientific contacts had shown him a single article from the scientific journal *SCIENCE*, in order to demonstrate the ethnic diversity of American research groups and the proliferation of multi-authored papers.

"But you didn't use it in that novel," she had protested.

"It would have been overkill. I just thought they might come in handy some day."

He hadn't lied. Some of the names were so unusual, it took Sabine only a few minutes in the library to find the article. She dropped that lead, not even considering it worth mention to Berg.

When she found the next list Sabine almost passed it over, until she realized it consisted only of women's names. Sabine stared at it for a moment, then tapped the "Print Screen" button. She studied the printed copy another minute. Women's names. Another ethnic stew, to be sure, but Sabine was reasonably certain a group such as this had never appeared in the pages of *SCIENCE*.

What to do? This time, there was no consulting with Marx. Why? she asked herself. No answer presented itself, only a reluctance she knew to respect.

Miriam? She looked at the list again, and a small, weary shudder coursed up her spine. Guilt. She had kept so much from Miriam.

It would have to be Noah. Placing the sheet of paper carefully in the lower desk drawer, she turned off the computer and reached for the phone.

"How many did you encounter?" It was the sort of idle question people ask to drive a conversation onward.

Sabine shrugged. "Several dozen, I guess. Maybe more."

"And what sort of names were they?"

"Let me think. Margaret, Susan, Agnes, Mary—"

"Pretty pedestrian," remarked Noah. "You'll never find that in any notebook of Henry James."

Sabine found that she, too, was capable of defending Marx's literary standing. "There was a Berit, I think. And a Kyle, Maya. . . ." Suddenly she brightened. "And a Miriam. And Thomasina: isn't that Miriam's—"

"We know where these two came from," interrupted Noah. "But what about the others. Could they be the female characters in the Marx novels?"

Sabine straightened in her seat. "Not really," she mused. "Celestine, Charlea, Jocelyn, Olivia, Hilary. . . . No overlap that I can see."

A few days later, Noah paid her an advisory call. He found Sabine still laboring over the list. It was evident from the state of the other papers in the studio that not much writing had been going on.

"The list consists of forty-seven names and really falls into three categories. The conventional ones, Dorothy, Margaret, Susan. . . ." Sabine dismissed them impatiently. "The second group," she glanced at the sheet in her hand, "is a bit less common: Andrea, Jan, Arlene, Janice, Monica. . . ." Sabine would have noticed the sudden start in Noah, had she not been reading from her list. "But there are unusual ones and not just 'Thomasina.' Felicity, Ute, Tegen, Meredith. . . ."

During her recital, Noah had risen; he walked over to the bookshelf containing the many editions of Marx's novels. As he spoke, he slowly ran his finger along their spines. "I would advise you not to discuss this matter with Miriam," he said in an even voice. "It's a matter of tact; and it would be tactless in the extreme. . . ."

He stopped, as if another thought had crossed the first one. "I can think of two explanations for these names." He turned, his finger still touching the book spines, to face Sabine. "One that I wish were true, but am reasonably certain does not fit the circumstances. And one I would find deeply offensive, but suspect is correct."

"So what's alternative A?"

Noah stepped away from the bookcase and moved around the desk to perch on it before answering. "Collecting names, like Henry James. Writer's business."

"And why does that not appear to fit the circumstances?"

"There are too many common names."

"And alternative B?"

For a long moment, Noah just stared at her from his seat on Marx's desk. "A list of mistresses, conquests, trysts, one-night stands. . . ." He spoke slowly, in a monotonous voice, his gaze now fixed on the floor.

Sabine nodded. "You're right. It's B."

He looked up. "You sound very sure."

"Why else would there be repetitions? Two Margarets; two Andreas; three Marys; a Sue and a Susan. Of course, they aren't listed next to each other. So you might say he had forgotten that one or the other name had already been entered. But three times? And with a name like Mary?"

Noah was nodding to himself, his eyes back on the carpet. But Sabine was not finished. She was ready to drive the final nail into the coffin of her conviction.

"There is something else. Each name also has an initial: Andrea C.; Mary U.; Monica S."

This time, Sabine caught the naked shock in Noah's expression.

Sabine usually fell asleep easily, but this night proved hopeless. The guilt she had been fending off for months seemed to have rebounded upon her redoubled. She had not pursued the Monica question with Berg. What would have been the point? She had understood, suddenly, the letter she had found, and knew in a painful instant to whom it had been addressed. And in the same moment, the complexity of her situation became clear to her—worse, the knowledge that she had been in the center of this mess for months, intent on her own schemes, oblivious to the possibility that she might be caught up in something much larger—and much worse. What, if anything, did the Berg-Monica-Marx triangle have to do with the pairing of Noah and Miriam? Sabine got up, put on a warm robe, made herself a cup of herb tea, and dug out the photocopies of the files she had delivered months ago to Marx in San Francisco.

The letter she composed, over seven pages long and single spaced, she never mailed. Instead, she sent Marx a brief note to the effect that she had only one more question before wrapping up her manuscript. She was confident he would call at the appointed hour.

"You wrote you wanted to check out some material dealing with a cemetery scene," he said warily.

"It was in the package I brought you."

"So what's the question? You've already admitted months ago that you'd read it all."

"True. But at that time, I thought I was reading scenes for a novel. The great sex novel of Stephen Marx, but written in the name of Mann, because Marx hasn't had much sex . . . in his recent novels. Some of the scenes were even original: the mango fork, for instance, in that beach scene where you rubbed a juicy mango over the woman's ass after twisting the bottom sides of her one-piece bathing suit into just a thin rope, thinner than a Copacabana bikini, you said—"

"That's quite a memory you have." His voice was soaked in sarcasm. "Or did it make such an indelible impression on you?"

Sabine was in no mood to let such cracks pass by unchallenged. "'The resulting tether practically hidden in the cleft between her buttocks.' Don't flatter yourself that your purple prose is etched in my memory. I'm reading from the page in front of me." There was a pause on the line, during which Marx thought he could hear paper shuffling. But all Sabine said was, "I had never heard of mango forks. I had to go to Tiffany's to track one down."

"You would."

"And I will concede the appropriateness of the phallic imagery conferred by that extraordinary central tine of the fork, considering how it's apparently used to penetrate the mango's kernel. I'll even grant you that the cemetery scene was . . . original."

"Get to the point. I'm sure you didn't ask me to call you to pay me some compliments."

"All right. To the point: these scenes aren't made up. They're from real life, aren't they?"

"Fiction is often autobiographical, even though it doesn't contain much biography."

"You asked me to get to the point. I'm now asking you to do the same. Aren't these scenes with the women from real life— *their* lives?"

"What if they are?"

"I recall a discussion between us about privacy."

"Ha! You're a good one to talk about that subject."

"I'm now talking about intruding into the privacy of living people, not supposedly dead novelists."

"Are you suggesting I'm giving away their names and addresses? Or hip and bosom measurements?"

Sabine clenched her fist. She was not going to let him make her lose her temper. "What about Felicity Samarand in the cemetery?"

"What on earth do you know about her?"

"There is a list of forty-seven women, all first names, with last initials. The only one without belongs to a woman called Miriam. Included in the list is Felicity S., whereas your cemetery scene stars one Joy Samarand. Now guess, how many Samarands there are in the Manhattan phone book."

It serves me right, Marx cursed himself, to think of revenging myself in such a sophomoric fashion.

"I take it your silence means concurrence. Now one last question: who is Dr. Amoroso?"

"A sixty-four-year-old character by the name of Achilles Luftig."

"I don't mean in your manuscript. I saw a few pages featuring your Achilles. I mean in real life; and what drives him?"

Marx hung up. It was their last conversation.

Sabine took a long, hot shower as if she wanted to cleanse herself of some persistent dirt. She had finished tying a towel around her wet hair in a turban; still naked, she stepped in front of the full-length mirror to examine herself. Such inspections are everyday occurrences in thousands of Manhattan bath- or bedrooms, but for Sabine, this one was different. Slowly turning, first to the left and then to the right, so she could see her full breasts and firm, jogger's thighs and calves in profile, she pretended to be a man. How fuckable am I, she asked herself. Why had Stephen Marx never made a pass? Had it been tact or caution or . . . ? He wasn't exactly her type, but was the converse also true?

Sabine had no complexes about being sexually unattractive; she could tell from the way men looked at her. Overt approaches were fewer than her physical appearance might have merited, but that, she knew, was the result of signals she conveyed, of barriers she erected. And when it came to final consummations, she explained their paucity with the truism that most men in New York were insensitive jerks.

Standing turbaned and naked in front of the mirror, Sabine thought of Felicity Samarand, also known as Joy. Except for her unusual height, Sabine had no visual picture of her. In his notes for *Doctor Amoroso*, Stephen hadn't given any physical description. Was it to protect some portion of her anonymity which he seemingly was so ready to violate through blatant disclosure of her last name? Felicity was probably Sabine's age. How was she prepared to take the sexual initiative? In principle, a woman of Sabine's generation knows she has the right—and perhaps even the political obligation—to initiate sexual encounters with men. But she also knows, as women have known always, as her mother surely told her, and perhaps as her own limited experience has demonstrated, that most men in her world are not ready for that sort of come-on. The risks of rejection are very high indeed. Certainly, both women and men lay a lot on the line in terms of their self-image, both physical and mental, when they proposition someone. Nobody likes to be turned down, but Sabine knew, as again so many women know, that men are conditioned to take such risk, accustomed to envisioning and experiencing success. Women, other than hookers or call girls, rarely have successful direct propositions in their sexual portfolios, and each attempt is likely to be threatening. Sabine was certain that most women of her age would be too cripplingly self-conscious to proposition a man with whom they'd never been sexually involved.

During the past four years, Sabine had been tempted; not once, but twice. But in the end, she had resorted to behavior in which women are so adept: conveying the message that they wish to *be* propositioned, thereby preserving what they have been taught to protect at all costs, the male ego. So how did Felicity Samarand manage to carry it off? Was her desire that strong? Did she feel she had to maintain an ego of her own? Or was the scene in which she led him to the cemetery a fantasy? And the other forty-seven women? What aspects of their sexuality would eventually be dubbed within the covers of *Doctor Amoroso*?

Standing naked in front of the mirror, Sabine realized that there was a part of Stephen Marx she, his biographer, had never seen and never would.

23

Sabine had reached the stage in a writer's labors where not only the light at the end of the tunnel, but even the landscape beyond it are visible. With the self-assured naiveté of a first-time author, at the start of her project she hadn't even looked for an agent, but, with half-finished manuscript in hand, had marched straight into the offices of Marx's former publisher to end up, after a few weeks, with a contract. The publisher correctly assumed that given the paltry advance accepted by Sabine, there was little to lose and much to gain: a biography of Marx, so soon after his death, could not help but stimulate sales of his novels. Months had passed since that initial visit, with the Marx biography now virtually finished. No firm publishing date had as yet been selected, but Sabine changed all that with one further appearance.

On March 15, Sabine walked into her editor's office with a new chapter in hand. Only ten pages in length, its page numbers ran backward. The chapter itself was numbered 0. Within minutes, she had convinced the editor to read it in Sabine's presence; less than an hour later the two women were closeted with the editor's boss. Sabine was lucky. The publisher's catalog was still at the printer. A quarter-page announcement could still be inserted by cannibalizing a few lines here and there from other, more extensive promotional descriptions of other books.

In the light of the new chapter's content, the publisher accepted without objection—in fact with fervent nods—Sabine's request that it be published under a pseudonym. "Sabine Diehlsdorf" was a complicated name, and to the trade and public of no promotional value. "A. S. Boswell" was not only easily spelled, it was familiar; the publicists would love it.

On the face of it, the projected low-key entry into the Autumn catalog looked like a sure pass to rapid oblivion via the remainder bins: no blurbs, no biographical sketch of the author, no promised book tours or promotion, no indication of advance shipment of bound galleys to book reviewers. To top it all, the biography had not even been introduced at the annual sales conference, because that had been held months ago. And if the sales people hadn't been revved up, how would bookstores be convinced to order such a low-key item? The full title of the biography in big letters, accompanied by a photograph of Stephen Marx, was about all a skimmer's eyes would notice in the catalog. The print size projected for the author's name and the few descriptive lines seemed almost microscopic.

All this was done with the connivance, indeed at the insistence, of the chief publisher himself, who hadn't reached honcho status by orchestrating deliberate infanticide with new books. With Boswell's *The Resurrection of St. Marx*, he plotted a PR campaign as novel as Sabine's reverse page numbering of her new chapter. In his opinion, it was only necessary to have a critical mass of the right people read page 0 of chapter 0 at the same time.

Under ordinary circumstances, Sabine should have been ecstatic about the speed with which her book was now rushing toward the outside world. Yet she hardly noticed, because that very speed made further procrastination on the one point that most concerned her impossible. She dreaded the idea of having to face Miriam and Noah.

"Noah, I must ask you for a favor," she announced in a tone so funereal that even the telephone could not hide her mood.

"You sound terribly depressed. What's the matter?"

"I need to see the two of you . . . together."

"Of course."

"This evening?"

"Impossible. If you want to see Miriam and me together, you need to be prepared for two complicated calendars—especially Miriam's. I'll have to check with her first."

"Noah, it's urgent."

"I'll call you back."

They compromised on a breakfast date the following day at the Marx residence. Sabine had printed two copies of the new chapter to expedite reading.

"Please read this. I'll be back in half an hour to explain."

Sabine gave them forty-five minutes. Pressing the bell, she felt even more apprehensive than she had at her first appearance before Mann's door in San Francisco. She was prepared for an explosion, for tears, for cold fury, for "bitch," "viper," "rat," "swine," or perhaps, from Noah, a "scoundrel." Instead, the open door framed Miriam wagging a finger in a gesture which at worst might be described as admonishment.

"What a fox! But have you had breakfast?"

For a moment, Sabine wondered if Miriam had actually read the chapter, but a look at Noah Berg, surrounded by her pages on the breakfast table, convinced her that the explanation lay elsewhere. He seemed less effusive, his look equivocal.

"I can't wait to hear the rest of the story, because there must be more to it. You know what I told Noah when I read this?" Miriam pointed to the scattered sheets. "He and I would never have met if you had disclosed this story right at the beginning. But why did you wait until now? You could have told me a few months ago—certainly after the divorce."

Sabine had nearly recovered her equanimity. She was ready to answer the last question, but Noah gave her no chance.

"I suspected it," he said quietly.

Sabine was aghast. "All along?"

He shook his head. "Only recently, but in retrospect, I should have caught on earlier. You really did know too much about Stephen Marx."

"It had to be more than that," she murmured. "I had access to a lot of material."

Noah nodded. "Earlier this year one of the national magazines had a competition for best short story. I was a member of the jury. One of the final ten stories, 'The Stallion's Voice,' should have won hands down, but in the end, the editor turned it down. He was wary of potential legal complications."

"What has that got to do with Sabine's chapter?" exclaimed Miriam. "I want to hear her story—"

"I'm almost finished," he cut her off. "'The Stallion's Voice' dealt with a famous, muscle-bound movie star with a hopelessly high-pitched voice. He always had to use a dubber, whom he refused to meet. By paying an anonymous voice, the star felt he owned it. One day he met his voice—"

"You mean the author was Mann?"

"I suppose it could have been a wild coincidence. I wanted to ignore it. I didn't want to delve into other secrets lurking behind Mann. I'm not even sure I want to know now."

Sabine knew what he meant, but Miriam didn't. "Darling, I am now divorced and we're together. But I'm still curious what happened to my former husband. And relieved that he isn't dead. Where does he live now? You didn't say so here." She lifted one of the pages.

"You mean you want to meet him?"

"Don't be silly, Noah."

Sabine explained that she had no intention of disclosing his whereabouts—not to them or anybody else.

"It took a long time for me to convince myself that as Stephen Marx's biographer I have to divulge how he decided to . . ." she searched for a diplomatic word, "end his existence as Marx. But D. Mann is living and I see no reason why I should interfere with his privacy."

Noah shook his head dubiously. "The day your book hits the bookstores, reporters will be chasing after him."

"I'll cross that bridge when we get to it, which is still a few months away. They won't send out any bound galleys—"

"I can't believe that." Noah, the professional reviewer, looked astonished. "How will they get the book reviewed in time for the publication date?"

"They won't." Sabine was eager to explain how an action, spelling evident disaster to a reviewer, would be turned to her book's advantage. "This chapter is being printed separately, somewhere overseas. It will be bound with the rest of the chapters at the very last minute. No one will suspect its existence."

"Is that why you call it 'Chapter 0'?" asked Miriam.

"Partly. But I also like the idea of an ur-chapter." She grinned sheepishly. "I stole your 'do it backward' idea."

"Is that why you numbered—"

"Precisely!" Sabine was relieved to see the conversation assume such a different character—addressing the future rather than past. "In printed form, this chapter will be exactly ten pages long. By numbering the first page as -9, the next as -8, and so on, it will be a like a countdown. At the count of zero, on the last page of this chapter, the Marx biography takes off."

"Gimmicky, but clever."

Sabine grinned at Noah. "There's more to it. Chapter 0 with the negative pages will also be bound separately. On the day before the official publication date, this chapter will be sent to wire services, newspapers, magazines, and the like. The publisher expects most news articles to appear the following day, at which time they will send copies of the complete, bound book by Federal Express to all major book reviewers. That ought to give them plenty of incentive to read quickly and to *publish* their reviews."

"Clever. You realize, of course, that I could beat the entire competition. I'm the only one, other than your publisher, who has now read the *entire* book starting with page -9."

"You wouldn't, Noah. Would you?" For a moment, Sabine looked shocked.

He laughed. "I can't review it at all. It wouldn't be ethical, although it would be the ultimate backward approach: assuring yourself of an outstanding review by using the critic as your private editor," he made a mock bow. "No," he said, "the secret will stay here."

"In that case, I'll let you in on another."

"But why?" exclaimed Noah, after hearing that Sabine intended to publish as A. S. Boswell. "I *know* you've got a good book. And with *that* preamble," he tapped the pages by his side, "your Marx biography is bound to become a best-seller. Your reputation, Sabine Diehlsdorf's, will be made as a biographer. Agents and publishers will come flocking to you, asking you to write another one. Just wait and see." He leaned back, giving her a now-answer-that-one look.

This was the second time she'd been asked that question. In the publisher's office, it had become clear to her in a flash that any answer would do. The moment she had explained her wish to allude to the biographical prowess of James Boswell, they were hooked on the promotional angle of a supposedly genderless, anonymous author revealing the secret of another such personality. But Noah and Miriam deserved the full answer.

"Because I don't want to become a biographer."

"But why, Sabine? You are a born biographer. Like Miriam, who is a born chef and, as we'll all learn soon, also a born writer in another special genre."

Sabine raised both hands, palms flat out, as if she wanted to push her questioners away. "If I'm anything, at heart I'm a reporter. I like to watch and observe, outside the public eye. But I'm also a hunter. Miriam," she leaned across the table. "Your former husband said it well. In *Gasps of Delight* he described the joy of hunting: the discovery, the chase, the capture. In that novel Stephen applied it to an art collector, to the erotic pleasure of acquisition." She looked briefly at Noah. "For some, it's probably a justification for womanizing, but for others, like me for instance, it describes the pleasurable part of journalism."

"Of some journalism," interposed Noah.

"Of *my* type of journalism. But there is more to my decision. For the last year and a half, I have been totally immersed in the life of another person. There was practically no emotional time for my own life. It's only now, after finishing this chapter," she reached over, assembling the scattered pages and stacking them, "that I've realized I have to focus on my own life. You know what provided the blinding flash of insight?" She gave a brief, sarcastic laugh, while looking at the ordered stack of pages in her hands. "After finishing the whole manuscript, after having lived with Stephen Marx for months on end, I have come to the realization that I really don't know him; that I never will; and that this must apply to most biographers if they are truly honest. It's a feeling I'm unlikely to experience as a journalist in the numerous small hunts of many different quarries." She took a deep breath. "Don't get me wrong. I don't regret for a moment having worked on the Marx biography. It was my outward-bound exposure, and to a large extent you two made it possible. But like most such experiences, they don't have to be repeated to benefit from the lessons learned."

"So what do you have in mind once the book is out?"

"Look for another apartment."

"But you don't have to move out right away," protested Miriam.

"I do. It will always be Stephen Marx's place. I suppose I'll ask *Sports Illustrated* for a full-time job."

"*Sports reporting?*" It was hard to mistake the dismissive nuance in Noah's tone.

"Before you pooh-pooh the sports pages, just ask your editor who pays the bills: book reviews or the sports section? But you are right: I don't plan to spend the rest of my days doing that. The *S.I.* job is excellent training, and I need some money before any book royalties start coming in. But then I want to turn to investigative reporting. I'm pretty confident I'll land a job when I state in my application that I am A. S. Boswell."

"I'm impressed. What do you think, Miriam?" Noah reached over and patted her hand. "You haven't said much."

"You moved me, Sabine. I wish I had done as much planning when I was your age. But I might as well disclose a secret of my own, which only Noah has shared so far. We're getting to be quite a secretive trio. Let's move over into the living room."

Miriam sat next to Noah on the sofa, one arm around his shoulder. She pointed to the easy chair across. "I want to see your face, Sabine, when you hear what I have to say. Noah knows all about it, so I don't need to look at him. I can just squeeze him."

Sabine grinned. "I bet I know what you're about to tell me."

Miriam turned to Noah. "Did you tell her?"

"I told her nothing."

"So you really guessed?"

The straightforwardness of Miriam's question, her total lack of coyness, threw Sabine off. She had expected some form of marriage announcement, or at least a formal engagement. Now she retreated.

"I'm not positive. So why don't you tell me."

"My book is nearly finished and I am really pleased with it. And not just the soufflé chapter." Again she hugged Noah. "I've always admitted that my first heroine was Julia Child, but I wasn't satisfied with just another recipe book. I became interested in the cultural and historical antecedents of ethnic cuisines in America." She rolled her eyes in mock despair. "'Antecedents!' I never used the word in conversation until I started to write. That's when I came up with the 'can you do it backward?' question that you have heard me spout about so often. In part, it's just funny—maybe even cute. Though not too cute, I hope. But there are serious dimensions to that question."

She didn't know it, but she'd started to lose Sabine's attention. What is she driving at? wondered Sabine. What's secret about it?

"Take the Japanese emphasis on presentation; or the Chinese principle of harmony, which can even be applied to the soup at the end of a Chinese meal. If they use a chicken, every part of that chicken will appear at various stages of the meal until the finale, when you get the essence of it all: the chicken broth. The Japanese will serve the broth early on, but add a chrysanthemum blossom."

Noah's facial expressions fluctuated between bemused affection and incipient impatience. "Darling," he finally interrupted, "you can show Sabine your manuscript where she can read it all. Tell her your secret."

"You're right. Sabine, I'm also going to publish my book anonymously! There you have it."

After a moment of shock, Sabine's response turned boisterous. She jumped up to hug Miriam. "This is getting infectious. First Stephen, then I, and now you. Noah you're next."

Noah raised his hand. "Not I. My nuggets of wisdom will continue to be issued under the name of Noah Berg. Except for my N.B. column, and that hardly counts, because everyone knows who is putting it together."

"So what made you do it? And what is your pen name?"

"One question at a time. First, what made me do it? One day, Noah showed me a letter to the editor of the *Times Book Review* by Marianne Wiggins. That really did the trick."

"Marianne Wiggins?"

"The former wife of Salman Rushdie. She's a fiction author in her own right, but even after her divorce from Rushdie, reviews of her books always identified her as 'Rushdie's former wife.' The crowning blow was struck when one of the reviews of her book was accompanied not just by one, but two pictures: one of Salman Rushdie, and the other of the Ayatollah Khomeini. Now just imagine what would happen to a book by Miriam Marx when the news from that chapter of yours hits the fan."

"Miriam, be fair." Noah patted her arm. "And calm down. You had made that decision weeks before you heard the news from Sabine. Your husband's reputation and mysterious death would have been enough to convert you into another Mrs. Rushdie. But you did have another reason. Don't blame me entirely."

"I'm not blaming you. I'm *crediting* you. But he's right." Miriam turned her focus back on Sabine. "I also want to pay tribute to someone, which brings me to your second question: my pen name."

"Which is?"

"I haven't completely made up my mind, but I'm very close to a decision. As a matter of fact, why don't you give me your opinion?"

"I can't." Sabine was getting impatient. "Not unless you finally decide that I can be trusted with the information."

"All right! Choice number one: 'L. E. N. Fant.'" She spelled it, making it plain she was dealing with three initials. "In addition to Julia Child, the queen of recipes, there is a culinary writer, as distinguished from recipe collector, whom I have admired for years: M. F. K. Fisher. So I thought I'd pay homage to both of them by generating three initials from the French *l'enfant*."

"I better tell you right away," interjected Noah. "To me, it seemed a bit too obvious, even corny—"

"Not more so than my A. S. Boswell," interrupted Sabine.

"How very true," observed Noah. "But how does that make *l'enfant* less so? And 'Fant' is rather wanting in euphony."

"He's prejudiced," laughed Miriam. "Even after I showed him that no less a wordsmith than Henry James had *two* entries each for 'Mant' and 'Tant' in his list of names."

"Lists of names by other authors are bound to lead into swampy territory," said Noah. "You haven't offered Sabine any choices. How can she express a preference?"

"My wise guy Noah is right. Choice number two is 'Judi Challi.'" She waited a few seconds for the name to sink in—long enough to test its sound and flavor, but too short to decipher its origin. "The final one is 'Jill D'Acuhi.'"

Noah spelled it; and the manner in which he did so—quickly, securely, and proudly when it came to the apostrophe—gave him away.

"They were Noah's suggestions. So which do you prefer?"

Sabine hesitated. "'Jill D'Acuhi' is clearly the most original . . . and 'Judi Challi' has an intriguing Middle Eastern ring. They sound as if they have a common base."

Noah leaned forward. "Not bad, Sabine. You're getting warm."

"I give up. Are they supposed to mean anything?"

"They are anagrams based on 'Julia Child.'" Noah made no attempt to disguise authorial pride.

"Very clever. Especially 'D'Acuhi.' It has panache; but will it sell books?" Sabine couldn't resist sounding commercial.

The morning Sabine had dreaded so much had ended on a humorous note. She had started to pack the loose pages of her urchapter in her backpack. Noah stopped her.

"Something just occurred to me. A pseudonym isn't going to shield you forever. Not unless you're willing to go to the lengths Stephen did. And even that didn't protect him from you."

"So?"

"Suppose they don't find Mann—"

"I hope to God they don't."

"Even worse. And I'll bet they don't: he's had more experience at this than you. But they'll certainly find you; and then they'll grill you: prove that Stephen Marx is still alive."

Sabine struck her forehead with her open palm. "I completely forgot. I've one more thing to show you."

Sabine bent over the coffee table and spread out several glossy prints. Miriam picked up one, Noah another.

"Who is this?" she started, then breathed, "Oh my God. Noah look at this picture! It's Steve!"

"I'm looking," he muttered. "I've got one of my own."

"I've never seen him with a beard." She reached for the remaining photographs, inspecting each before handing them over, one at a time, to Noah. "His hair is much longer. And glasses! He always bragged about his 20/20 vision."

Sabine threw the knapsack on the couch before sitting behind Stephen's desk. When she'd left that morning, she had been seriously contemplating that she might have to move out this very day. Her eyes swept slowly over the room. It had been her home for a longer period than any other place in Manhattan. It felt like home. Yet it was still Stephen's place, in fact even more so, because most of her psychic and emotional life during the past year had been spent with him right here. Who had she become, this past year? She and Marx were no longer the distinct individuals she had once imagined. Few subjects remain heroes for long to their biographers. Given the circumstances under which they'd first met, Marx had not even started as a hero; he'd been more of an adversary who interested her in the sense that reporters are interested in journalistic quarry. There were periods when he'd almost turned into villain, but now she wasn't so sure. Totally terminating one life to embark upon another is a heroic step. She felt justified in disclosing that step, but not in rendering a judgment or offering an explanation. Marx's closure had turned into Mann's beginning. But that beginning and its sequel could only be authored by Mann and not by a Boswell.

The telephone rang. It was Noah.

"Sabine, there were two things I wanted to tell you this morning but couldn't in the presence of Miriam. What I want to say may come across as a lecture, but it is meant as a warning, as a friend's words of caution. The biographer's highest function is interpretation, which does not necessarily involve total disclosure. Especially when dealing with a living subject."

"Why are you telling me this?"

She could tell he was hesitating—by the pause, and the false start. "As you know better than anyone else, I have my own agenda. Don't be tempted by Marx's list of female names. And unless you want to interfere unduly with Mann's life, don't disclose where he lives."

"I have no intention of doing so. Why even raise the question?"

"Then destroy at least one of the photographs. I could tell why you took it: you wanted to establish the precise date of your meeting. This is important reportorial material, but biographical overkill. With that photograph, you provided two coordinates—the name of the play and the date—with which even a book critic could locate the Curran Theater anywhere in this country within minutes. Fortunately, Miriam didn't notice, because she was too excited to look at Stephen. And I would be the last one to misuse the information."

"I'll get rid of it, Noah. I promise."

24

Dear Saint,

Tomorrow morning, I am moving out of your apartment. With Miriam's consent, your telephone is being disconnected. We all accept that Stephen Marx is gone for good.

You and I have not been in touch for quite a while. The purpose of this letter is to alert you to two changes in your biography—one in the title, the other in a new chapter.

The full title is *The Resurrection of St. Marx: In My End Is My Beginning*. You are unlikely to be surprised by most of the text. But to do justice to the T. S. Eliot subtitle (which I kept from you even though I had been toying with it for many months), one more chapter had to be written. It comes at the very beginning, is numbered 0, and is by far the shortest. It is also the most important and will, undoubtedly, come to you as a shock, because I have decided that it is impossible to write a biography of Stephen Marx without disclosing that he is still living as another person. Some people will consider your staged disappearance devious, cruel, possibly even narcissistic; but others are likely to concur with me that you have paid and are paying a personal price which justifies evaluating Marx's non-physical suicide as a much more complicated gesture. Chapter 0 contains only a bare outline of the facts. I leave justification and interpretation to the individual reader. I can offer you one consolation, small as it may be: nowhere have I disclosed the whereabouts of D. Mann. Since that is not the name by which you lead your ordinary life, you should be safe. In addition, I will surely be contributing to Mann's material well-being: people who haven't read *Middles* are bound to want to do so now.

The official publication date is this coming Friday. The day after tomorrow, the new chapter is being distributed by *our* publisher to the various news media. Therefore, you can expect initial coverage of your biography to occur in the news section, most likely on the front page, rather than among the book reviews.

Stephen Marx is an extremely good novelist—probably an important one—and certainly a complex person. But deep down I consider him a shit. As Marx's biographer, my dilemma was how to construct a silk purse out of a sow's ear. Marx, undoubtedly, would have preferred my starting with a silk sow, but that is probably the inherent desire of all living subjects of a biography. You have at least two brains—St. Marx's and D. Mann's—and maybe another one to come; but I have never been able to find the heart. Since a heartless existence is impossible, I conclude that, deep down, I do not understand Stephen Marx.

In particular, I do not understand Marx's relation to women. I have to admit that the list of women's names aroused my curiosity; it provoked other reactions as well. My consultant, Noah Berg, and I surmised that it must be a list of your lovers—forty-seven of them. According to Miriam, who, incidentally, is unaware of that list, the first years of your marriage were solid ones, in the best sense of that word. I deduce, therefore, that the bulk of that list dates from the last decade, averaging around four women per year. I suppose there are many men who will just shrug their shoulders at this factoid, but to a woman who matured sexually during the AIDS era, four women per year means one new lover every three months—in other words a classic womanizer. I am at a loss to understand this. All I can do is speculate.

As a woman, I am acquainted with the various species of the genus *womanizer*: gradually developing ones; born again types; the late bloomers; and, of course, the born womanizers. The present evidence from the West Side of Manhattan points to Stephen Marx as a late bloomer, but I am somewhat puzzled about Donald Mann in San Francisco, even though he is not the subject of my biography. My limited personal exposure to Mann would never have led me to classify him among any species of that genus. Hence, I offer for your reflection another working hypothesis, which at least in part is based on discussions with Noah Berg about literary styles.

Some contemporary authors, of the Philip Roth or Norman Mailer variety, are preoccupied with style, while others primarily situate their imagination in the contemporary milieu of material reality (business scandals, legal hanky-panky, espionage). You are an interesting hybrid, who has chosen for each book an important subculture, with style still in mind. Your recent excursions into the world of science and of art are first-class examples. You really seemed to have been able to immerse yourself into their tribal customs. I should know, because I read your novels with great care and checked out your research activities with people who knew, foremost with Miriam. But with one exception, a nun, all your important characters were men and all your realities essentially male.

So here is my speculation: at some stage of your literary career, you recognized this deficiency in your fiction and decided to make women your subject. But the only way you thought you could enter their reality was through sexual familiarity. I shall be honest and admit that I felt very revengeful about such exploitation of sexual intimacy for the sake of research, because to me it is not the route to knowledge of women *as* women. In most of fiction, as in everyday life, the role of women is considered solely in relation to men. Thus, I suspect that *Doctor Amoroso*, if it is ever launched, will fit into that conventional mold.

You will note the absence of any questions in this letter. When I move tomorrow to a new address, I will have a post office box for my mail, and an unlisted phone number, so there is no way for you to contact me unless you're willing to risk writing in care of my publisher, who also happens to be Marx's. But I do leave you with a memento of our last meeting in San Francisco: the attached photo, of which I have kept no copy, because I need none. I am unlikely to forget you.

Sabine

25

Sabine,

I'm not a hypocrite; hence the absence of the usual "Dear"
before your name. Maybe there is a god looking out for me,
because yesterday, I woke up exceptionally early. Thanks to *Middles*, my standard of living has risen to a level that includes home
delivery of the *New York Times*. I opened my door around 5:30
AM and . . . I am sure you can guess the rest.

As soon as I finished reading "Novelist Marx 'Resurrected,'" I
tried to call you to see whether I could commit murder over the
telephone. But *my*(!) phone, Stephen Marx's only remaining connection to New York, had already been disconnected—an act
whose symbolism did not escape me. Only then did I realize that
even if you had wanted to alert me (which I doubt), you could not
have done so. I have been changing my post office box every few
months, and the last change occurred just a few weeks ago. In a
way I am glad I could not reach you. Instead, I had thirty-six
hours worth of reflection before writing this letter in a small
motel somewhere on the West Coast.

Luckily, Marx's photograph was not on the front page. Even
more fortunately, the *San Francisco Chronicle* carried no picture
as part of its article. Still, there are enough *Times* readers in San
Francisco that the chances of someone recognizing me are more
than finite. I still lead a Spartan life, although it is now fully
dedicated to writing, so it only took a few hours to pack my
belongings into a small U-Haul van.

It is amazing what thirty-six hours by oneself can do to one's
psyche. I shall continue to hole up out here in the sticks until
your news story has blown over. You may actually have presented
me with a test—a type of self-immolation—to which I would not
have subjected myself, had it not been for your violation of what
I took to be a bargain between us.

I shall now do something that will surprise both of us: address Sabine Diehlsdorf without a single interruption, an experience one cannot have with you face to face. Is it not ironic that the only truly open statement you will ever have received from me is my very last communication to you? To which you cannot reply; and which, in any event, comes too late for A. S. Boswell (nudge, nudge) because her book is now out.

To me, the ultimate truth is fiction. In ancient Greece, whenever lawyers met after some interesting case, they teased each other with "What if that had happened?" "What if he had done . . . ?" "What if . . . ?" Supposedly, that was the origin of fiction. In any event, that is how I write. I do serious research; I collect the evidence; and then I proceed with "But what if . . . ?" It is a god-like feeling, creating people and situations, passing judgment upon the creatures of your imagination. But unlike a god, I am very sensitive to judgment of my own work. Preoccupied with wanting to know what people *really* thought, I felt only posthumous evaluations would give me that insight.

Most people are bound to judge my staged death as crazy. The two persons who knew the facts, my friend Ambrose and you, thought me heartless, a verdict to which I plead nolo contendere. D. H. Lawrence said, "You have to have something vicious in you to be a creative writer." I am certain that "heartless" can be substituted for "vicious." Comedians always get a laugh when they claim the brain as their second most cherished organ. Doesn't the audience always know that the heart is not the other one? But ask the question seriously. Would Pavarotti not cite his voice, Picasso his eye or hand, Chanel her nose? What professional would list the heart?

Although I may have thought of my "sailing accident" initially as a stunt, it turned into something much more serious. Starting a new life as genderless D. Mann became extraordinarily important to me, because it permitted me to consider some literary experiments I had not performed before—experiments I would like to see evaluated (here I go again with my obsession!) uncontaminated by comparisons with "the oeuvre" of Stephen Marx.

A digression: is the world worse off if an author dies or had never lived? With a Shakespeare surely. But not with most writers, including Stephen Marx. I considered that question in my interviews with scientists during my *Cohen* phase. With them, the answer is more often "yes." Scientific research is a collaborative activity, even among bitter competitors. Their work builds on that of others. Even a mediocre scientist can boast that he sees farther than some famous predecessor, because he is standing on his shoulders. By contrast, our trade is solitary, not cooperative, and generally not progressive. Genius among authors is frequently self-deluding narcissism—important to the person, but not to society.

Let me now return to why I was so murderously angry when I first discovered what you had done. It was not just the violation of a tacit agreement, presumably done to further your own personal ambition (what right do I really have to question such motive?). By resurrecting Marx, you have destroyed the anonymity of Mann: given him a history, a body—a gender—an act I found unconscionable. That sexless authorial mask has become so important to me that you have forced me to undergo another self-immolation. I would not have done so, because it is more convenient to continue to deal with an agent and a publisher who have accommodated themselves to my desire for total privacy. Starting over a third time is a hassle, but I now recognize also its compensation. For someone so preoccupied with judgment, there is something reassuring about being evaluated de novo.

Why is the loss of gender so important? Because the relation of the reader to the gender of the author has a great deal to do with the way a book, and especially a novel, is read. Of course, that is also true of ethnicity, but with gender it is overpoweringly so.

I have become very interested in the "voice" of an author (another reason why dubbing intrigues me). I, for instance, have never written a novel in the first person singular, although many writers have done so because of the inherent attraction, combined with the challenge of coping with the limitations of such a style. But do you know of any novel where "we" was used in the true first person plural sense, rather than as the royal "we" of scientists or politicians? Siamese twins might qualify. It is one of my current experiments.

Let me address the subject of *Doctor Amoroso*: it was the last question you ever asked—one that convinced me not to subject myself further to your intrusiveness. The title implies a Don Juan, which my character indeed is. But his voice is hardly heard. Instead, I dissect him in terms of appearance, morals, strengths, and blemishes, almost exclusively through the voices and eyes of his women lovers. Even the eroticism is considered solely from the woman's viewpoint. For me to know whether I succeeded, it is indispensable that the reader be ignorant of the author's gender.

There is nothing more I wish to tell you about me as a writer, but I shall end by addressing your last question, "Who is Dr. Amoroso?" without answering it.

When I first arrived in San Francisco, not knowing yet that I would never return to New York, I led a virtually celibate life. I did so deliberately, because I avoided every form of intimacy so as not to give myself away. But after a few months of such life, and after gradually acquiring the psychic skin of D. Mann, I continued in that asexual mode. I felt like a libertine, who had now joined a monastery and was proud that he actually managed to cope. Dr. Amoroso's disciplined writing was like daily cold showers and prayers.

And one last quotation, this from Thomas Berger, whom I admire: "My real life is unbearable to me unless I can escape from it into fiction."

Saint

Coda

Jill D'Acuhi's *Can You Do It Backward?* proved to be the cookbook sensation of the year. It took perhaps three days for the press to penetrate her incognito—Miriam enjoyed the game of hide and seek, she said, but what was the point if no one ever caught you? In one TV show after another—from Jay Leno to Oprah—Miriam found herself bombarded by double entendres related to the title of her book. Her unexpected talent for repartee gained her, within months, her own D'Acuhi show on television—the premiere featuring the reincarnation of a historic banquet offered on 13 September 1513 to the Medicis in Rome and discovered by Noah in an Italian Renaissance account. The Medici feast reportedly ended with scented toothpicks, but commenced in true "backward" fashion with pinenut cakes, marzipan confections, custards in little pots, figs, and sweet wines.

Miriam's catering establishment continued to bear the Marx name, but her private checkbook bore the legend "Noah and Miriam Berg" with her Second Avenue address.

Following the release of the Stephen Marx biography, the publisher of *Middles* had to reprint Mann's novel twice before sales dropped to previous levels. According to publishing scuttlebutt reported in the *Village Voice*, over the course of five months Mann's publisher had received no fewer than seven manuscripts over the transom, all purportedly written by D. Mann. Three came from Los Angeles, two from San Francisco, and one each from Vancouver, Portland, and Fargo, North Dakota. According to the *Village Voice*, all were turned down. The paper also claimed that an out-of-court settlement had been reached between Marx's publisher and Mann's, since the former had held the right of first refusal to Marx's next novel. Since Mann had been shown to be Marx, *Middles* should have been published by them.

Two years later, a first novel, *Doctor Amoroso*, without blurbs or much promotion, made it onto the best-seller list for a few weeks, followed by a paperback auction sale in six figures. Many reviews commented on the refreshingly novel, erotic, female voice of an author named D. Janus.

For a few seconds, Sabine Diehlsdorf, an investigative reporter with the *Village Voice*, considered contacting the publisher of *Doctor Amoroso* about writing a piece on that anonymous author. But then she recalled that Janus was also the Roman god of all beginnings, and she wasn't ready to start all over again. So the temptation passed.

Carl Djerassi is a professor of chemistry at Stanford University. His books include the novels *The Bourbaki Gambit* (Georgia, 1994) and *Cantor's Dilemma;* the autobiography *The Pill, Pygmy Chimps, and Degas' Horse;* and essay, short story, and poetry collections. Djerassi has been awarded the National Medal of Science in 1973 (for the synthesis of the first steroid oral contraceptive), the National Medal of Technology in 1991 (for novel approaches to insect control), and the 1992 Priestley Medal, the highest American award in chemistry. He is also the founder of the Djerassi Resident Artists Program, an artists' colony near San Francisco that supports working artists in various disciplines.